THE
ORPHAN'S
MOTHER

BOOKS BY MARION KUMMEROW

Not Without My Sister
A Light in the Window
From the Dark We Rise
The Girl in the Shadows

THE
ORPHAN'S
MOTHER

MARION KUMMEROW

bookouture

Published by Bookouture in 2022

An imprint of Storyfire Ltd.
Carmelite House
50 Victoria Embankment
London EC4Y 0DZ

www.bookouture.com

ISBN: 978-1-80314-390-3
eBook ISBN: 978-1-80314-389-7

To every person who loves and cares for a child

LODZ /LITZMANNSTADT, NOVEMBER 1944

Emma picked up another log and put it on top of the eight logs already in her arms. Once she was upright, she turned and walked toward the small house she and her family called home.

She opened the door and entered the cozy living room with the large cast iron stove sitting on the wall between the living room and the kitchen. This was the coldest winter she could remember and it became increasingly hard to buy wood to heat the stove. Thankfully her husband had made provisions for the cold, cutting and chopping extra wood the last time he'd been on leave. As always, when she thought about Herbert, her heart squeezed. He was somewhere out there in these arctic temperatures fighting against the Russians.

"Mami, come and play with us," her son Jacob called out. His hair was tousled from sleep, as he walked down the stairs. Her youngest was four years old and was the spitting image of his father, with the blond hair, blue eyes and those adorable dimples in his cheeks.

"Go to your room and get dressed, breakfast is almost ready," Emma said. "Where is your sister?"

"Coming." Sophie emerged behind her brother, fully

dressed in a dark-blue ankle-length dress with woolen panty-hose. Three years older than Jacob, she was Emma's pillar of strength in these hard times. A diligent, serious and obedient girl, who was mature beyond her age.

"Set the table for breakfast, will you?"

Sophie dutifully walked into the kitchen. Emma watched her daughter moving about, while she kneeled down to feed the oven. Something had to give. The situation was getting increasingly worrisome. Rumors were spreading far and wide about the abominable crimes the Soviet soldiers were committing. She was not only afraid for herself, but even more so for Sophie, a pretty blonde girl who was entirely too young and innocent for what might await her. Kindling the fire, she thought about her options. There weren't many.

"Mami, where are my socks?" Jacob shouted down from his room.

If only her son were as neat and tidy as her daughter. "Look beneath your bed," she called and asked Sophie, "Would you please go upstairs and help your brother?"

"He should really learn to be tidier, he's not a baby anymore." If Jacob was a tiny copy of his father, Sophie took after her mother. It wasn't only her looks, she'd also imitated Emma's phrases and behavior, down to the frown of her brows.

"I know. But he's still small. Please, go. I have to finish preparing breakfast."

Just as soon as Sophie trotted off, someone knocked on the door. Emma wondered who could be visiting this early in the day.

"Emma, are you there?" Recognizing the voice, she went to open the door for her heavily pregnant friend.

"Luise. Come inside. Where's Hans?" Luise's son Hans was Jacob's best friend.

"He's with my mother-in-law. I needed to have a quick talk with you." The undertone in Luise's voice was frightening.

"What's so important that you had to come over before breakfast in this horrible weather?" It had snowed overnight and there was a stiff wind coming from the north, causing Emma's cheeks to sting with the cold bursting inside through the open door.

"Did you hear the latest about the Russians?" Luise asked, while Emma finished kindling the fire.

"Not this morning. Where are they?" The front was advancing fast, and despite the strict ban on fleeing, many of their friends and neighbors had left their homes to try their luck in the West, since everyone agreed it was preferable to fall into American, British or even French hands than Russian ones. She and Luise had talked numerous times about packing up and heading west, but since neither of them had immediate family who would accommodate them, they hadn't gone through with their plan.

"They are approaching fast. It seems it'll only be a matter of days until they reach us."

"Oh dear, come and tell me in the kitchen." Emma cast a warning look at her friend, urging her not to go into details where Sophie might overhear them. As soon as she closed the kitchen door behind them, Luise shared the news, while Emma stirred the porridge.

"It's bad. They say the Red Army is less than thirty miles away and the Wehrmacht is retreating fast. Despite all their brave fighting they can only hold up the Ivans for so long. It seems for every killed Soviet soldier, ten new ones show up. I really don't know where they take them from."

"Well, the Soviet Union is huge. Their country reaches far beyond the Ural Mountains all the way to the Pacific Coast. I guess they get new soldiers from all these hinterlands whenever they want."

Luise sighed. "The thing is, my mother-in-law has dug out a second cousin who used to live in Aachen, near the Low Countries. We don't even know if she's still alive, but Agatha insisted that we should at least try and find this cousin of hers."

"Really actually leave Lodz?" Emma felt a sharp tug at her heart. This was the place she called home, as had her parents and grandparents before her. She knew no other place.

Throughout the city's checkered history, when it had changed hands more times than anyone cared to remember, Poles and Germans had lived and worked more or less peacefully side by side, making it the "Manchester of Poland". Lodz had become synonymous with the thriving textile industry, which bestowed great wealth on the industrial owners, mostly Jews, and gave work to the city's population.

The good times lasted until the end of the Great War, when the fastidious Versailles Treaty had handed over her beloved hometown to the newly founded Republic of Poland, also known as the Second Polish Republic. Suddenly the Poles had been out for revenge.

Emma had only been five years old, but her life had changed forever. Gone were the happy, carefree times with beautiful dresses and fancy birthday parties. Instead she remembered nothing but the dulled mood and continuous struggles, culminating in the hyperinflation of 1923 and the downfall of the formerly thriving economy. A hard time indeed.

She got married and had borne her first child, when the tide turned once more and it felt as if luck was finally shining down on Lodz again. In 1939 Hitler brought the Reichsgau Wartheland—to which Lodz belonged—home into the German Reich, expelling what they called the Jewish bloodsuckers and installing good Germans in all-important positions.

Emma smiled at the memory of the joyous celebrations. Half of the city had been out on the streets dancing and singing after the Wehrmacht had freed them from the Polish yoke. Herbert, her husband, had taken her out and whirled her around until she collapsed breathless in his arms.

"Now everything will get better for us," he'd promised her.

And he'd been right. Lodz had been renamed Litz-mannstadt and had become the center for the war production of textiles for Hitler's Third Reich. People had work again and could afford small luxuries that hadn't been possible during the harsh interwar years.

Strange as it sounded, for her family the war had been a blessing, at least in the beginning. Her gaze fell on the rather dilapidated hut of her neighbors, a Polish couple. They hadn't danced when their city had been liberated.

For them, it hadn't been a blessing and they detested the Germans. No wonder, they were subdued then, but were now giddily awaiting the Red Army to free them. How much had changed in the past five years.

Would her neighbors be the ones to break out into joyous celebrations soon?

Luise's voice interrupted her musings. "It's not getting any easier with the days passing. Anyway we can return once the war is over and everything has settled down."

Deep down in her heart Emma doubted that anyone who left could ever return. "Maybe you're right. But how will we go? And how are our husbands going to find us?" Luise's husband Gustav was in the Wehrmacht just like Herbert and neither of the women knew exactly where their men were fighting.

"We can send a letter with the *Feldpost* to them both."

"We could." Although Emma doubted the military mail system would work reliably for much longer, she nodded, because what else was there to do?

"And on how to go... Did you hear Marianne is leaving with her children?"

"No. When?"

"Tomorrow morning."

"What? But how?" Since the *Statthalter* had forbidden anyone to show cowardice before the enemy by leaving the city, the trains would only take soldiers or the odd high-ranking civilian with proper travel permits.

"Here's the thing." Luise lowered her voice to a conspiratorial whisper. "She has arranged to meet with a bigger trek about ten miles out of town. They have some horse-drawn carts and are willing to take them. You know, strength in numbers."

"I never thought Marianne would flee." Emma was torn between wanting to follow in Marianne's footsteps and wanting to stay at home, hoping the Russians weren't half as bad as everyone said.

"Mami? The table is ready." Sophie peeked her head inside and Emma took the time to watch her daughter closely. At seven years, she was still a child and had just started her second year at school last fall. Her face was gaunt from not getting enough fattening food, yet she still looked pretty with her big blue eyes, the soft curled-up lips and her blonde hair braided into two long pigtails.

"Call your brother, I'm almost done." With an apologizing glance at Luise, she stirred the porridge once more, before she took the pot from the stove. "Are you leaving, too?"

Luise writhed uncomfortably. "Not yet. But my mother-in-law... Well, we should discuss this in detail without prying ears."

"I'll come over later to talk."

"We have to run errands in the afternoon."

"Then I'll pop over before noon. See you."

Emma gave her friend a one-armed hug, before she scurried back to the living room, where both her children were sitting at the table, waiting for their porridge. She loved them both with all her heart. Sophie was the older one, neat and tidy, responsible and a big help with the chores, while Jacob was a little whirlwind, who rarely did as he was told, but conquered everyone with his cute looks. One of his big smiles combined with a mischievous gaze from his blue eyes and she melted into a puddle at his feet. She knew she should be stricter with him, but he was such a lovely boy and still so young.

"Mami? Can we eat now, I'm hungry," Jacob asked.

Emma pushed aside the worries plaguing her and pasted on a smile. "I'm coming just now." A few moments later she sat down with them, dispensing equally small amounts of porridge into their bowls, which earned her a disgruntled look from Sophie. There was never enough to satiate their hunger, since both of them were having a growth spurt and were always hungry like a pack of wolves.

After breakfast the children joined her in the kitchen, Sophie helping to clean the dishes, while Jacob sat there playing with his building blocks.

"Can we go outside and play in the snow?" he asked.

"Maybe later. First we could go over to Hans and Luise's house, what do you think?"

"Yes! Yes!" Jacob hopped up and down in glee, toppling over his construction work and making a right mess on the kitchen floor. Instead of collecting his building blocks, he got up and started putting on his shoes that Emma had last night stuffed with old paper and put next to the stove.

"Jacob. Put away your toys first!" She did her best to sound stern.

"I don't want to. Why do I always have to tidy up? I'll come back later to play with them anyway."

Emma couldn't deny there was a certain logic to his words and worked hard to suppress the smile wanting to break out on her face. Jacob was her sunshine, and without him all these hardships would be so much more difficult to endure. Not even Sophie had the ability to make her forget all her sorrows the way he could.

Thinking of what might happen to one of her wonderful children sent painful stabs into her heart, so she quickly pushed those disturbing thoughts away, trying to figure out what the best course of action was. To stay or to leave.

Either way, many hardships lay ahead for her family, therefore she soaked up all the joy she could get right now to draw on later when she'd need the strength to see them through to the other side.

2

POSEN, JANUARY 1945, 120 MILES WEST OF LODZ

The empty crib stood in the corner. Irena couldn't bear the sight anymore and fled the room into the kitchen of her tiny house. There, she took a shallow breath and looked out the window over the kitchen sink, wrapping her arms around herself.

Snow lay on the ground and the gray sky overhead promised more to come in the next days. The chilly temperatures outside mirrored the feelings in her soul. Nothing but despair, sorrow and hopelessness. She had felt that same way every single day for the past year, since the fateful events had smashed her dreams, her future, her very happiness.

Despite the Nazi occupation she and Luka, her husband of four years, lived more or less unbothered on the outskirts of Posen. Luka was a well-respected doctor in the Catholic Hospital, where she also worked as a nurse in the children's ward.

Even the Nazis needed doctors and nurses, so they usually didn't harass them or make their lives otherwise difficult. As long as the hospital administration catered to every whim of their new masters, life was bearable. Sure, they had let go all of their Jewish colleagues way back in the first years of the occupation, but apart from that, it was more or less business as usual within the thick walls of the former convent that had been converted into a hospital in the seventeenth century.

A lone tear ran down her cheek unchecked as her mind replayed the events of that fateful day about a year ago:

After a long, but rewarding, shift in the children's ward, Irena walked across town to visit her midwife for a check-up. Like most first-time parents, Luka and she were not only overjoyed, but also incredibly nervous, and she couldn't wait to hold her bundle of joy in her arms.

In her second trimester, she had already begun to feel the baby's movements inside her. Every time she paused whatever she was doing for a moment and put a hand on her belly, she found herself silently conversing with her baby.

Still smiling with joy, she rounded the next corner and ran straight into a ruckus. Apparently some rebellious youth had painted the *Kotwica*, the emblem of the Polish Home Army consisting of the letters PW and the sign for the resistance movement, on a statue.

Several German SS officers strode about, obviously looking for retaliation for such disrespect of their authority. Irena immediately stopped in her tracks, because it was always best to stay clear of trouble. Even those who were not involved might get arrested or worse. As she turned on her heel, the SS tightened the cordon around the square she was about to cross. Rushing back in the direction she'd come from, she bumped into a soldier wearing the detested black uniform with the skull on the shoulder flaps.

"Excuse me, please, I'm sorry," she stammered, but he'd already taken out his truncheon and started battering her with it. Falling to the ground from the impact, she rolled up into a ball and whimpered, "Please, stop. Please."

He wouldn't relent and worked himself into a frenzy, raining blows down on her legs, back, head, and stomach, while she lay there using her arms to protect the unborn baby until she passed out.

"Can you walk?" a female voice whispered into her ear.

It took Irena a few blinks until she finally forced her eyes open and looked into the concerned face of a girl who couldn't have been older than fifteen. She nodded. "I think I can."

"They gave you quite the beating. Still, you can consider yourself lucky. Because you passed out, they didn't put you on one of their trucks to take you God knows where." The girl made the sign of the cross, before she stretched out her hand to help Irena up.

A horrible pain stabbed Irena's belly, and then another one. She folded her hands across the bump and put on a brave face, resolving to return home, build up the fire and take a warm bath, thinking everything would be fine. Luka was a doctor, so he could tend to her wounds and would give a note to Matron that Irena needed a few days rest to recover.

Yes, everything would be fine.

Irena wrung her hands and returned to the present. Nothing had been fine. Two days after the awful beating, she'd lost her child and had felt like she was crying inside ever since. Due to complications from the miscarriage, she'd been forced to stay in the hospital for weeks and by the end of it, the doctors told her she'd never be able to fall pregnant again.

After their verdict, it was as if a black hole had opened up and swallowed Irena's soul. Nothing seemed to make life worth living anymore, not even her beloved Luka, who cared for her, binding her ribs, tending to her wounds, and cradling her in his arms while she wept endless hours for the loss of their baby.

How could she ever recover from this blow of fate? Not even her work at the children's ward was able to bring a smile upon her face. Every time she looked at a child, all she saw was the one she lost. Every day in her life had turned into an ordeal, until she could take it no more.

Gathering up all her courage she had asked Matron to transfer her to another ward, but the woman had refused. In the throes of this horrible winter, when more undernourished children arrived at the hospital daily, suffering from nasty respiratory infections and pneumonia, Matron simply couldn't spare an experienced nurse like Irena.

She raised her head, looking at the snow with unseeing eyes. The end of the war was near, everyone knew this—yet Irena could find no joy in this fact. Her soul was too consumed by her own grief.

From the radio the governor's voice droned, strictly forbidding every German citizen from leaving their villages. She sneered. Much good his orders did, since the Red Army was crossing Poland with lightning speed to free them from the Nazi's yoke and thousands of German families left their homes to flee westward, ban or no ban.

The refugees worsened the public health situation by bringing infectious diseases to an already weakened and suffering Polish population. Irena shook her head, it didn't do any good to think about the poor coughing children in her ward.

But then her emotions overwhelmed her and she cried again, bent over the kitchen sink, holding onto the faucet as the only thing to ground her in the here and now. How many times had she wished to follow her sweet baby to wherever it was now? One glimpse of his perfect little body was all she had. All she would ever have.

Waves of sobbing shook her shoulders as she reminisced about her and Luka's dream to have a family of their own. A sweet little baby to take care of, to nurture, and to raise into a responsible adult. And they'd come so close... Another sob wrecked her skinny body.

Laboriously standing straight, she wiped her cheeks with her fingers and went upstairs to the bedroom where Luka still slept. There, her gaze fell once more on the empty crib sitting in the corner, the constant reminder of what she could never have. She knew she should have discarded the crib already, but despite the grief it caused, it gave her a strange sense of belonging—of a better world before all of this happened.

Again, she lost the tenuous hold on her emotions and bitter tears ran down her cheeks as her sobbing awakened her husband. Overwhelmed she crumpled to the floor, banging her knees, but not caring about the pain. If anything, it distracted her from the boundless grief dwelling within.

Luka climbed from the bed and picked her up, cradling her against his chest as he returned to the bed. He laid her down and then climbed in behind her, wrapping her tightly in his arms and pulling the covers over both of them.

"Shush, Irena. I know it hurts..."

"Why?" she cried.

"Not everything happens for a reason, but maybe God has different plans for us."

"Whatever his plans might be, I hate them, I hate God!"

"Shush, you mustn't talk like that. We should be grateful that you survived."

"I'd rather I had not..." She gave a sigh filled with utter desolation.

"You can't talk like that. I need you. The children in the ward need you." Luka stroked her back in long and calming movements.

"I... I can't do this anymore. I see their eyes and wonder what our little boy would have looked like."

The doctors hadn't let her cradle the dead baby, so all she'd had was that one glimpse of him. A boy. Pavel. That's the name she'd given him. For everyone else, this baby had never existed and didn't deserve a name, but for her, she carried him deep in her heart. Forever.

3

LODZ /LITZMANNSTADT

"Bang, you are dead!" Jacob sprung from his cover behind a bush and used his fingers to imitate a gun pointing at his friend Klaus.

"No, you didn't get me. I killed you first!" Klaus protested. Several other children came running toward them, jumping at each other and forming a ball of legs and arms. Nobody knew who was the first to use a snowball as ammunition, but soon enough all of them were involved in a good old-fashioned snowball fight.

"Ouch! That wasn't fair!" Hans yelled, when a snowball with a core of ice hit him against the temple.

"All is fair in love and war," the perpetrator, a boy of about eight years, answered.

"What is that even supposed to mean?" Hans grumbled, doing his best not to break out in tears, an angry red mark showing on his temple.

"Shouldn't you have your mother look at that?" Jacob asked him.

"Nah... she'll only scold me. She always tells me not to be so wild. She loves your sister, you know?"

"Sophie?" Jacob simultaneously adored and hated his older sister, since she was so much more grown up and knew so many things, but also wanted to boss him around all the time.

"Yes. My mom's always 'Sophie this, Sophie that. I wish I had a big girl like Emma does to help me' blah, blah, blah."

Jacob giggled. "My mother is the same. Tells me to take a leaf out of Sophie's book. Paah! Who wants to be like a girl? We're made to fight wars, not to tidy up our rooms!"

"Right you are!" Hans had taken the opportunity and formed another snowball while Jacob was talking and now shoved the cold stuff way down his neck.

"Hey! That's unfair. You'll pay for that."

Jacob launched at his friend, who was already running away and taunting him, "Catch me if you can!"

Just then one of the mothers ventured out into the yard and yelled, "Klaus, Maria, we have to go."

Klaus ran up to Jacob and in an unusual show of affection, he embraced him so hard that both of them toppled into the snow.

"What was that for?" Jacob asked.

"I have to go now."

Sure, it was annoying that his mother was making him leave so early, but that was no reason to be so upset. "Tell her you want to play with us again tomorrow," Jacob said.

Klaus shook his head and sudden tears spilled down his cheeks. That's when Jacob saw Klaus' mom talking to his mom. When the two women hugged, he knew something was amiss and he asked, "What's wrong?"

"We're going to my aunt's house tomorrow. I don't want to, but Mommy made me pack up my clothes and favorite toys. She said I have to be really good and that it was going to take lots of days to get there."

Jacob didn't like this news and frowned. "When are you coming back?"

"Mommy didn't say. I overheard her talking to Granny. Both were very afraid of the Russians. They think I can't hear them whispering, but I do."

Jacob nodded. He'd been eavesdropping every night when his father was home on leave, but since then there hadn't been talk about the war or the Russians in his house. Because to whom should his mother talk, when he and Sophie were supposed to sleep? Sometimes Luise came over, but the women always closed the door to the kitchen so he couldn't listen in.

A tremendous suspicion rose in his chest. Was his mother lying to him when she said everything would be fine?

"Klaus, I'm waiting!" Klaus' mother called.

"Bye." Klaus reluctantly got up and gave Jacob a sad little wave.

"Bye." Jacob waved back, a frown on his face. He watched his friend disappear and then he turned to watch his mami speaking with Luise and some other women.

"Jacob, are you playing or not?" Sophie interrupted his thoughts.

He turned and watched as she twirled the stick she was using as a gun.

"I'm playing." With that, Jacob darted behind a barren tree. Several of the other children on his side joined the renewed play and after another twenty minutes, it was decided by the mothers that it was getting late and too cold for them to remain outside.

Later that evening over dinner, Jacob asked his mother, "Why did Klaus have to leave?"

She rubbed a hand over his head. "His mother has an aunt who lives a few days travel away from here. She invited them to come live with her and they've decided to go."

"Is that because of the Russians?" Jacob asked.

"Why would you say this?" his mami asked in a measured tone.

"Klaus said the Russians are coming. Are they coming here? Are they going to hurt us?" A small tremor of fear laced his words, despite his determination to be brave. His mother hugged him close and then pulled Sophie to her other side. She looked different without her usual bright smile, and again, fear pulled at his heartstrings.

"I don't know what's going to happen, but we might have to leave as well someday. Right now though, I don't want you to worry about that. Alright?"

Jacob looked at Sophie and they both nodded. He knew his mami loved him and would never let anything bad happen to him. In any case he still had Sophie. His sister might be annoying at times, but in dire straits he could always count on her.

POSEN

Irena bent to tuck the sheet and blanket around the little girl, ensuring she would stay as warm as possible in the large children's ward. The hospital had seen another influx of little patients over the last few days. A horrible freezing cold was moving through the city, and many children had taken it badly, since most families were running low on fuel and food.

"Irena, if you'll finish tucking this row in, I'll go start on the babies," her colleague said.

"Thank you," she said gratefully. A faint reminder of her former smile appeared on her face as she remembered the joy she'd always felt working with children, something she'd all but lost since miscarrying her own precious baby. As time passed the debilitating stab to her heart every time she saw an infant was easing off, but it still was a relief when her colleague took care of them.

She nodded and moved to the next bed, where a scraggy little boy lay with full-blown pneumonia. She gave him a Thermos with warm water to drink for the night, impressing on him not to lose it and then administered a spoonful of the precious cough medicine.

Even as she fed him the syrup, she felt a pang of guilt, because he most likely wouldn't make it through the night and she should have saved the medicine for a child with better prospects. But his big, round eyes full of pain compelled her to at least try and alleviate his coughing. He swallowed dutifully and grimaced at the awful taste, before he fell back onto his pillow. Irena tucked the sheets around his frail body, sending a prayer to heaven before she continued down the line of cribs and beds, giving each child the same loving attention, if only for a minute or two.

The poor little souls had nobody else but her to give them a kind word, because parents weren't allowed in the hospital except during visiting hours. Although she could understand the reasoning behind that rule, she and her colleague sure could have used the help of some mothers to prepare all the children for the night.

She was almost back to the doorway when one little sob gripped her heart and sent her feet moving back to the third row. A tiny girl sat upright on her bed, her thumb in her mouth, and her large eyes wet with tears.

"What's wrong, lovey?" Irena asked, reaching out a hand and feeling for fever.

"I want my mommy." The girl removed her thumb barely long enough to utter the words.

"Your mommy had to go home. She'll be back tomorrow morning. You should get some sleep and show her in the morning how much better you are."

The girl burst into harrowing sobs, causing her coughing to pick up until she was gagging on her own phlegm. In an effort to calm the distraught child, Irena reached out and hauled her into her arms. The little one promptly wrapped her arms around Irena's neck and laid her head on her shoulder.

She rocked back and forth with the child, rubbing a tender hand in a circular pattern on her back. Only when the sobs subsided and the little body relaxed in sleep, did Irena carefully place her back in the bed and tuck the covers around her.

It was the smallest ones who didn't understand what was happening that broke Irena's heart. They came to the hospital, hurting, sick, malnourished, and scared. When their mothers left, some descended into complete panic, aggravating whatever illness ailed them. In their weakened conditions, a simple cold could become life-threatening. The nurses did what they could to ease their suffering and help them recover, but too many children and babies would spend their last days in the hospital surrounded by strangers.

Matron always told her to dissociate herself from her patients' suffering or one day she'd collapse with a broken heart under the emotional strain. But how could a heart that had been shattered into a million pieces ever break again?

No, Irena poured everything she had left into the children at the hospital. Every little smile or grateful glance gave her a glimmer of love that helped piece her heart together and maybe, one day, she'd be whole and happy again.

Her shoulders treacherously shivered and she furtively glanced around before she swiped her tears away. It wouldn't do any good for anyone to see how much she still suffered. On silent feet she slipped from the ward, switching off the light and closing the door behind her.

"I'm so tired," her colleague said.

"Me too." Twelve hours on her feet caring for the patients was draining physically and emotionally and she would love nothing more than to drop down right there and then. But she gathered her strength and waved a goodbye to the night nurse taking over, before she stepped out into the stinging cold for her long walk home through darkness and cold.

The Nazis had imposed a strict curfew, but as a nurse she had a special permit to walk home at night. Still, she'd rather not run into a patrol, because the sight of a German SS man in his black uniform still made her panic.

If only the Red Army would hurry up to liberate Posen and get rid of their hated oppressors. Maybe then, her own life would take a turn for the better too. Just as she did every morning and every night, when she walked past the cathedral, she stopped for a moment and sent a prayer to heaven. "Please dear God, give me the miracle of having my own child."

5

LODZ /LITZMANNSTADT

Two days later Emma met with Luise, her mother-in-law Agatha, and several other women while the children were playing outside.

Agatha was the oldest of the group and had naturally taken on the role as leader. "For the sake of our children and grand-children, we must leave Lodz, sooner rather than later."

"We can't. The *Statthalter* hasn't—" Elvira objected.

"That lying prick has evacuated his own family weeks ago, claiming they were visiting family in Berlin over Christmas," Karin said.

"That's not forbidden." Luise had a mouse-like frightened expression on her face.

"So why haven't they returned?" Karin asked.

Emma agreed with her, but was too afraid to speak out. The entire conversation they were holding in this room was trai-torous. If the authorities ever found out, they might all be hanged for the crime of cowardice in front of the enemy.

Agatha looked at the half-dozen women gathered in the room and cleared her throat. "You are all much younger than I am, and none of you was a mother right after the last war ended.

Believe me when I tell you that neither you nor your children want to be here when the Russians arrive."

"I'm not sure they will hurt—" Luise said, but Agatha silenced her with a raise of her hand.

"After everything we've heard from places that have already fallen to the Russians, there's no doubt what will happen. The Poles will jump on the opportunity to take away what belongs to us German citizens, and mark my words: none of us is ever going to see this home again. If we leave now, we can at least save our lives."

"That old hag is crazy, Hitler will never allow this," Elvira whispered, but nobody believed her. Every woman in the room knew that it was only a matter of time until Germany lost the war.

The onslaught of Red Army troops all across Prussia, Pomerania and the General Government of Poland was so overwhelming that not even Propaganda Minister Goebbels could whitewash it. Everyone knew that 'strategic regrouping' meant 'retreat' and 'tightening the frontline' was a euphemism for 'running from a superior enemy'.

The fact was, their beloved homeland was lost. Though nobody dared to openly admit it, only a few delusional women still believed there would be a fortunate turn in this war.

"But how would we leave?" Emma gathered all her courage to ask. "All trains going west are strictly military transport only."

Agatha pursed her lips. "I have a plan, but first I have to know, who wants to leave? If you'd rather stay, that's entirely up to you, but then you should quit this gathering now."

Emma was amazed at the old woman's guts. "Isn't she afraid of someone telling on her?" she whispered to her friend Luise.

"She's always been fierce, but I guess that now she really doesn't care about the authorities and their threats anymore and has decided to take the fate of our community into her own hands."

It seemed strange, after being ruled by men in uniforms for most of her life, that suddenly a haggard old woman should be their last salvation. Like every mother she knew, Emma wanted to do right by her children. She fought a short inner struggle, whether she should go against the *Statthalter*'s orders and flee the city. In the end, the thought of her sweet Sophie being raped by a Russian was the image that made her say: "I'm in."

All heads shot around to look at her, but then, one by one, all the women, except for Elvira pronounced the willingness to leave the home of their ancestors, where Germans had lived for centuries side by side with Poles, for an unsure and dangerous future.

Once Elvira had left the room, Agatha began to lay out her plan.

Emma had been up most of the night packing her family's belongings. She sighed, since she'd never imagined it would be so hard to condense their lives into two suitcases. Before the decision to flee, she'd never appreciated how many things she owned. Packing only the most essential warm clothes, blankets, and her jewelry, already filled the suitcases.

With a heavy heart she retrieved the family album to put it back onto the shelf. Cold sweat ran down her spine as she held the heavy book in her hands. This was her life, her history, her memories, her everything... yet it had to stay. The remaining space was better used for food, because nobody knew how long they would be on the road and when they'd be able to buy groceries again.

Opening the family album, she smiled at the first photograph: Herbert and she on their wedding day, looking as if they didn't have a care in the world. Back then, they probably hadn't, at least nothing compared to what she faced now.

The awfulness of her situation hit her like a punch to the

stomach. She was fleeing the only home she knew for an uncertain future in an unknown place, leaving everything and everyone behind, including her beloved husband who had to stay and fight against the Russians.

A tear rolled down her cheek as she ripped the wedding photo from the page, along with three other images: one of her parents; one of Sophie on her first day of school, looking so smart in her dark-blue skirt and starched white blouse, carrying a huge school cone in her hands; and her favorite picture of chubby-faced Jacob on his first birthday. Then she stored them in a thin notebook she used to jot down important things.

Before dawn she slipped into the nursery where Jacob and Sophie were sleeping peacefully and took a minute to observe their angelic faces. During the last few days, she'd been full of energy, preparing for their impending flight, but now she had second thoughts. The trek westward would be fraught with so many risks and dangers. Her heart squeezed painfully as she tried to make sense of her opposing emotions.

Each alternative had their own perils, but was she taking the best course of action for her two beloved children? Would following Elvira's example—staying and hoping the threat of Russian conquest would not be as bad as feared—result in a better outcome?

Deep in her heart she knew they needed to get away from Lodz, but she also feared the strenuous journey. She wondered whether her sweet little Jacob would be able to keep up. Yes, he was a vivacious boy who could run around like a wind-up toy for hours, but he was only four years old.

She sighed. She'd talked this over in private with Luise and her mother-in-law. It was too late to back out now and leave her friends hanging, though. Altogether six women, fifteen children and babies, and two old men would form the trek of refugees heading west.

Each family had paid a fee to participate in the trek and

with this money Agatha had not only bribed police, to make sure they wouldn't be asked for travel permits at the city border, but had also paid a carpenter for two sturdy carts timbered from wooden furniture that would allow each family to put two pieces of luggage on top.

The adults had to take turns dragging the carts. The march was what bothered Emma the most. Two hundred and twenty miles to Frankfurt an der Oder, where apparently it was possible to cross the Oder River into mainland Germany.

Naturally, they hoped to find a running train service westward much earlier than that, but they most likely would be on the road for several days, if not weeks. It was the worst season to go on an endeavor like this, in the middle of January, when the coldest of winter—and this year's was the most frigid winter in ages—was yet to come, but Agatha had insisted that waiting until February or March was not an option if they wanted to have a fighting chance to outrun the Red Army.

When the wind came from the right direction, she could hear the artillery fire and every day it seemed to get louder. Despite being deathly afraid, the noise told her she was doing the right thing here. Whatever awaited them on the journey, it was better than waiting like trapped mice for the Russians to eat them alive. The time had come to get her family to safety. She woke her children, ignoring their drowsiness, and explained to them that they were going to leave their home.

"But I want to stay," Jacob whined, while Sophie shook her head and said, "And what about Papa?"

Emma put on a brave face as she explained. "He'll find us as soon as he can. But right now, Lodz is not safe for us and we need to go someplace else. Just for a while."

"I'm not going anywhere without Affie." Jacob pressed his stuffed animal against his chest.

"Of course, Affie will come with us. He's part of the family, right?"

Jacob was mollified and put on the clothes she'd laid out for him the evening before. Sophie walked over to her pile, and then gave a shriek.

"You don't expect me to wear this?" She gingerly picked up a pair of gray pants and held them under Emma's nose with an aghast expression on her face. "These are boys' clothes. Why can't I wear my own dress?"

"Oh, sweetie, it's going to get very cold and your pretty dresses are not very practical," Emma tried to reason with her, but she could see the stubborn wrinkle forming on her daughter's forehead and she cut any possible resistance at the root. "You'll wear the pants whether you want to or not. Understood?"

Sophie glared at her, but didn't dare to contradict her mother and put on the used clothes, which Emma had exchanged for a silver candleholder the day before. She didn't tell her daughter that wearing boys' clothes would serve another purpose beyond keeping her warm, if the worst came to pass. Indeed, she had toyed with the idea of cutting Sophie's long blonde hair to fully disguise her as a boy. For now though, she'd hide her braids beneath a woolen cap. If—and Emma prayed it would never come to that—the Russians caught up with them, she could still cut her daughter's hair.

After preparing two bowls of porridge, she stored the remaining foodstuff in one of the suitcases and gave a last glance at the house that had been her home since she'd got married almost a decade ago. She and Herbert had shared so many happy moments in here, among them Sophie's and Jacob's births. Her throat constricted. It was a truly frightening prospect to leave Lodz for an unknown place and future. She missed her husband so much. After his last leave, she'd not heard from him again, despite sending letters to his *Feldpost* address religiously every week.

No news is good news, she told herself, finding comfort in the belief that Herbert would find them after the war. She had written to him, letting him know they had to flee, in riddles of course, as not to alert the censors about their illegal intentions, and would let him know their new address as soon as they had settled down somewhere. Just in case, she'd also left a note for him in the house, carefully choosing the hiding place. It couldn't be too obvious, because she fully expected someone else to move in as soon as they were gone for good, and not too well hidden either. She'd finally settled on the ledge in the structure sheltering the firewood against rain, where he stored his axe. She was sure if he came here, he'd want to retrieve the tool whose shaft he'd whittled himself.

"Hurry, children. Luise and Hans will already be waiting for us."

"Hans is coming? How smashing!" Jacob said.

Sophie rolled her eyes, pretending to be a grown-up. It didn't last more than a few seconds until she asked, "Are any of my friends coming, too?"

"Erna and Gretl."

"What about Karin?" Sophie inquired about her best friend.

"I'm sorry, but her mother has decided to stay."

Sophie looked crestfallen.

Emma stroked her daughter's hair. "We can't choose who's going on this trip with us."

"Well at least I'll have someone to keep me company. And Karin can always join us later on, can't she?"

Emma didn't have the heart to disappoint her daughter, so she lied. "Of course she can. Once we have arrived safely, all your friends will probably join us."

Sophie gave her a stern look and put her hands on her hips, adopting a posture Emma herself used frequently when scolding her children. "Mami, you make it sound as if we're going on some fun trip for the weekend, but in reality we're running away from the Russians. I'm not a child anymore, you know!"

"You certainly aren't." Emma had to suppress a smile, since her daughter was such a bright girl, too bright for her own good at times. But she had neither the time nor the inclination to admit that Sophie was right, especially since Jacob was listening. She signaled her daughter with a side-glance that this wasn't a topic for little ones and said, "There's no reason to worry. Can you please put on your coat now?"

About two blocks down they met the heavily pregnant Luise, Agatha, and four-year-old Hans. Together they walked along the main road until they left the town behind. About another half-mile down the road, Emma spotted a group of people waiting.

"That must be our trek," she said.

"I hope. I'm already tired of carrying our suitcase," Luise answered.

Despite her arms hurting from carrying their own two suitcases, Emma offered, "Shall I help you?"

"No, no. I'll manage. Once we reach the group we can put our luggage on the cart."

Emma gave her a reassuring smile, although she was greatly worried. The cart would only take their luggage, which they had to drag behind. Worse, she noticed, how both Hans and Jacob were already getting slower, moaning that they'd had enough. She sent a prayer to heaven and said in a chipper tone, "See that group over there? Who reaches them first, wins."

"What is the prize?" Jacob asked with a much brighter face.

"I'll tell you once we are there."

"That will keep them going for a little while more," Luise whispered. "But what happens a few hours from now?"

"We'll need to take turns carrying them."

Agatha must have listened in to their conversation, because she said in a tone that brooked no argument, "We might have to let the small children take turns riding on the cart. But not before I say so."

Normally Emma wouldn't let the older woman boss her around, but right now she was grateful to have someone taking charge. Since Agatha didn't have small children of her own, she was less prone to let emotions cloud her judgment and would surely have the well-being of everyone in mind.

As they approached the waiting group, Emma marveled at the huge carts and at the same time worried how they would be able to drag them. The two old men accompanying them didn't waste time with formalities, and went to work right away, stowing everyone's belongings on top of the two carts.

Both Luise and Emma handed over the two allotted suitcases per family without a problem, but another woman with three children showed up with a total of six suitcases.

"Only two," one of the men said, starting a lengthy argument with the complaining woman.

Emma elbowed her friend and whispered, "Look at your mother-in-law."

"She's not amused," Luise said as they watched how Agatha walked over to the recalcitrant woman and ordered, "Choose two of the suitcases to ride on the cart, the rest must stay here."

"No I won't. Do you know how many things I had to leave behind?"

"We all had to leave things behind." Agatha put her hands on her hips, demonstrating she wasn't the least bit intimidated.

"By the way, who gave you the right to give orders here?" the woman riled.

"You. When you paid the fee to participate in the trek I organized. So, you either leave the four extra suitcases or you'll have to carry them. What shall it be?"

The other woman grumbled, making no move to do as she was told.

"We're running late. Arnold and Rainer, go ahead and stow

the rest of the luggage and then we're off. It doesn't do to dawdle and risk being held up," Agatha said and the two men continued their work without further delay. As soon as they were finished, the sulking woman quietly handed them her two biggest suitcases and distributed the rest between herself and her children to carry.

The carts that had seemed so huge when empty, suddenly looked frail and tiny, burdened by all the stuff stowed on top. Agatha organized the adults into pairs for dragging. "Luise and Emma you're first. Every turn is one hour, and then we switch. Now let's get going, we need to make the most of the few hours of daylight we have."

Emma took up the rope and pulled, but nothing happened. "Dear goodness, that beast is heavy!"

"Wait, we do it on three." Luise counted, "One. Two. Three." Together they threw themselves forward and after several long seconds of delay, the heavy cart gave a little jump and began gliding across the icy road.

"Puh. Once it's in motion, it's not that hard to pull," Emma said, even as she was heaving like a locomotive.

"Then let's pray to God it never comes to a standstill."

Emma glanced over to her friend and whispered, "Let's pray to God that we stay alive."

6

Jacob kicked at a lump of ice in the road, but it wouldn't move. He kicked harder and then hopped a few steps at the searing pain shooting from his toes all the way up to his knee. "Stupid stone!" he muttered under his breath.

"Jacob, stop dawdling," Sophie chided him from twenty feet in front of him. She had stopped walking and was staring at him with her hands on her hips and an irritated scowl upon her face. It was so annoying, since she had seemed to have taken it upon herself to patronize him whenever Mami was too far away to do it herself.

He caught up to her and declared, "I hate this! I don't know why we had to leave. We've been walking forever."

Sophie grabbed his arm and gave him a little shake. "Stop your whining. We had to leave because it wasn't safe anymore."

"You two, stop talking and keep walking," one of the adults traveling with the caravan ordered them.

Sophie turned, still holding Jacob's arm, and dragged him forward as they hurried to catch up with their mother and Luise, who were keeping Hans between them.

"You're going to get us both into trouble," Sophie accused him, squeezing his elbow for emphasis.

"Ouch!" He yanked his elbow away, grinning with glee when his rash movement caused his sister to stumble. "Stop bossing me around," he ordered her with narrowed eyes.

"I'm the older one and Mami has put me in charge of you."

"Jacob! Sophie! Come here!" their mother yelled, and they ran to her side, keeping pace with her as she didn't bother to stop or even slow down.

"How many times have I told you to stop fighting? We have a long way ahead and we need to conserve our energy."

"My feet hurt," Jacob interrupted her. "And I'm hungry."

Sophie sighed. "Jacob's right. When do we get a break and something to eat?"

Their mother gave them a tired smile. "Soon."

Jacob didn't believe her, because she'd been saying this same thing all day long, so he asked, "When?"

"Soon."

"But how soon?"

"Very soon."

"Can I at least have something to eat?" Jacob tried again.

"No, sweetie, all our food is on the cart and we can't make everyone stop for us to get you some bread. You'll have to wait until we rest. It won't take long."

"Can I at least hold your hand?"

She smiled. "Sure, sweetie."

"I want your hand, too," Sophie said and Jacob couldn't help but stick out his tongue at her, before he rushed to grab his mother's free hand that wasn't pulling the cart.

"Oh, Sophie, you're such a big girl already, you can manage on your own." His mother's voice sounded tired as she answered.

Jacob couldn't enjoy his small victory, because a cough tore through his chest. After walking an eternity beside his mother he got bored and removed his hand from hers.

"Wanna play, Hans?"

Hans nodded and the two of them searched for sticks, which they could use as weapons, when one of the men approached them and said, "Why don't you search for more sticks and give them to me? We'll use them to make a nice fire at lunchtime."

Jacob and Hans went off in the search of sticks and were so hooked, both of them forgot about being tired and hungry. But several hours later, he sidled up to his mother again. "Mami, how long do we have left to go?"

"Not long. We're almost there."

"Will we have another nice house just like ours?"

"I don't know yet, sweetie."

Jacob had a faint suspicion that his mother wasn't telling him everything, but he was too tired to mull over it. Around noon the group finally stopped to rest. The women distributed bread and the men made a fire from the sticks the children had collected.

It smoked and smelled awful, but at least Jacob could sit down and warm his frozen feet. Someone gave him a cup of hot tea. He wrapped his red fingers around it to thaw them and then swallowed the liquid, savoring every swallow that ran down his throat, bringing much needed heat to his insides.

The very moment he'd finished his cup, Hans' grandmother called everyone to get going again. He ignored his hurting feet and the cold in his bones for as long as he could, because every time he slowed down his pace, one of the adults scolded him and told him to keep up and to stop dragging his feet.

"Mami, I can't walk another step," he complained, puffing air and watching how it turned into clouds of smoke.

"Just a little bit longer."

A child sitting on top of the sleigh caught his attention. He squinted his eyes and moments later cried with outrage, "Hans is riding on the cart! I want that too!"

His mother put on her stern look and said, "Hans was very tired."

"I'm tired, too."

"I know, sweetie, but you're my big boy and you can keep going just a little while longer."

"But why can't I go on the cart?"

"The two of you are too heavy, so only one can go at a time. But I promise, your turn is next."

"When?"

"Soon."

"I'm cold."

"I know." She took off her own scarf and wrapped it around his midriff.

"No way I'm wearing a woman's scarf and looking like a girl!"

Strangely, his mother didn't insist and wrapped the scarf around her own neck again. "If you get any colder, you can have it, alright?"

Sometime later, when he barely knew how he was still trudging along with his leaden legs, his mother finally said, "Jacob, sweetie, it's your turn to go on the cart."

With her help, he climbed on top of the suitcases and settled into the dip his friend Hans had just vacated. It was by no means comfortable, but he didn't care. From up here he had a great view over their caravan and he even managed to give a Sophie a gleeful look, because she wasn't allowed to ride the cart. Served her right, since she always insisted on being so much bigger than he was.

"Where's Affie?" he suddenly asked.

His mother rummaged in the back of the cart, before she

handed him his beloved stuffed monkey. He instantly felt soothed.

"Ready?" his mother asked, and he nodded in reply. "Hold tight. I don't want you to fall off."

"I'm not a baby anymore!" He cast her a dark stare. Did she actually expect him to fall off a cart? He leaned back against a big suitcase, enjoying the vantage point, when a sudden yank set the cart into motion and he all but toppled over. Fighting to keep seated he snatched a glance at Sophie's smirking face.

That morning the group of refugees had seemed rather small, but now they were spread out for as far as his eyes could see. He excitedly pointed out all the things along their path, talked to the birds, wishing he could fly along with them and when it began to snow, he tried catching the snowflakes with his hands, watching in awe how the little stars melted on his bare hands.

After a while he got bored. Sure, it was better sitting up here than having to walk, but it was also getting awfully cold. He could barely feel his feet and legs anymore and wanted to stomp to get some warmth into them, but there was no space, and truth be told, he feared he might fall down from the heap of luggage if he moved too much.

So, he waited. After a while his eyes became heavy and he fell asleep. Suddenly, the cart jolted and he barely held onto the rope securing the suitcase beneath him.

"What's happened?"

"Nothing, sweetie, we've arrived," his mother said.

"Is this our new house?" He peered around, except there was nothing to be seen. Just a few trees and dark figures kindling a fire.

"No. But we'll stay here for the night."

His mother couldn't be serious. Where was the house? A bed? A fluffy blanket? Or at least a table and chairs? Had she forgotten about dinner? It was probably best to remind her of the urgency of the situation. "I'm hungry."

"We'll make a soup as soon as we can get the fire burning."

Another, more pressing need made itself known. "I have to pee."

"Over there." She pointed to a low hedge near the road. That in itself was rather strange, because usually she would force him to use the bathroom and sit down properly, so he glanced at her again, just to make sure.

"What are you waiting for? Go over there and pee."

Jacob straightened his stiff limbs and climbed laboriously from the cart, before he hobbled off to the hedge, where a few other boys were already taking care of business. Once he arrived there, the need had taken on a sudden urgency, but his cold fingers were too stiff to open his zipper.

He was near to tears, fearing an accident that would make him the mockery of the other boys, and so decided to tear his pants down without bothering to first open zipper or button. His mother would be furious when she noticed, but he'd rather receive her scorn than being called a pee-pee.

On his return to the group, he moved as near to the fire as the adults would allow, but even after drinking his soup and eating his bread he still felt hungry, cold and tired. Sniffing, he wiped his nose with his hand and coughed several times. This adventure wasn't turning out half as exciting as he'd expected. In fact, it was quite nasty.

"It's time to sleep," Mami said after she collected his soup bowl.

Jacob stared into the pitch-black darkness and goosebumps arose on his skin. "Out here?"

"I'm sorry, but we couldn't find a shelter."

"What if there are monsters?"

"Monsters don't exist," Sophie said, not looking too confident herself.

"How do you know?"

"Because I'm smart."

"You can't be sure." Jacob wanted to believe his sister, but he was so afraid of sleeping in the darkness. "What about ghosts?"

"There are no ghosts. Even if there are, I'll chase them away for you."

"Wolves? Bears? Foxes? Or robbers?"

Finally she seemed to understand the gravity of their situation, because even in the dim light cast by the fire, he noticed her go pale.

"See? I told you it's dangerous out here. Mami, please can we go somewhere else? I don't like it here."

But his mother shook her head. "I'm afraid that's not possible." She took the blanket from their suitcase and laid it out on the ground, before she told them, "You two, cuddle together and I'll tuck you in."

"What about you?" Sophie's voice was but a faint whisper.

"I'll be right with you after cleaning the dishes."

She always has to tidy up, even out here in the middle of nowhere, Jacob thought, pressing Affie tight against his chest. Second later he felt Sophie's arms around him and the reassurance of his big sister's presence caused him to relax and fall asleep. He loved her to pieces despite the way she often annoyed him and right now he wouldn't have traded her for anyone else.

He felt like he'd barely closed his eyes when his mother was shaking him awake. "Jacob, it's time to get moving."

"I'm still tired," he whined, refusing to open his eyes.

"I know, sweetie. But we have to leave, it's morning already."

Jacob coughed once and rolled to a sitting position, opening his eyes to slits. Much to his surprise, the sky was showing a faint blue deep down on the horizon, whereas the other side was still dark. He must have slept longer than just a few minutes.

"How much longer do we have to travel?" he asked.

"A few days."

"Days! I thought we'd arrive at our new house soon."

"Shush, now. Be a big boy and let's get walking or we'll never arrive."

7

POSEN

Irena rubbed her hands across her lower back. The other shift nurse hadn't shown up and she hadn't had the heart to go home and leave the children's ward without supervision. She had one more hour to go until the next day's nurses arrived and she could finally leave to catch some much needed shut-eye.

Conditions in Posen were deteriorating on a daily basis, and with the Red Army rapidly advancing westward, the Nazis had become increasingly jumpy. What was worse, a horrible cold held the city in its grip and, due to war damage to the power plant, not enough electricity was being produced, so even the Catholic Hospital suffered from frequent outages.

Just as she settled on the cot in the nurses' lounge, the groundskeeper knocked on the window. Irena stifled a groan and got back on her hurting feet. "What is it, Mister Nowak?"

"Has Matron arrived?"

"No."

"Anyone?"

"The day shift isn't due to come on for another forty-five minutes." He should know that after working at the hospital for many years.

"So sorry, Nurse Irena, but there's been another power outage."

"I noticed." She had heard the emergency generator spring into action a while ago, which happened a lot these days.

"You better keep these handy." He handed her a box full of assorted candles in all colors, shapes and conditions of being burnt down.

Irena squinted her eyes at him, her tired brain slowly processing what was happening. "But what for? The generator—"

"Won't be working much longer." He cast his eyes downward. "We have diesel for about another hour and I haven't been able to get provisions anywhere in town. The Nazis have restricted any kind of fuel only for critical infrastructure."

"And since our hospital caters only to Polish patients, we are not critical," she said with a desolate sigh. "If only the Red Army would hurry up."

"Can't be long now."

As much as she waited for the liberators, she also knew that every day that passed would mean the death of thousands. "At the current pace, we'll all freeze or starve to death before they arrive."

"Now, now, Nurse Irena. We still have the candles. Will you inform Matron and I'll hand out candles to the other wards?"

"Sure, and thanks for all your work, Mister Nowak."

He gave a curt nod and disappeared into the dark hallway where even the emergency lights had been switched off. Irena lit a candle and did the same with the lights in her ward. The remaining power had to be saved up to enable life-saving operations.

Returning to the cot, she lay down, listening to the coughing, sneezing and whining in the children's ward, ready to get up whenever something unusual happened. Her eyes closed and she fell into a light doze. Images of the hordes of refugees pouring into the city on their trek westward appearing in her dreams. But she found she couldn't commiserate with the women and children leaving their homes for what they hoped would be a better future in central Germany. Because she truly and thoroughly hated the Nazis, military and civilians alike, and couldn't wait to see the last of them. It wasn't only her own tragic fate that had turned her bitter, but also the casual racism of civilians who considered the Polish people inferior to them.

Soon after the Wehrmacht marched into Poland, they'd closed all secondary schools for Poles, claiming that a people of servants didn't need more education than basic reading, writing and calculation.

As if that wasn't enough, they'd forced them out of any positions with decision power, given them lesser ration cards, and brutally persecuted anyone who uttered a critical word against their new masters. The Pawiak prison in Poland's capital Warsaw was just one infamous example of the atrocities committed against the Polish people.

What had given these once high-and-mighty people the right to come into her city, putting an additional strain onto the resources that didn't even suffice for the current population? The children's ward was filled to the brim and they already had to send the less severe cases home.

The sound of a horrible coughing fit broke through her doze and she perked up her ears, but then the ward fell silent again, save for the usual, mumbling, sniffing and snoring. Irena was worried. The children weren't having just the usual winter ailments. This was something more severe. Some kind of respiratory illness that was sweeping through the city, attacking the young, the old, the undernourished. Small children seemed especially vulnerable and with the shortages of medicine, there was only so much they could do.

Since the day shift nurses could arrive any moment now,

she got up to finish her report on the night's occurrences, so she could finally go home, crawl under her eiderdown and sleep for twelve hours straight.

She had barely started, when she heard footsteps coming. Her initial smile quickly turned into a grimace of horror when the steps approached—much too loud for her fellow nurses— and a pair of SS soldiers barged into the room, filling the entryway with their menacing presence.

It took Irena every ounce of courage to sit still and ask, "May I help you gentlemen find something?"

One of the soldiers pushed forward and asked in broken Polish, "All your patients Polish?"

"Yes, your administration designated this hospital to cater only for the local population."

"Release them. We need the space."

"What? Why? No, these children are sick. They need medicine and..." Irena stopped talking when the other soldier left the nurse's room and walked toward the nearest bed, where he grabbed the sleeping child, a boy around the age of ten, by the shoulders and tossed him to the floor.

Protectiveness for her charges overtook her fear and she rushed to the child's aid. "Stop! What are you doing?"

The other soldier stepped directly into her path, pulling his revolver from his side holster and leveling it at her head. "These children need to go. Now."

Turned into a statue, Irena couldn't move. Her only reaction was a slight nod. It took an eternity, staring into the muzzle before she found her voice. "Please, don't hurt them, I'll do it."

"Right away." He scrutinized her from head to toe and added in a slightly kinder tone, "Get them dressed and into the reception hall where their parents can fetch them. I want this ward cleared out, cleaned and ready for German patients in thirty minutes."

Fear snuck up her spine, as the memories of her abuse at the hands of other SS soldiers came rushing back, nevertheless somehow she managed to hold her ground and say, "I'll do as you wish, but just please don't hurt them. Within the next ten minutes, the day shift nurses and Matron will arrive to help with your orders."

"Good." The two men left, no doubt intent on repeating the same threats in the other wards of the hospital.

Suddenly, it all made horrible sense. The Nazis needed the hospital beds for their own people and weren't hesitating even for a second as they threw out all the Polish patients, who they considered inferior anyway. Once more she silently prayed for the Red Army to hurry up and liberate them.

She walked to the row with older children and said, "I'm so sorry, but we have to evacuate. Your parents are informed and will be picking you up from the entry hall downstairs. Who is able to get up without help?"

About a dozen children raised their hands.

"Put on your shoes and coats. Once you're finished you sit upright on your cot so I know who is ready to leave. Understood?"

The children nodded.

One girl asked, "What will happen if I can't get up?"

Irena gave her a warm smile. "I'll organize someone to help you. Don't worry, everything is under control." She shuddered at the lie, because she had nothing under control and was probably as frightened as the children were, if not more. "Your parents will soon be here, don't you worry."

"Where are my shoes?" a boy who'd been rushed in last night, asked.

"Stored beneath your bed, together with anything else you brought with you. And now hurry up, we don't have much time." Irena clapped her hands and turned to walk to the next row of children, when she all but bumped into Matron.

"What on earth are you doing, Nurse Irena?"

"Thank God, you're here, Matron." Irena wanted to weep with relief, since Matron was so much better at organizing an evacuation than she was.

"I just arrived and what do I find? The entire ward in uproar and you telling the children to get dressed?"

"I'm so sorry, Matron." Irena was near tears from exhaustion and worry. "Just ten minutes ago, two SS men came and ordered me to expel every single patient from the hospital, because they need the beds for Germans."

Matron's eyes shot furious glances and she said, "You immediately stop doing this foolish thing. They can't do that, we're a hospital. Let me talk to them."

Irena slumped on the nearest cot, a pang of guilt tugging at her heart. Matron was right and she had overreacted. The Nazis could not simply come here and evacuate a hospital. She had scared the children to death without reason. But only five minutes later, Matron returned with her lips pressed into a thin line, the nurses of the day shift walking a few steps behind.

"We'll evacuate. Hurry up. They say that everyone who's left in the ward in"—she gazed at the big clock hanging on the wall—"twenty-one minutes will be shot." After giving instructions to the nurses which row of beds to take care of, she turned toward Irena and asked, "I take it you stayed here overnight?"

"Yes, Matron. Natalya didn't arrive in the evening, so I took over for her."

"That's very laudable. Unfortunately I can't send you home just now, because we need every helping hand to get the children out of the ward and everything cleaned up."

Too tired to protest, Irena simply nodded and dashed off to the area Matron assigned her. She bundled the babies into their coats or blankets, stuck the card with their names and birthdates onto them and carried the first two down into the reception area next to the entrance door.

The area was filling quickly with patients from other wards.

In her despair she simply pressed each baby into the arms of a comparatively well-looking female patient. "Here, make sure it gets delivered to the parents. I'm off to fetch more."

The news had evidently spread like wildfire in town and by the fifth trip she made downstairs, a crowd of people waited on the front steps, wanting to take their loved ones home. Matron and several helpers did their best to organize the crowds and deliver the patients to their families.

After they'd whisked out the last little patient from the children's ward, Matron told Irena, "You can leave now and get some sleep. I'll send a messenger for you if I need you sooner, but otherwise I still expect you to return in the evening."

"Yes, Matron."

As Irena walked away from the hospital, barely able to keep her eyes open, she clenched her fists in the folds of her gown. This time as she passed the cathedral, she prayed for the Nazis to receive their just punishment, and in an act of utter defiance of her Catholic faith, she added, "For every child that has to die because of their heartless actions today, I wish for a hundred SS men to be brutally slaughtered."

8

HEADING WEST FROM LODZ

Her bones feeling like frozen ice, Emma snuggled closer to her children. She and Agatha were lying on the outside of their little group, cuddling Luise and the three children between them for added warmth.

They had pooled their clothing and blankets to protect them as best they could, using one blanket as a mattress and the other one as a cover in addition to wearing all their clothes one over another.

She reached out her hand and found Sophie soundly asleep, but little Jacob's forehead was radiating heat, while he constantly moaned and coughed. If they didn't reach Posen soon, she feared for the worst. Her little boy simply couldn't hold out much longer. While riding on top of the sleigh gave his legs a rest, he also complained that it was so much colder up there.

Sophie stirred and whispered, "Mami? Is Jacob very sick?"

"It's just a cold, sweetie, nothing rest and a warm bed won't cure." She brushed her hand across Sophie's cheek. Her fearless, brave daughter had kept up with the pace of the adults, day in day out, without much complaining.

"Will he die?"

Tears sprung to Emma's eyes and she had difficulty keeping her voice steady as she answered, "No Sophie, he's a tough little guy. As soon as we're in Posen we'll get him some medicine and he'll be just fine." *If we ever get to Posen. And if we can find shelter and food.*

"You know, Mami, he annoys me a lot, but I don't want him to die, ever."

Emma had to smile at the admission. Her children often fought like cat and dog, but when it counted, they stuck together like bosom buddies. "Don't worry, sweetie. Jacob will annoy you for years to come."

"I love you, Mami," Sophie said in a sudden outburst of emotion and for a split second Emma had an inkling of the horrible sorrow her daughter must feel.

"I love you too. We'll get through this together."

Emma lay awake for a long time, pondering whether taking her children on this trek from hell had actually been the best solution. Should they have stayed at home and waited for the Red Army to arrive in the hope things wouldn't get as bad as everyone believed?

She bit her lips, fighting against the panic rising inside her. Everything she had done was for the well-being of her children. Sure, she was afraid of being raped herself, but just the image of one of the soldiers bending over her innocent little daughter made her gag. No, whatever hardships they had to endure, anything was better than falling into the Russians' hands.

As dawn lit up the sky, the people in the caravan woke and began moving about. Ten days into their journey, they were running low on everything: food, strength, warmth and even courage. Emma got up to light a fire, so they would at least be able to melt snow and make hot water to drink.

Agatha sidled up to her. The old woman was astonishingly

tough, making her the only person in the caravan who looked the same as she had prior to the journey. But maybe this was only because so many wrinkles had been etched into her face over the years that there was no place for more.

"I need to talk to you," she said and took Emma aside. Gazing into her haggard face made Emma squirm.

"Sure. What's on your mind?"

Agatha cut right to the chase. "Luise is about to have her baby."

"What now? That's not possible. She has two months left to go." Emma felt a searing pain cut through her chest. If the baby came now, it would not survive. Images of both Sophie and Jacob as newborns came to her mind, and for several seconds she felt as if she were drowning, fighting desperately for air, since she couldn't bear to contemplate her friend losing a child.

"I'm afraid it's going to be a matter of days, a week at most." Agatha furrowed her brows. "We have to consider the possibility that neither she nor the baby will survive the birth."

"Dear God..." Emma tore her eyes open in shock. "What can we do?"

Agatha didn't bat an eyelid. "There's nothing we can do, except to hope that we reach Posen and find a shelter to stay in. Our family might have to abandon the trek, though."

Emma gasped. How could Agatha be so... so... devoid of emotion over this? Had she forgotten how it was to be a mother?

"You're Luise's best friend, and therefore I wanted to ask you whether you'd be willing to stay with us too, until the baby is born."

"Of course I will."

"Don't take this decision lightly, because after everything we've heard, it might not be pretty."

That must have been the understatement of the year, because just the day before they'd been outpaced by a caravan of horse-drawn carriages headed to Posen. They'd talked a few minutes and had received frightening news.

Lodz had now been captured by the Red Army just a few days prior, and apparently the Poles—under the benevolent eyes of the Russians—were having a feast hunting down their former German masters. Nothing was too cruel and depraved to satiate their lust for revenge. They didn't even stop at violating small children.

"I will stay with you, whatever happens," Emma assured the other woman.

Agatha squinted her eyes, before she continued. "I'm too old or I'd do it myself, but there's one more thing I have to ask you."

Fear that was icier than the cold wind chilled Emma's soul. "Anything."

"If Luise doesn't make it, will you take care of Hans and raise him as your own?"

"Me? But why?"

"Knowing Hans is in good hands will help me to keep a clear mind." Agatha still showed no sign of emotion, but must dearly love her grandson or she wouldn't see the need to make arrangements for his future. Hoping she'd never have to make good on her promise, Emma said, "Of course I'll take him in, but it won't come to that. Luise is strong and she will survive."

A bloodcurdling scream cut through the air and made Emma jump. "What's happened?"

"No-no-no-no." The scream morphed into a hopeless whimper.

Emma rushed over to where the sound came from and found Gretl's mother bent over her child. One glimpse into the girl's bluish-white face was enough to grasp the harsh reality. Gretl's weakened body had literally frozen to the ground during the night.

A shudder ran down Emma's spine, since Gretl was the same age as Sophie. She'd been a healthy thing until she'd sprained her ankle during the first days of their journey and from then on her condition had been on a downward spiral, beginning with a cough, followed by a fever... A more violent shudder racked Emma's body as she thought, *just like my little darling*. Jacob's cough had been getting worse, and then the fever... She bit back a sob, since there was no use in crying. For that, she'd have enough time once they arrived in safety, but right now she had to stay strong for her children. Fighting her despair, she swore to herself to make sure they survived this ordeal, even if it was the last thing she did in this life.

Agatha caught up with her and, practical as always, didn't waste time taking the issue in her hands. "There's nothing we can do for the girl. Get her undressed and we'll leave her here covered with some snow."

Gretl's mother jumped up, ready to scratch out Agatha's eyes as she accused her, "How can you be so cruel? You... you... awful witch!"

Emma involuntarily held her breath, fearing an outburst after the insult. Agatha, though, merely raised an eyebrow and said with the same commanding tone she always used, "Your daughter is dead. We can't take her with us, and we can't dig up the ice for a proper grave."

"But why would you deny the child a last act of decency and expose her body?" another woman chimed in.

"For all that's holy! Your religion must have ruined your brains. Our job is to protect the living, not the dead. Her clothes could save another child from freezing to death tonight. And now, do as I say, because we must be on the road in half an hour, if we ever want to reach Posen."

The scolding seemed to have the desired effect, because nobody uttered another word and went to do Agatha's bidding in silence. Emma understood the reasoning behind her words, nevertheless she loathed the old woman for her harshness. What if the dead girl had been Sophie? Would she be able to undress her darling and dump her in a ditch?

She couldn't bear to think about that and busied herself collecting clean snow to melt over the fire, before she distributed hot water to the children gathering around her.

Neither Jacob nor Hans had come around and she asked Sophie, "Be a good girl, and bring this to your brother and Hans. And see to it that they drink every last drop."

"Yes, Mami." Sophie looked down at her hands, holding the two cups, then up again at her mother, and whispered, "No bread?"

Emma shook her head. She couldn't bring herself to voice an answer, since she'd distributed the last of their provisions the night before. If they couldn't buy food soon, they'd all starve in this godawful Polish winter.

Since leaving Lodz, nothing had worked out the way it had been planned. They hadn't found shelters for the night, hadn't been able to stock up on food and to add insult to injury they'd been forced to deviate from their route twice already, because either the road was blocked or there was fighting ahead.

"We should have stayed at home," Sophie murmured, close to tears.

"No we shouldn't." She wouldn't tell her daughter all the things she'd heard, although after talking to the other trek the day before she had come to the conclusion, that whatever horror awaited them on this journey, nothing would come close to the treatment they would have received in their hometown.

"It's time to leave," Agatha announced. The caravan set into motion again, all of them hoping to reach a place of safety in what was left of Germany—alive.

Emma fell in step beside Sophie and Luise, to pull the cart with Hans and Jacob atop.

"We should be reaching Posen by nightfall," she said.

"I hope we'll find shelter there." Luise was but a shadow of herself and Emma suddenly feared that Agatha might be right and that her friend's life might be in danger. She really shouldn't be out and walking all day in her condition.

"Let me help." Sophie must have had the same idea, because she put her hand on the rope and released Luise from her dragging duty. Both boys were in such a bad shape, they couldn't walk on their own and had to ride on the cart all day, placing an extra burden on those who pulled it.

Jacob's spasmodic coughing cut through the air and once again gripped her heart with fear. Her sweet little boy was sick, cold and hungry. And worst of all, she couldn't remedy any of this. Not until they reached Posen, a city that was supposedly still in German hands, where they might find shelter, at least for one night.

"Are you sure he won't die?" Sophie suddenly asked.

Tears sprung to Emma's eyes and she had difficulties keeping her voice steady as she answered, "Of course, Sophie, he'll pull through. Like I said, it's just a cold."

"You said the same about Gretl." Sophie's lip was quivering treacherously. She always tried to appear a grown-up, but at the end of the day, she was just a child.

"Your brother is a fighter." Emma glanced back to Gretl's mother who was walking a few yards behind them, and recoiled at the utter desolation of her expression. Her face was etched in grief and she shook her head with every step, murmuring unintelligible words.

"Poor woman," Luise said. "I couldn't imagine, if..." She didn't finish her sentence, because she believed it was a bad omen to speak about bad events before they happened.

Emma involuntarily wrapped herself tighter into her coat and looked at Jacob, who lay on the cart. His pale forehead contrasted awfully with his bright red cheeks. Despite cuddling against Hans, both wrapped in whatever clothing they'd carried with them, he was shivering. Every so often his bone-chilling coughing cut through the frigid air, and each time her heart broke a little more.

9

"They're sending four more children up," one of the nurses called out to Irena, who was working to get the fever of a little girl to break, but so far, nothing had made a difference. The child's chest rattled with each labored breath she fought to take. If she didn't start responding to the medication soon, there would be yet another empty bed in the ward.

She talked to her patient in Polish, but the anxious girl didn't understand her. For a moment she pondered whether to ask one of the SS soldiers guarding the entrance to translate, but dropped the idea almost immediately, because the thought made the hairs on her neck rise.

Smiling, she stroked the girl's head and put a cold cloth around her calf. Maybe that would get the fever down. If only she could tell the girl what she was doing, and reassure her, whisper some words of comfort into her ear.

"Shush, everything will be fine," she said in a soothing tone.

"*Wo ist meine Mama?*" the girl demanded to know in a whining tone.

Even without speaking German, Irena knew what *Mama* meant, and she answered, "Your Mama is waiting outside. She couldn't come in, because the hospital is so full, but she loves you very much."

With watery eyes, the girl cried once more, *"Wo ist meine Mama?"*

"Shush, you need to rest."

The scream of another patient at the other side of the ward sent Irena rushing over, but the guilt of not being able to comfort the little girl stayed with her. Out of spite, she had always refused to learn German; now she regretted her stubbornness. It turned out that her silent resistance didn't hurt those she wanted to punish, just her innocent patients.

Since the SS had taken over the hospital a week earlier, the beds had filled up with German patients. Despite her hate for the Nazi soldiers, Irena continued to work as meticulously as always. It wasn't the children's fault. They were innocent and depended on her care.

More and more German refugees from out of town were showing up in front of the hospitals and the scenes taking place were heartbreaking. Desperate mothers, begging the SS men to take in their babies, because it was their only chance of survival.

Usually the SS furtively glanced at the mother's papers and if she was German, they called a nurse to take the baby from her, since visitors weren't allowed in the hospital anymore, due to the overflow of patients.

Some parents returned home, but it seemed the majority didn't have a home to return to, so stayed in hastily erected refugee tents in the nearby park. Even though Irena had wished for God to unleash eternal evil on the Germans, seeing the scenes of bawling mothers desperately holding their children up to get into the hospital, tugged at her heartstrings.

Not for the mothers so much, as for the innocent children caught up in this evil war.

The door to the ward opened and a young auxiliary nurse came inside with one toddler on each arm. Irena met her in the middle of the room with a shake of her head. "The babies are in the room down the hall."

"It's completely full, Irena. That's why they sent me here."

"How can that be?" she asked, because yesterday there had only been half a dozen children in that room.

"Things have gotten so much worse. The Red Army is closing in and those Germans are fleeing for their lives."

"Without their children?" Irena asked in disbelief.

"It seems they don't have any food to feed them or ways to keep them warm. So they dump them outside on the steps and leave, perhaps in the hope we'll take them in, nurse them back to health and they can return for them in spring. Some have a note with their name and birthdates, but others don't even have that."

"Oh dear God." Irena couldn't fathom how any mother would just leave her child. Although, when it was the only chance at survival, perhaps? She refused to let her thoughts go down that road. If she'd had a child, she'd have never let it go.

"Where shall I put them?" the auxiliary nurse asked.

Irena looked around and then pointed to the far corner. "There. You'll have to put the two of them into one bed." She shook her head and murmured, "When is this going to end?"

"I don't know. The adult floors are filling up too. I overheard one of the doctors mention influenza."

"That's all we need! As if the war isn't enough to deal with." Influenza was a death strike to many thousands each winter. It was highly contagious and in the crowded refugee shelters it would run rampant among the weak and undernourished children.

Irena spent the rest of her shift moving from one bed to another. The cooks brought up bread and some sort of broth, but most of the children were too weak to eat, and had to be fed. Fevers spiked. Children threw up. Babies cried and needed comforting.

Once she'd made her rounds and attended to the last child, it all started again. To make matters worse, her fellow nurse hadn't shown up again that morning, so Irena was on her own with the never-ending work. When her shift finally ended, she was drained, physically, mentally and emotionally.

"You can't imagine what's happening outside," the night nurse coming to relieve her said.

Irena shook her head, indicating she couldn't bear to hear more sordid details about the situation in the city. Instead, she proceeded to give her colleague detailed instructions about each one of their current patients, hoping she'd find all of them alive when she returned in the morning.

"Wishing you a calm night," she said and put on her coat, hat and gloves.

"I doubt it. You get some sleep, tomorrow will only be worse."

Irena walked down the long hallway, filled up with coughing, sneezing and wheezing patients waiting on chairs or even on the cold stone floor. Extra beds obstructed her way, so she had to weave through the onslaught of patients, doctors and nurses coming her way.

She barely avoided the collision with a rolling bed, when a bleeding soldier was hurried to the operations room. For a second, she stared with unconcealed hate at his black SS-uniform with the skull on the collar, before she jumped aside. She certainly didn't envy the doctors and nurses who worked in the adult wards, forced to attend to their very oppressors. At least her patients didn't have blood on their hands.

As soon as she stepped through the hospital doors, a gush of cold wind reached her. She took a deep breath to dispel the stench of sickness from her lungs. Digging her hands deeper into the pockets of her coat, she made her way through the front yard, avoiding the gazes of the masses beleaguering the hospital, trying to get their sick relatives inside.

She recognized a neighbor and his wife, but there was nothing she could do, since the SS had made it very clear that only German patients were to be allowed inside. So she hunched her shoulders forward, her eyes on the frozen ground in the hopes nobody would recognize her.

As soon as she left the yard behind, she walked down the main street toward the part of town where she lived. Several minutes later, she passed by the park with the tents for refugees. She hadn't been prepared to see the immeasurable suffering: a mother carrying her baby in her arms, its lips a deep blue against the pale skin, and no spark of life in the open eyes. Crying, sobbing, and hollow-looking women wherever she looked, along with children that seemed walking corpses, nevertheless were not poorly enough to be admitted to the hospital.

She increased her pace, intent on getting away from this grim place as fast as she could, but the image of the desperate mother holding her frozen baby followed her all the way home. Irena could imagine how that woman must feel, because she'd felt similar ever since she lost her own sweet child. The dormant grief reared up, knocked the breath out of her lungs with its horrible pain and made her eyes water.

10

Jacob didn't understand. He'd begged his mother to let him ride on the cart, because his legs had hurt so much. But up here he felt even more exhausted and all he wanted to do was to sleep. Mami had wrapped him tightly in all kinds of girls' clothing, and he'd been too weak to protest. Not even when she'd put her red scarf around him and Hans, had he been able to croak out a single word.

With chattering teeth he moved his toes and fingers to keep them from getting numb, while at the same time he was sweating so much, his undershirt was completely soaked. Even Affie had become sick, his moist fur smelling foul.

Every so often his mother unwrapped him and stuffed newspaper beneath his shirt to soak up the sweat. He both loathed and yearned for these moments, because it would mean that for some time he'd be dry, but on the other hand, it always brought an unwelcome gust of icy air.

"Mami, how long until we arrive?"

"It'll be soon now, my darling. Just hang on, will you?"

He nodded, too tired to ask further questions. Leaning to his side, where Hans was sleeping, he gasped in shock.

His best friend looked awful: the face greenish-white with the exception of the red dots on his cheeks. A fear colder than the icy wind took hold of him as he considered that Hans might be dead. With some effort he elbowed him, but nothing happened.

"Mami! Hans is dead!" he screamed and all but toppled from the cart when it came to an abrupt standstill.

Luise came racing and picked up her son with the most aghast face Jacob had ever seen in his life. Tears streamed down her face, as she murmured incoherent words, pressing Hans' body against hers, until he drowsily protested.

"You're not dead. You're alive. My Hans, my darling Hans." Several seconds later she turned around and glared at Jacob. "What did you say that for? Did you think that was funny?" She kept scolding him, not even taking a breath to give him the opportunity to answer.

Jacob thought she was making too much of a fuss. So what? He'd been wrong. Shouldn't she be happy that Hans was still alive, instead of shouting like a madwoman?

Finally Luise stopped berating him and put Hans back on the cart. Jacob instantly felt better, when Hans grinned at him, but the next moment, Luise showed up beside Jacob.

"Whatever did you make such a cruel joke for?"

"It wasn't a joke!"

She seemed to unravel directly in front of him and before he knew what was happening, she slapped him hard on the face.

"Ouch!"

"That'll teach you to misbehave," Luise said and he feared she'd slap him again, but thankfully Hans' grandma stepped between the two of them and said, "Enough of that. I'm sure Jacob didn't do this on purpose. Now did you?"

He'd always been afraid of the strict old woman and stammered, "No... yes... I mean... I thought... he *was* dead... I elbowed him, but he wouldn't move."

"You did nothing wrong," Agatha said in the kindest voice he'd ever heard from her and then turned toward Hans' mother, who'd completely lost it. She was sobbing frenetically, while she sunk onto the frozen ground in front of his eyes.

Her utter discomposure left him feeling bereft, because if the adults didn't have control over the situation, what chances did they have of ever reaching a safe place? Yet, he couldn't avert his eyes from the spectacle unfolding in front of him: a hysterically bawling woman, who kept calling out "My darling Hans", until she howled a high-pitched scream that pierced his marrow and bone. "Oh God! My baby!"

Her screaming alerted his mother and Sophie, who'd walked ahead, probably to collect sticks, and seconds later they appeared next to them. Jacob was too exhausted from the bedlam to follow what happened. The last thing he saw was his mother's worried face as she and Hans' grandma helped Luise to get up. His eyes closed, even as he listened to Luise's wallows and Agatha's soothing words.

He woke, because the cart jerked vicariously, holding on for dear life, as the entire load with him atop careened. Tearing his eyes open, he yelped for help.

His mother, who was pulling the cart side-by-side with Sophie, turned her head and said, "Hold on, Jacob, it'll be a rough ride. We paused quite a while, and now we'll have to double the pace to catch up with the rest of the group."

Jacob saw neither Luise nor Agatha around, and fear grabbed his heart. Glancing over to his side, he noticed with relief that Hans was still tugged in tightly with him.

"Why is he allowed to lie all day on the cart while the rest of us have to pull him?" Sophie asked.

"Sophie!" their mother called out. "Your brother is sick."

"I'm sick too..." She gave some phony coughs. "I want to ride on the cart like him."

"Please, Sophie, you're my big girl, you can do this. Jacob is still little."

"He's only little when it suits him. And you... you love him more than me..."

That was news to Jacob, since he'd always suspected Sophie was his mother's favorite child.

"That's not true, I love you both the same."

Sophie, though, wasn't appeased easily. "He's the reason we're lagging behind. Because of him we'll never arrive. I hate him! I wish we'd left him at home!"

"Sophie, please," Mami said, but his sister let go of the rope and stormed off. It was the first time he'd seen his mild-mannered sister quite so upset and her words cut deep into his soul. It *was* all his fault. Without having to drag him along, everyone in the group would already be somewhere safe. Big, fat tears rolled down his cheeks.

"Sweetie. That's not true. Sophie is just on edge because of how tough this journey is. We all are." His mother tried to console him, but he didn't believe a single word she said. When he didn't reply she looked ahead again, pulling the cart all on her own. If only he could get down and help.

Misery and guilt washed over him. Sophie was right. They'd be so much better off without him. He stared into the whitish-gray sky and let the tears fall.

Over the course of the day he carefully observed how his mother, Luise, Agatha and sometimes even Sophie were taking turns pulling the cart and it became increasingly clear to him, that he was the cause of all their hardships.

Mami often changed the hand on the rope, making a pained face and rubbing her back or massaging her shoulder. When Sophie took the rope, she was heaving like a locomotive after just a few minutes.

Jacob so wished he was the older one and could help, but he could barely manage to breathe through his sniffing nose and the violent coughing spells that became ever more frequent, leaving him wheezing and feeling dizzy.

At noon the entire group stopped to rest for a while and distribute the only provision they had left: hot water melted from snow. They had joined with another trek, at least that's what he guessed, because half of the people milling about, he'd never seen before.

"Drink this." Mami held out his cup for him, but he was too weak to hold it in his hands and she had to do it for him. "My poor darling. We'll arrive in Posen before nightfall and there we'll find you some medicine and food."

"I'm not hungry."

"That's just the fever. As soon as the doctor sees you, you'll be hungry, again." She smiled at him and stroked his hair, but he noticed the twinge of sadness in her expression. And it was all his fault. If only he was bigger, stronger, healthier... They should never have left their home... Or at least they should have left him there. He wasn't going to make it anyway. So what difference would it have made?

He closed his eyes again, not wanting anyone to see his tears.

"Please God. Let me die, so Mami and Sophie can travel faster."

Emma's heart hurt with grief as she watched her travel companions from the group they recently joined put an old lady to her last rest in a ditch. The ground was frozen solid and all attempts to dig a grave had been useless, so they covered her with snow and branches from nearby bushes.

She had to tear her eyes away from the scene, if she wanted to hang on to her sanity. Luise still hadn't recovered from her hysterical breakdown, behaving like a ghoul, clamoring about Hans and the baby she was about to have. Agatha had her hands full just keeping her in line, on top of her responsibilities as leader of the trek. Although they had joined with another, bigger group, she was still in charge of their subgroup.

No, Agatha couldn't afford the luxury of being affected by her emotions. She had to keep a clear mind to ensure the survival of the remaining twenty people who'd left Lodz almost two weeks ago. They'd already lost three.

Everyone hoped that one day, when the war was over, the dead could be given a proper burial, although Emma feared that might be wishful thinking. The bodies of the unfortunate ones who died fleeing from the Red Army would soon be forgotten to

all but their loved ones who remained—if there even were any
survivors. There would be no funeral processions. No graves to
mark. Nothing.

Sophie sidled up to her and put her hand in Emma's.
"What's gonna happen in spring?"

"In spring?" It seemed so far away. "By then we'll be with
Agatha's cousin."

"No, I mean, with her." Sophie pointed at the makeshift
grave, where the daughter of the deceased was saying a prayer.
"Won't she melt?"

"She's dead, my darling."

"I know. But won't everything thaw and she'll peek out from
the ground like a scarecrow frightening the passersby to death?"

Emma looked at Sophie and would have laughed if the situation weren't so sad. "I hope not." Deep in her heart though she
knew that by springtime this old lady wouldn't be the only
corpse littering the landscape and most probably by then people
would have gotten so used to the sight that they wouldn't find it
frightful in the least. "We should get moving again. Agatha said
if we keep our pace we'll reach Posen tonight. They say it is still
in German hands and the SS are doing their best to feed and
house all the refugees coming through."

"So we can get Jacob to a hospital?"

"I hope so. I'm worried about him. He's deteriorated so
much today, while Hans seems to be on the mend." More and
more Emma found herself talking to Sophie as if she were an
adult. Her daughter had matured so much during the past
weeks on this horrible trek. It was shameful to admit, but a
seven-year-old had become her most trusted companion, the
one person she shared many of her worries with.

Emma knew she shouldn't put this burden on Sophie, but
truth be told, she herself was teetering on the brink of collapse
and had no one else to confide in. Certainly not distressed Luise
who had withdrawn into herself, worrying for her unborn child,

and not Agatha who had worse troubles to attend to. Gretl's mother was a wreck since the death of her daughter, leaning heavily on Erna's mother. The two men in their trek constantly strategized with the new group about where the current fighting was and if this way was better than the other one.

Sophie pressed her hand, as if she'd been reading her thoughts. "Don't worry, Mami. We're doing the right thing and everything will be just fine once we arrive in Posen."

Tears sprung to Emma's eyes at the kind words her daughter uttered, but even more at her own failure of being a good mother. It should be her consoling Sophie and not the other way round. "You are right. We should never give up hope."

After the rest, Emma took up the rope again, and Sophie came to her aid. Currently most of the pulling was done by her, because Luise was too weak to help. Agatha did the best she could, but the old woman was frail and while she never complained, Emma often witnessed how she furtively rubbed her hips and knees whenever she felt unobserved.

She remembered previous winters with Sophie and Jacob, when they'd go out with a sleigh, swishing down the nearby hill and trudging up again. If she survived this horrid journey she never again wanted to use a sleigh or handcart in her life.

After another hour, Jacob coughed violently and she turned around to look back. He was scrambling to get upright and between coughing fits, whimpered, "Mami! Mami! I can't breathe!"

"Can you pull alone for a moment?" she asked Sophie. Starting the cart was the hardest part, so she preferred to keep it moving, however slow that might be.

Sophie nodded with exhaustion in her gaze, keeping the cart moving, while Emma dropped back to walk beside Jacob. "You shouldn't get so upset, sweetie. Lie back, again." Her hand felt for his forehead that was glowing with fever despite the frigid cold.

"But... how...?" He struggled to get enough oxygen into his lungs.

"Easy, Jacob. Take a slow breath." She pushed her hand beneath the blanket to reach for his and chills ran down her spine, because it was so cold. Rubbing his fingers, she murmured soothing words of comfort, but he wouldn't calm down.

"Mami..."

"I'm right here, sweetie. Tonight we'll arrive in Posen and we'll get you some medicine. I promise."

"Mami..." He kept struggling and Emma sensed there was something other than his sickness that bothered him. "Mami..."

"Yes, my darling?"

"How... how will Papi... find us?"

She brushed a frozen strand of hair off his forehead and pulled his hat down lower over his ears. "Don't you worry about that right now. Your papa is very smart, and he'll come looking for us just as soon as he can. But you have to get well first. Can you do that for me? Take a nap now and by the time you wake up, we'll have arrived in Posen. There we'll sleep in a nice, warm house and get as much food as we want."

His eyes lit up at her description of what awaited them and she hoped she wouldn't disappoint him. But she'd do anything to keep his spirits up, so he would continue to fight against that awful cough.

When dusk settled over the country, they finally saw the silhouette of Posen appear on the horizon. On the outskirts of the city, a control post manned by SS stopped their group.

"Destination?"

"Posen," said Rainer, one of the two men traveling with their group.

"You hiding any Wehrmacht stragglers?"

Rainer flinched. "No, *mein Herr*, only women and children

apart from Arnold and myself." He waved at Arnold to step forward.

The SS soldier peered at the men, before he nodded, obviously deeming both of them much too old to be a deserting Wehrmacht soldier.

"Town of origin?"

"Lodz."

For a split second empathy crossed the soldier's face. "Papers?"

For each family, one person stepped forward and presented their papers. After scrutinizing them, the soldier handed them back. "Can't be careful enough. We're not allowed to take in people deserting their hometowns, but since Lodz is temporarily in the hands of the Soviets, civilians can take shelter with us meanwhile."

Emma bit her lip so as not to give him a snide remark. Were there really people delusional enough to believe this was a temporary setback and soon enough the Wehrmacht would push the Russians back to where they came from? Even many months ago, her husband Herbert had confessed—in the safety of their bedroom—his fears of Germany losing this war.

His whispered warnings to her, to get herself and the children to safety if the Red Army approached had ultimately been what tipped the balance in Emma's decision. Joining the caravan with Agatha and the others had seemed the safer option, despite her fear of the unknown. Once things settled down after the war, she'd find a way to let Herbert know where she was.

"Follow the main street until you get to the city park. There's a temporary reception office from the local authorities. Once you register with them, you'll be assigned a place in one of the tents and receive coupons for the field kitchen."

A tent? Emma was dismayed since she'd hoped for an actual

house where Jacob could have a warm bed to recover from his awful cough.

"Please, my son..." she said, but the SS man waved her onward.

"Go and register. They'll answer all your questions."

It took less than ten minutes to arrive at the registry office, which was just a small tent with two women sitting behind a flimsy desk, filling lists, handing out temporary residency cards and coupons.

"Please, my son is very sick," Emma said.

The woman barely looked up. "The entire town is sick."

"He's coughing so badly, I'm afraid he'll die if I can't get a doctor to see him."

Finally the woman looked up and saw the heavily pregnant Luise with hunched shoulders standing next to Emma. "What about her? When's the baby due?"

"It could be any minute now." It was a white lie, because it should be six more weeks, but Agatha had said it would be sooner.

"You're relatives?"

Again, Emma lied. "Yes. Our husbands are cousins. And this woman," she pointed to Agatha, who looked like an octogenarian and not the healthy sixty-year-old she'd been at the beginning of the journey. "She's her mother-in-law. In total we're six: three adults and three children."

The woman sighed. "There's not much I can do for you, but I'll assign you to one of the tents in the back, those are the most protected from the wind. And"—she handed Emma a pink slip of paper—"show this to the guard at the hospital and he'll let your son inside for an examination."

"Thank you so much!" Emma could have hugged the woman. She clung to the paper that she hoped would be Jacob's salvation.

In the assigned tent they found three empty beds, one for

each adult. Once they were settled Emma turned to Agatha and asked, "I have to leave and get Jacob to the hospital. Can you take care of Sophie for me?"

Agatha nodded. "Of course. But you better hurry, because if the baby comes, someone needs to help me with the birth."

Emma blanched, cold sweat trickling down her back. The old woman did not actually expect her to replace the competent assistance of a midwife or a doctor during a birth? She picked up Jacob, who was too weak to even move his head and rushed out in search of the nearest hospital.

The guard at the entrance to the refugee camp didn't want to let her pass, despite showing him the pink slip, because it was shortly before curfew. She desperately pleaded with him, fearing Jacob might not survive the night without medicine, and was about to throw herself at the guard's feet, when he finally relented.

He let her leave, giving her directions to the Catholic Hospital that was only a five-minute walk down the main street.

About halfway there a coughing fit wrecked Jacob's little body and woke him from his fitful sleep. Even through the many layers of clothing she'd wrapped him in, she could feel the heat emanating from his skinny body.

"Mami... can't breathe," he whimpered.

Her heart constricted. She could not, would not, loose her little boy. Not now, when they'd finally reached Posen, would she let her little boy die literally in front of the hospital. Pounding her feet on the gravel, she mobilized the last of her energy, racing toward the hospital whose silhouette she could see a few blocks down the road.

Just as she arrived, it began to snow again, and a big flake settled on her nose. Back at home she might have been delighted and would have gone outside with her children to build a snowman or watch them fight a snowball war. Here though, it was yet another nuisance. She pressed Jacob harder against her chest, shielding him from the icy gusts coming along, while she elbowed her way through the overflowing front yard to the huge entrance gate.

"Papers," the SS guard asked and she showed them to him. "What's wrong with the child?"

"He's been coughing so hard, he can barely breathe."

The guard looked undecided, apparently weighing whether Jacob's condition was severe enough for him to be let inside.

"Please. I'm afraid he'll die!" Emma barely held back her tears, ready to pounce at the soldier if he wouldn't allow her son inside the hospital that might save him.

"Everyone tells me this," the SS man answered, looking down at Jacob, who peacefully snuggled against her chest. "He seems quite fine to me."

"He isn't! He's coughing out his lungs! Look, we've been on the road for weeks with barely any food or rest, never mind warmth. You must let him in."

"I'm afraid, without a doctor's recommendation I can't."

In her anguish she hadn't remembered the pink slip. Now she fumbled for it in her pocket and held it out to him. "The nurse at the refugee camp sent us here."

"Well then," he sighed. "Wait over there." He indicated a place a few steps aside, where three women with small children in their arms were already waiting. Then he turned his attention to the next person.

Several minutes later, a woman in a long black coat arrived on the steps, jumping the queue of waiting people to be admitted. She pulled down her hood, revealing thick, dark hair braided pretzel-style around her head.

"You. Take these children with you," the guard ordered the woman, who was apparently a nurse.

"Sure. Let me have a look at them," she answered in Polish. Having lived all her life in Lodz, Emma spoke the language quite well.

"No. Take them with you right now," the guard commanded.

Emma didn't miss the nurse's mutinous look, before she turned around to the four waiting women, just as Jacob had another coughing spell. The nurse looked at the gray pallor of his face, put a hand on his glowing forehead and asked Emma, "How long has he been coughing like this?"

"A few days." Emma wanted to explain so much more, but the queue forming behind her indicated the urgency.

"You really should have come earlier, it sounds like a severe bronchitis, possibly pneumonia."

So as not to appear like a negligent mother, Emma defended herself, "We've been on the road for weeks, fleeing from the Russians."

"Well, you shouldn't have started this war in the first place," the nurse murmured between her teeth, although Emma couldn't be sure she'd actually said such sacrilegious words, because her voice had been so low.

The nurse seemed to forget that it had been the Poles who started the war. Hitler himself had said it in his speech: "This night for the first time Polish regular soldiers fired on our territory. Since 5.45 a.m. we have been returning the fire, and from now on bombs will be met by bombs."

Louder, the nurse said, "I'll take him in, what's his name?"

"Jacob Oppermann."

"Come back tomorrow to see if he's made it through the night."

"What?" The nurse's casual cruelty left Emma gasping for breath. "I have to go with him. He's just four!"

"No visitors are allowed beyond the main floor, because of the influenza virus. Come back in the morning and ask for him." With these words, the nurse took Jacob from her arms and cradled him against her chest. "You'll have to be strong, little man."

Jacob, of course, didn't understand Polish and began crying as soon as he realized a stranger was holding him. Emma hurried to reassure him. "Jacob. This nurse is going to take care of you, so you'll get healthy again. Promise you'll be a good boy and I'll visit you in the morning."

He looked back at Emma with longing and fear in his little eyes, and she gave him a last kiss on his heated cheek, before the guard interrupted. "Now, hurry up, nurse. There are more patients waiting."

"I'll be here in the morning. I love you, Jacob," Emma called after him, and then he was gone. Her only consolation was that the nurse had been holding him with so much love. Despite her apparent hate for the Germans, Emma knew deep in her heart, that the woman would do everything in her power to treat him. Within a few days she could hopefully take her son home again.

Except, she realized, she didn't have a home anymore.

12

Irena cradled Jacob against her chest with one arm, while another desperate mother shoved a baby into her other arm. "I'll send someone to fetch the other children," she said, before she rushed off toward the children's ward upstairs.

It wasn't normal practice to pick up children on the steps leading to the entrance door. But what was normal these days? With the Red Army closing in, the German occupiers were getting ever more frantic, and with refugees arriving in droves, there simply wasn't enough personnel in the hospital to properly register the patients.

If the mothers decided—and many already had—that both parties had a better chance at survival if they left their babies on the steps of a hospital or a children's home, then there was nothing they could do anyway.

Although Jacob's mother had not looked like she'd ever give up her son. No, her fierce expression had suggested she'd rather die than be separated from him. Despite her being a German, Irena felt sympathy. She hoped the little boy would make it. The first night in the hospital was usually the crucial point at which it became clear whether a patient would survive.

Unfortunately this had become common wisdom just recently, when only the worst-off children were admitted inside. The guards had strict orders to send everyone away whose life wasn't on the line—possibly to return at a later time, hoping it wouldn't be too late by then.

Never in her life had Irena seen so much suffering. The daily death toll tugged at her soul and drained all the energy from her. Many years ago she'd trained to be a nurse to help the sick, but nowadays it seemed all she could do was keep them company as they died. The baby in her arms began to cry and Jacob joined right in.

"Shush, the two of you." Normally her soothing voice had an effect on her patients, despite the language barrier, but not today. Ever since she'd left her house that morning the entire world seemed to have turned upside down. A palpable tension lay in the air, heavy enough that Irena could feel it pressing on her lungs and making it difficult to breathe.

The desperate crowd in the hospital yard seemed to be more desolate than the days before, caught in a collective whimper, clamoring for someone to help their loved ones. It was such a miserable sight that Irena gave a deep sigh when she'd escaped into the comparative quiet of the hallway.

As soon as she dropped off the baby in the infant ward, she felt the tension again: dozens of bundles screaming at the top of their lungs, lying side by side. She rushed away as fast as her feet would carry her, rocking Jacob on her hip. He relaxed a bit and stopped whimpering.

"I'll get you some medicine and hang your clothes up to dry."

His face was blank, indicating that he didn't understand a word she'd said. Unfortunately, that had become commonplace in the wards. Unlike the older German children, most of those born after Hitler's invasion hadn't been taught a single word of

Polish, the supposedly inferior language of a subhuman Slavic race.

Irena, though, had refused to give up her heritage and learn German, just to spite the occupiers. If they wanted something from her, they should learn *her* language. It was her country, after all. Now that decision was backfiring on an hourly basis.

"Shush, little man. Everything will be just fine," she said in a melodic sing-song voice, knowing that children responded well to songs, never mind the language. At last the boy smiled at her, indicating his growing trust.

As soon as she arrived in the children's ward, she peeled him out of his damp clothes, shaking her head at the ragtag mixture of scarfs, towels and torn pieces of cloth and paper he was wrapped into. The Germans surely had fallen deep. *Pride comes before a fall.*

She hung his clothes onto the clothesline crossing the ward from one end to the other—another first that would have her training instructor turn in her grave. Unfortunately it was the only practicable solution, since most new patients arrived dripping wet from sweat and snow.

Jacob whimpered again as she sat him down in a bed with two other children. It almost broke her heart when he reached his scrawny little arms out to her and began coughing spasmodically.

The poor child, separated from his mother, unable to understand a word she said. She wiped him dry, wrapped him into a towel, for lack of proper clothing, and tucked him beneath the blanket with the other children.

Later, she'd get him some broth or at least hot water before the next meal was distributed. She forced herself to walk away, since she couldn't allow herself to get sentimental with her patients, as there were many of them—too many.

Each of the little ones needed her care dearly, so she had to distribute what little time she had as evenly as possible. During better times, before the war, she would indulge in the luxury of sitting beside the bed of a very sick patient, to read him a book or recount a story.

"Irena, can you help me over here?" Margie, a young nurse in training, called, her eyes showing how overwhelmed she was.

If it was difficult for an experienced nurse like Irena, how much worse must it be for a novice in the field?

"Coming," she replied. As she passed by the tea kitchen she called inside, "Could you bring hot soup to the new patient in bed twelve?"

"No soup left."

"Then hot water. He needs to get warm, and quick."

"On my way."

Irena didn't wait to watch how the volunteer grabbed a cup and brought hot water to little Jacob. She had more urgent things to do. "What's the matter?" she asked Margie.

"I don't know where to put this one?" She held a child of maybe four years in her arms with ugly red spots on her face.

"Heaven help us! If those aren't the measles! Just what we need right now. Take her into the broom closet."

"The broom closet?" Margie stared at her as if she'd lost her sanity.

"We've put two cots in there to quarantine the contagious cases."

"Oh..." Margie trotted off with the poor mite in her arms. Her parents shouldn't have brought her here, since she'd surely catch some respiratory disease in addition to the measles.

Irena shook her head. All of her new arrivals were undernourished, suffering from hypothermia and in severe distress. During a short lull, she ventured outside to take a breath of fresh air and eat a sandwich she'd brought from home.

The sky was heavily clouded. A snowflake landed on her face and then another one. Winter had come early this season and she couldn't remember it ever being this cold.

Giving a heavy sigh, she gathered her skirts and returned inside to complete her shift, making sure she looked after each of her little patients, handing out hot water, giving medicine to the worst cases, dressing them in their dried clothes and making sure they stayed warm.

As she reached the end of the ward, her gaze fell on the angelic face of a little girl. She lay on the bed in her white night-gown, her blonde hair draped around her head like a golden halo. She looked supernaturally beautiful, peaceful even. Tears filled Irena's eyes even before she stepped to the girl's bed, because from experience she knew that only real angels would look this celestial.

She closed the girl's bright blue eyes and told the ward assistant to take her to the morgue. When he came to retrieve the girl, a stabbing pain seared through Irena's heart. Another senseless sacrifice in this awful war. Just like her own little darling boy.

13

Emma returned to the refugee tent, finding her group settled on the cots, eating hot broth that had been distributed by the camp kitchen. Amongst her sorrows over Jacob's health, she'd completely forgotten her hunger, but now it returned with a vengeance.

Tears of relief stung at her eyes as she watched Sophie sitting with Hans, who finally had a rosy color in his cheeks once more, and was even able to hold the cup of soup all by himself. A pang of envy hit her soul as she watched the pair. This should be Jacob sitting next to his sister, not some other boy, but the same moment she felt guilty for her thought. Hans was her son's best friend and she should be happy for him and for Luise, who was leaning against the bedrest, her forehead sweaty and her face a grimace of pain.

Emotionally drained, Emma's entire being swirled with the conflicting emotions she felt: gratefulness for being given shelter in the tent, a cot and food, along with astonishment that they had actually arrived in one piece. But also fear about the uncertainties during their next leg of the journey, combined with anguish over Jacob's health. She staggered from the impact at realizing that this was far from over.

"Sit down." Agatha appeared out of nowhere, holding two steaming cups in her hands. She handed one to her daughter-in-law and after a glance at Emma's tired expression, gave her the other one. "Here, eat. How is Jacob?"

"Bad enough that they need to keep him overnight." Dejection took over and Emma was thankful for the mug to hold on to. It gave her something to occupy her hands and fight the emptiness spreading inside her. Today was the first day since Jacob's birth that she wouldn't tuck him into bed at night, read him a story or kiss him goodnight. She wanted to weep.

Agatha must have sensed her despair, because the old woman, who wasn't known to show public affection to anyone, put a hand on her arm and said, "He'll be fine. The Catholic Hospital has a good reputation. I heard it's under German administration now. They'll make sure the doctors and nurses do everything to get him well again."

For lack of a spoon, Emma took a sip from the broth, the hot liquid running down her throat. It was such a heavenly feeling, she closed her eyes to follow the soup's path all the way down into her stomach. Several more sips followed the first one and with time, the liquid warmed her bones from the inside, sending searing stabs into her thawing toes. Even the pain felt heavenly and she welcomed it. Together with the bodily heat, her spirits returned, too.

"I'm sure he'll be fine. They told me to return tomorrow during visiting hours and ask about his progress."

Agatha nodded kindly, although the next moment her eyes squinted with worry when Luise gave a grunt between gritted teeth. She bent forward to whisper into Emma's ear, "She is not well. Her contractions have started already."

"What, now? Here?" Despite Agatha's warning just a few days ago, Emma had hoped it would happen much later. It wasn't Luise's first one, but the conditions in the tent left a lot to be desired for a birth. "We need to get her to a doctor."

Agatha shook her head. "You were at the hospital. If it's as full as they say, no doctor has the time to come and see a pregnant woman in good health." Luise's health wasn't exactly good, although in comparison to the many desperate, coughing, wheezing and sneezing people out there, perhaps it was.

"So, what should we do?"

"I already made inquiries. Two of the women in the next tent have each birthed twelve of their own children and are well versed in the business. They have both agreed to come over when the labor starts in earnest. I also arranged with the kitchen for hot water and a set of clean towels."

A heavy burden fell from Emma's shoulders, since Agatha had this under control. "Is there anything I should do?"

"Just get the children out of the way. Childbirth is no business for them."

Emma nodded, wracking her brain where to go with Sophie and Hans, since it was much too cold outside and the night had settled over the city. "I'll keep them busy until it's bedtime. Let's hope they are exhausted enough to sleep through all the noise."

"We will get through this together," Agatha said and turned toward Luise. "How often are the contractions coming?"

"Maybe ten or fifteen minutes apart."

"Then we still have time."

Emma turned to Sophie and Hans, who both looked at her with expectant eyes.

"How's Jacob?" they both asked in unison.

"He's in the hospital and they're giving him medicine. I'm sure he'll be fine. Tomorrow I'm going to visit him and either then, or a few days from now, he can come home with us."

Sophie gave her a horrified stare. "Is this our new home?"

"No, my darling, it isn't. We're only staying here until Jacob is healthy enough to continue our travels." *And Luise has recovered from having her baby.*

"I wish we could leave this place right now!" Sophie burst out.

"And we will soon, there's no need to worry," Emma said. Without Jacob falling sick, they'd be first in line to board a train to central Germany in the morning. But there'd be other trains. A few more days surely wouldn't make a difference.

"You're only saying this to calm me down. I'm not a child anymore, I know quite well what will happen when the Red Army captures us." Emma blanched while her daughter continued to talk. "You always think I'm little, but I'm not and I listened to the other women talking about those things. How awful the Red Army soldiers are and how they force themselves on every female, even little girls like me. How they tear them apart from the inside out, because they are much too big for them. How they stab their eyes with a bayonet when they scream. How they cut off breasts to use as trophies. How they slice up bellies and throats after they're done with them." Sophie broke off, tears streaming down her face. "I don't want to be torn into pieces and have my eyes cut out."

"Shush, Sophie, shush." Emma hugged her daughter, who was much too mature for her tender age. "Haven't I always protected you? I won't let them hurt you."

"Pah," Sophie said through her tears. "You want me to believe that? There's nothing you can do. They have guns and we don't."

Emma sighed. Even if she had a gun, how much use would it be against a battalion of Russian soldiers? Its only purpose would be to give Sophie and herself a merciful end before the Russians could have their way with them.

"We should get some sleep, while we can. A few days of rest here in this warm tent with sufficient food will serve us well for the next leg of our journey."

Sophie nodded with a miserable face, but soon enough exhaustion overcame her scrawny body. She cuddled against Emma on one side, while Hans already slept on her other side. That's when Emma's gaze fell on Affie, hanging from a clothesline to dry. Poor Jacob would be so lonely without his stuffed friend. She'd have to remember to bring Affie with her when she visited him in the morning.

She stayed awake a few more minutes, worrying what the future held in store for them. If they couldn't get on one of the trains going west from Posen, they'd have to walk another hundred something miles until they reached Frankfurt an der Oder. Rumor had it that from there, train services into western German cities were running on a regular basis.

From everything she'd overheard, it was best to be conquered by the Americans or British, so Aachen was a good choice, even though it meant having to cross all of Germany from East to West. She'd never let Sophie know, but deep down in her heart, she was scared to death.

14

Jacob woke with a start. It was dark in the room, apart from dim night lights near the floor. Sitting upright in his bed, he felt for his Affie, but his toy wasn't there. Sometimes he went for a stroll at night and Jacob would find him on the floor next to the bed, because he was too small to clamber up.

What worried him more was that his mami's place was empty as well. He rolled to the other side, bumping against a small body. His mami would not abandon him. Ever. Although that person was much too small to be her. Still, he gave a big sigh of relief that at least Sophie was with him. Mother must have gone somewhere. Maybe to get food, or whatever things she did when her children were asleep.

He snuggled tighter against Sophie, wrapping an arm around her bony frame. Seconds later he recoiled with a shriek when he noticed her hair was cut short like his own. When had that happened?

Sweat broke out on his forehead and he had another coughing fit. Not as violent as the ones before, but still awful enough to press all air from his lungs and send a searing pain into his tummy muscles.

"Be quiet! And get off me, I want to sleep!" the person in his bed half-yelled at him.

Jacob's heart drummed against his ribs. That voice definitely was neither Sophie's nor Hans'. So, where was he? Who was the person sleeping next to him? And most importantly, where was his mami?

Big, fat tears rolled down his cheeks. Quietly at first, then louder, he sobbed, "Mami! I want my mami! Mami! Where are you?"

People around him moved and told him to be quiet, but he couldn't. Frightened to the bone, he made the effort to sit up and get off the bed, determined to search for his mother. Just as soon as his naked feet hit the cold floor, a woman came rushing toward him. "Will you keep quiet? You're waking all the other children."

She looked like a nurse, although he didn't remember having seen her before. Her German had a very peculiar accent, a lot like the Polish maid they'd once had in Lodz, not even that long ago. More fear seeped into every single one of his cells, when he suddenly remembered the gruesome journey and lying in misery on top of that cart.

The nurse gave him a spoonful of awful tasting medicine, which did nothing to reduce his panic. His mother must have left him here, because he'd slowed them down too much. Sophie had blamed him more than once. If it wasn't for him, they could have traveled so much faster and would have reached safety with Hans' grandma's cousin a long time ago.

It was all his fault. Because he'd gotten sick, they had been forced to slow down. And now Mami had punished him for being such a bad boy and had left him alone. How often had she threatened him, when he'd dawdled at home: "If you don't hurry up, I'll go on my own."

Renewed tears streamed down his cheeks, as realization hit him. He'd dawdled and Mami had continued without him. "I didn't do it on purpose, Mami. Please, I never wanted to slow you down. Please. I'll always be a good boy, but please come back for me."

He sobbed and cried, yelled and screamed, coughed and sneezed until the old nurse with the short gray hair grabbed him from his bed and put him all alone into the cold hallway. "When you stop screaming, I'll return you to your bed. You understand?"

Nevertheless, he couldn't stop crying, because all of a sudden he was completely alone in this world. Without his dearest mami, his papi, and even without his oh-so-annoying big sister. What would he give to at least have her by his side. "Please, Sophie, I'll do everything you say, if you only come back. I'll never once argue with you and even do all your chores, but please, please, please, don't leave me alone."

His feet grew numb and exhaustion dried up his tears. He sank to the floor, curling into a ball and must have fallen asleep, because he woke when the nurse returned to carry him back to his bed. "No more screaming, you hear me?"

He nodded, too desolate to utter a word.

"Your mother will come to fetch you, when you're better. So stop crying, sleep, and take your medicine."

A little ray of sunshine lit up his soul. Maybe not all was lost. He determined to do as the nurse said and get well by morning. Then his mami would come and get him. Maybe she had not abandoned him after all.

In the morning, a different nurse, her brown hair braided like a crown around her head, made the rounds, took his temperature and made him swallow a spoonful of the disgusting medicine, before she distributed bowls of porridge.

"Where is my mami?"

"*Twoja matka odwiedzi cię później rano.*"

He didn't understand a single word she said. Once again

tears pooled in his eyes; he valiantly fought them back and tried again, "I want my mami!"

Again, the nurse responded something he couldn't understand and he began to despair.

The child next to him turned his head. "Don't be stupid. That nurse doesn't speak German."

"What did she say?"

"I don't know." His bed-neighbor was a boy about his own age. The tousled blond hair covered half of his head, while the other half was buried beneath dressings, along with his left hand and arm.

Jacob's mouth hung agape. "Whatever happened to you?"

"Shelling set our house on fire."

"Oh." Jacob closed his mouth, yet kept staring at the boy. "How long have you been here for?"

"Long."

"And your mami?"

"She comes to visit every day, but has to leave before noon."

Finally he remembered his manners. "I'm Jacob and you?"

"Erich. It's not that bad here. At least it's warm and they give you food. You had better get dressed though, or the nurse will be angry."

Jacob looked down at himself, noticing that someone had undressed him and wrapped him in a towel. Erich pointed at a neatly folded heap beside the bed.

"Thank you."

Usually, he was well able to dress himself, but today nothing worked. After several fruitless efforts, the nurse shook her head at him, before she yelled something across the room.

Moments later a girl about Sophie's age shuffled toward him and helped him get dressed. Once he was done, the nurse appeared again and talked to the girl, who translated for him.

"She says your mother will come back during visiting hours. But you'll have to stay here a few days before you can go home."

15

In the early hours of the morning, Emma woke up to an ear-piercing scream. Instantly alert, she shot up in the bed, checking on the two children by her side, who were both sleeping soundly.

Moments later she heard a slap and then a weak cry. She smiled and looked over to the corner of the room, where a woman held up a baby and put it into Luise's arms. "It's a girl."

Emma wriggled herself free from the children cuddled by her side, walked over to congratulate her friend and admire the newborn. There was no bigger miracle in the world than giving birth, and even in these difficult times, it was a tiny reason for hope.

"You did it," she said to Luise, stroking the baby's back. "Such a beautiful girl."

She well remembered when her own children had been born. Both times it had been a painful ordeal, but as soon as she'd held her newborn in her arms, she'd forgotten the pain and had been the happiest person on earth. Nothing could be compared to the feeling of finally embracing the tiny human she'd harbored under her heart for nine months.

Emma smiled, confident everything would turn out just fine. Jacob was in the hospital, getting medicine. Luise's baby had arrived, and soon they'd be on a train to Aachen, where they'd safely wait out the end of the war. She sent a prayer to heaven for her husband to join them as soon as the war was over.

One of the women who'd helped during the birth, shook her head, concern etched into her face. Emma couldn't ask her what was wrong, because in that moment Hans cried out, "Mami! Mami!"

"Shush. Your mami is over there. She just gave you a little sister. What do you think, should we go and say hello?"

Hans was immediately mollified and eagerly jumped from the bed, racing over to the other side of the tent, but she caught him in the last moment. "They are both very tired, so we have to be quiet."

"Alright." Hans nodded.

"Can I see the baby, too?" Sophie asked.

"Of course." Emma smiled at the memory of how Sophie had come into her room after Jacob's birth. She'd been a proud big sister, watching her little brother in awe. She'd even brought her favorite doll for him to play with and had been rather disappointed when Emma had explained to her that the baby wouldn't be able to play with dolls for quite a while.

"Then, what can he do?" Sophie had asked.

"Drink and sleep, mostly," she'd said and Herbert, who'd received leave for the birth of his new child had added with a grin, "And poop."

She missed her husband so much. At home she'd gotten used to raising her children alone, but on this hellish journey she really could use the comfort of his presence instead of having to worry about his safety, too. She shook off the feelings. This wasn't the time to get depressed. She had a family to take care of.

After leaving Hans next to his mother, she asked Sophie, "Would you like to go to the hospital with me to visit Jacob?"

"Do I have to?" Sophie's eyes clouded with abject fear.

"No you don't. I just thought you'd like to know whether he's getting better."

"Can't you tell me when you return?"

Emma sensed how her irritation with her daughter was getting the better of her and took a deep breath. When had Sophie begun acting up like a rebellious urchin? "Watch your mouth. That is no way to speak to your mother."

"I'm sorry," Sophie muttered. "I just want to stay here."

Emma was too exhausted to ask what bothered Sophie so much, so she let it go for the moment. Being on this awful march had changed so many things, had even turned her well-behaved, docile little girl into a rebel. She hoped this would sort itself out, once they reached safety, or she would never find a suitable husband to care for her.

"Well then, stay here. Agatha, can you watch over Sophie, please? I'm going to the hospital to find out about Jacob."

Agatha nodded. "Don't stay long though, it's not safe out on the streets."

She fetched Affie from the clothesline and walked to the hospital. Once there, the German soldier guarding the entrance wouldn't let her enter to go upstairs into the children's ward.

"Please, the friendly nurse promised that I could see him this morning," she begged.

"Which nurse?"

"I don't remember." Now she regretted not having asked for the name, but since the woman had only been a Polish hospital employee, she hadn't paid her much attention.

"Well, the nurses don't have any say here, anyway. You'd have to talk to a doctor."

"I'll certainly do that." Emma gave him a terse smile and made to pass into the hallway, but he put out a hand to stop her.

"Not now. This is the admission floor for emergency patients."

"My son is already admitted."

"That's what you say, but how do I know you're telling me the truth?"

Emma's patience was running low. "Please, I need to see him and make sure he's fine."

The guard raised an eyebrow. "Our good doctors are certainly able to care for their patients and don't need the help of an untrained civilian."

Did this guard have mush in his brains? She tried once more. "Please, he's only four and he doesn't speak Polish."

"What's that got to do with it?"

"Just... the nurse yesterday spoke only Polish."

"Because she's a simple nurse. The doctors mostly speak German. I assure you, your child is being taken care of, and now, would you please leave?"

Emma's shoulders hunched forward in defeat as she turned around to see a bloodied SS soldier being half-carried toward the entrance. The guard jumped down the stairs to help his comrades and without wasting a single second, Emma grabbed the unexpected opportunity with both hands and slipped into the hallway.

She asked for the children's ward and minutes later, she stood in the entrance to a huge room with dozens and dozens of beds. How would she find Jacob there?

"Jacob, sweetie? Can you hear me?" she called into the room filled with coughing and sneezing children.

"*Kto cię tu wpuścił?*" a nurse approached her, asking who had allowed her inside.

"The guards. I need to check up on my son," Emma lied.

"No visitors outside visiting hours," the nurse insisted.

"I was told visiting hours are in the morning."

"Not today."

Emma shook her head. Whoever had put Polish people in charge? "Please. We are traveling to Aachen. We are only waiting for him to continue our journey."

The nurse said in a much warmer tone, "What's his name?"

"Jacob Oppermann. He's four years old, blond hair. He was taken in yesterday."

"The new arrivals are over there." The nurse pointed to a row of beds beneath a line of clothes. Had nobody in this hospital the slightest idea about hygiene? Emma could only shake her head. These things happened if you employed Poles for a job, that's what her parents had always said. Apparently they were not smart enough for most work. It was yet another proof they came from an inferior race. She just hoped the doctor knew his job.

Every bed had a small blackboard where the name of the child was written in chalk. Much to her dismay she discovered that all beds were occupied by two, or even three children. The hospital administration really should know better.

When she couldn't find Jacob, she walked along the row of beds once more, this time reading the names on the boards. *Jacob Oppermann/Erich Drassel.* But there was only one boy in the bed; Erich she assumed.

"Hello, Erich, do you know where Jacob is? The boy who shared this bed with you?"

Erich opened his eyes and sleepily shook his head. "No idea."

Despair flooded her system and her knees wanted to give out beneath her. Gathering all her strength, she rushed over to the nurse and said, "He's not there!"

"Who? And what are you even doing here?"

Emma wanted to scream with frustration as she looked into the nurse's face and realized it wasn't the same one she'd spoken to before.

"Jacob Oppermann. My son."

"No visitors allowed here, ma'am."

The nerve of this woman to speak to her like she owned the world. Emma straightened her shoulders and said in her iciest voice, "I demand to know where my son is."

The nurse shrugged. "I'm simply obeying my orders. If you don't agree, complain to him." She pointed toward an SS-man who stood in the hallway and, alerted by the loud voices, came inside the ward, his rifle at the ready.

"I will," Emma hissed, although her confidence had evaporated all of a sudden. It was one thing to patronize a nurse, but a totally different one to demand an answer from an SS-man.

"Is there a problem?" he asked, pointing his rifle at the nurse.

"No, sir, I just explained to this woman that no visitors are allowed in here, since this is what the new hospital director ordered."

He nodded. "Go, do your work."

The nurse scurried away, leaving Emma alone with the officer.

"Please, Herr"—she looked at his shoulder lapels to find out his rank—"Sturmführer. I'm here to visit my son. But he's not in his bed."

"He'll be with the doctor for examination and will be brought back shortly."

"Can I—?"

"I'm sorry, but you must wait downstairs with everyone else." He must have noticed her dejected expression, because he added, "I assure you, our doctors and even the nurses do everything to help the children. But we have strict orders not to let anyone into the ward. Once your son is cleared to leave the hospital, you'll be informed."

"But we live in the refugee camp," she weakly protested.

"Hmm... Then you'd better come here every day and ask for him downstairs. But now I have to ask you to leave."

"Can I at least leave his stuffed animal for him? I'll need just a second," Emma begged the man. On his nod she raced back to Jacob's bed, where Erich had fallen asleep. She placed Affie on what she assumed was her son's pillow.

The guard had appeared beside her and said, "You have to leave now."

"I'm on my way. Thank you for your patience." Emma knew there was nothing else she could do.

Her shoulders hunched as she embarked on the walk to the refugee camp. She should be happy that Jacob was still alive, instead her heart broke for her little baby who was all alone in the hospital, waiting for his mami. At least Jacob would have Affie's company in bed. It was a small comfort, but better than nothing. Her poor darling didn't even speak Polish, and the nurses apparently had failed to learn German.

Upon her arrival, Agatha intercepted her before entering the tent. "The baby died."

"What? No?" That couldn't be true. She'd only been gone a matter of hours.

"Unfortunately, yes. The poor mite was too weak to suckle. She wasn't breathing properly either. We were lucky, though, and could get her baptized in an emergency ceremony."

"Poor Luise."

Agatha furrowed her brows. "She's not taking it well. We must leave this place sooner rather than later. Getting back on the road might take her thoughts off the baby."

Emma didn't think rushing her friend onto another walk in the freezing cold was the best way to deal with her grief, but if Agatha had made up her mind, it would be easier to move a mountain than make her change it. "When do you want to leave?" Her voice was but a frightened whisper.

"As soon as Jacob is back with us. Although"—she lowered her voice and Emma's heart froze over by the stern expression on her face—"you might consider leaving him behind."

"What? Leaving my son?"

"It wouldn't be forever, just until after the war."

"Never. I will *never* leave him behind. I'd rather die here than continue without him."

Agatha shrugged. "I know this is a hard decision, but you must do what is best for all of you. He might not recover fast enough... and he might be too weak to withstand the ordeal of our onward journey, since we don't know what hardships await us."

"Then I'll stay right here with him."

"You and Sophie might not survive if the Red Army captures you. Then he'll be on his own—forever."

"No. And this is my last word." Emma pressed her lips into a thin line, her entire being aghast at Agatha's suggestion. How could she leave behind her sweet little boy among strangers, just to save herself? No, she'd never betray his trust and love in such a heinous way. Not now and not ever.

"It's your decision to make," Agatha said.

Emma stared at the old woman, hatred for her coldness spreading through her cells. *I'm not going to abandon Jacob.*

16

Irena glanced at the clock and realized it was almost time for her to head to the hospital. She was working the late shift tonight and would have left already, if she hadn't been waiting for her husband.

Luka should have arrived home an hour ago. Being held up at the hospital wasn't unusual, but due to the escalating situation of the war, she was worried sick. After another glance at the clock on the mantelpiece, she put on her coat and hat. If he didn't show up within the next five minutes, she would have to leave without saying hello to him. With some luck though, she might pass him on the way to exchange a few words.

She pushed another log into the tiled stove to keep the house warm throughout the night. The huge antique stove with the green and white ceramic tiles was a sturdy construction, a chest-high cube with a tower-like smaller cube on top of it. The mantelpiece surrounding the tower could be used to keep food warm or to dry wet socks and shoes. Attached to the main stove was a small bench featuring the same green and white tiles, where two people could sit and soak up the warmth of the oven.

It was a true blessing, because with just two or three logs of wood it kept the kitchen and living room warm for up to twelve hours. Throughout the occupation she and Luka had been forced to sell most of their valuables for necessities, and the Nazis had come to steal the rest, but thankfully, nobody had ever considered to touch the tiled stove, since it was such a huge and heavy piece that it would take days to dismantle and reassemble in another place again.

She grabbed her shoes from the warm mantelpiece, before she walked into the kitchen to fetch the soup pot and place it up there to keep warm for whenever Luka returned home. Just as she turned around to leave the house, she finally heard heavy steps coming up to the door, and instinctively flinched. Since that awful incident last year, she couldn't help doing so, even though she knew it must be her husband.

With bated breath she waited for the dreaded knock on the door and slumped with relief when she heard the key turn in the lock.

"I was about to leave," she greeted him, pressing a kiss on his lips.

"I'm so sorry, my love. Seems the Red Army is approaching fast, because the Nazis have gone crazy with control posts. They asked me for papers five times between the hospital and here."

She felt her stomach grow queasy. Being held up and asked for identification was inevitable these days. Still, every time her knees grew wobbly and she barely made it through without collapsing.

Luka sensed her distress and put an arm around her shoulders. "Should I go with you?"

"That's sweet of you, but no. You must be exhausted and hungry."

"In fact, I am. But I can accompany you if it helps?"

"It's really not necessary." Luka needed his rest, since he could be woken at any time of the night to see a patient at home, and would still have to return to the hospital at six in the morning. Relief spread over his handsome face. She knew he would have done it for her, despite his utter exhaustion.

"Be careful out there. Keep a white handkerchief and a Soviet armband at hand, just in case."

"The Russians are that near?"

"Difficult to say. From what I gleaned along the way, they are gathering on the outskirts of the city."

"Thank God. They'll give the Nazis a good running."

Luka chuckled and shook his head at her. "I'm afraid it won't happen without a fight. If you hear gunshots nearby, try to somehow reach the hospital. The soldiers won't come shooting into there."

"Nothing will happen, Luka. I left your soup on the mantelpiece."

He kissed her again. "Godspeed. I'll see you in the morning."

Irena left their home and headed for the other side of the city, keeping her head down, using the side streets to avoid the checkpoints. Since it was a few minutes before curfew, she increased her pace. Despite having a special permit that allowed her to be outside at all times, she preferred not to run into a patrol. It was bad enough having to deal with the SS posted to *protect* the hospital.

Strangely enough though, today there was only one soldier at the entrance, where recently half a dozen had stood watch. Since he knew her face, he didn't even bother to see her employee card and beckoned her through with a tired wave of his hand. The ground floor teemed with flustered patients and relatives alike, so she quickly escaped upstairs into the relative calm of the children's ward.

"Have you heard?" Margie asked her the moment she entered the big hall.

"Heard what?"

"About the Russians. They have razed the outlying forts and are marching into the city, block by block."

"Good. I hope they send the Germans running."

"I sure hope so. We may not like Stalin and the Soviets, but I guess it's time to bury the hatchet," Margie said.

"Right. Nothing and nobody can be worse than the evil Nazi oppressors."

"My husband has said, once the war is over, the Soviets will retreat and Poland will be a free country again."

Irena knew that both the British and the Americans had promised to recognize Poland's sovereignty after the war—albeit with different borders. Apparently, part of Poland's east would be given to the Soviet Union as some kind of payment, although Irena didn't understand why Poland should have to pay, since they'd done nothing wrong. On the contrary, Poland and her brave people had fought tooth and nail against the Nazis, at great peril and loss to themselves.

Anyhow, in exchange they would receive vast areas that had belonged to Germany before the war. She shrugged. If that was what the politicians up there had figured out, there must be some kind of sense to it.

"We can only wait and see," Irena said, taking off her coat. She washed her hands and started her first round, hoping for a quiet night. Unfortunately, the moment she stepped into the heavily overcrowded ward, she knew she wouldn't have a single minute to sit down, let alone sleep, during the coming twelve-hour nightshift.

17

Emma had barely slept all night. There were so many reasons to be anxious. She prayed for Jacob to be on the road to recovery and sent him all her love hoping he'd somehow be able to pick up on it. The poor boy must be frightened to death alone in that hospital.

As the sun was rising, Agatha approached her. "Can you help me to fetch breakfast from the soup kitchen?"

Emma nodded, although she thought this was a strange request, since Agatha was perfectly able to do so alone. She slipped on her socks and shoes, and put on her coat over her nightgown. "Ready."

Once outside, Agatha didn't beat around the bush. "We have to leave. The Red Army are fighting their way through the city quarters and it won't be long until they reach us."

"How do you know?" Emma asked. As if to answer her question, artillery fire bellowed through the air. Both women froze in shock, since it sounded as if the shots had been fired right next to them.

"You'll have to make a decision. Go to the hospital and drag Jacob with us on the trip, or leave him there until after the war."

"I'm going to fetch him right now." Emma would never leave her son behind.

"You do that and I'll pack up our things. We will leave by noon at the latest."

"What about Luise?"

Agatha's face hardened, but she kept her voice without a trace of emotion. "She's not in the best condition, but she'll manage. I promised my son I'd take care of her and Hans, and that I will do. I'll do the same for you and your children. Because, make no mistake: you and I may be able to withstand the treatment these barbarians intend to dole out, but neither Luise nor your daughter will survive it."

Emma sighed. Agatha was right. She couldn't even bear to think about her seven-year-old daughter being ripped open by hordes of brutal men forcing themselves onto her.

Breakfast consisted of *Ersatzkaffee* and bread. Emma changed out of her nightgown and told Sophie, "Will you lend Agatha a hand, while I go and fetch Jacob?"

Sophie made a frightened face. "Are you coming back, Mami?"

"Of course, sweetie." She stroked her daughter's hair. "Meanwhile, you be a good girl and do what Agatha says."

Taking an extra shawl to wrap Jacob in, Emma left the tent and walked to the exit of the refugee camp. There were a lot more soldiers guarding it than there had been last night. A deep chill settled into her bones, as she determined not to let anything deter her from fetching her beloved son and then getting the hell out of this town.

One soldier stopped her. "Where are you going, ma'am?"

"To the hospital."

"Which one?"

"The Catholic Hospital."

"Sorry, but I can't let you go there. The Red Army has

conquered the city center, there's no way for you to reach the hospital."

"But my son is there!" She flinched at her own squeaky voice, trying not to succumb to the desperation that was crawling across her skin.

"I'm sure he will have been evacuated already."

"But where to?"

"I wouldn't know that."

Emma wanted to scream with frustration, though from experience she knew this wouldn't impress the soldier one bit and might get her into trouble. "My little boy is only four years old. He needs me. Please let me go and find him," she said in her calmest voice possible.

His face took on a compassionate expression, while he continued to shake his head. "I'd like to help you, ma'am, really. But orders are orders. No one leaves the refugee camp, except to be put on the evacuation trains."

She found a sliver of hope in his words. "I thought there were no trains for civilians."

"This morning we received orders to evacuate the entire town. Trains are arriving as we speak to bring you away from the front."

That was a worrisome change, because it made Emma realize the gravity of the situation. Up until now, the authorities had strongly discouraged, even forbidden, the civilians from fleeing the Reichsgau Wartheland. If they had decided to evacuate its capital Posen, the situation must be dire. It meant the Red Army had indeed arrived, and the war was as good as lost.

In a rare moment of clarity, Emma realized that she would never see her home again. Lodz lay to the east of the Wartheland, close to the border with the General Governorate of the occupied Poland, as it had been named after Hitler's liberation. The Poles—or the Russians—would cling to the freshly conquered lands for all eternity.

"Please, can I try to find my boy? I promise to be back in time for evacuation." Emma was beside herself, begging the guard. He wouldn't budge and forced her to return to her tent. There, she found Luise in a state of apathy, sitting on her bed and staring at the wall, while Agatha and Sophie were packing up what little stuff they owned.

"Back already?" Agatha said, raising one eyebrow.

"The guard wouldn't let me leave. Apparently they're going to evacuate the entire town starting this afternoon."

"How?"

"They're sending in trains to take everyone west."

"Thank God!" Relief showed on Agatha's face for less than a second. "Although this means the Russians must be nearer than I thought. We'd better hurry up." Agatha gazed at the cart stored behind one of the cots. "We might not be able to take that on the train. We should better decide right now what to take and what to leave."

"What?" Emma was too shocked by Agatha's practical thinking to consider her request.

"Look, I know this is a lot to take in, but we need to be clear-minded about our survival. If we get on a train, they might make us leave the luggage behind, therefore we'd better be prepared and repack our things into bundles for each one of us to carry on our backs."

"What about Jacob?"

"I told you before, you need to make a decision."

"I'm not going to leave him."

"Fine. Then stay, but at least let Sophie go with me."

Emma stared at the old woman, full of anger that she could be so cold-hearted, cruel even. Her heart was shattering into a million pieces at the thought of letting her little girl go, without knowing if she'd ever see her again.

"It's for the best. I'll make sure she's fine and she can help me to take care of Hans, since Luise currently isn't of much use."

Quivering, Emma shook her head.

"You know where to find us. You have the address of my cousin in Aachen."

Emma was still shaking, with sorrow, rage, and fear.

"Think about it." Agatha turned around, repacking their things into small bundles, leaving Emma feeling bereft.

How could she choose between her children? How could she even entertain the idea of letting one of them go? Nevertheless, as she busied her hands sorting their things and making bundles for each one of them, she had to accept that Agatha was right. Keeping Sophie by her side would be a liability. Alone, she'd be so much faster getting around and finding Jacob.

Sophie on the other hand, would be in the safest place possible, together with her brother's best friend Hans, his mother, and the capable Agatha. If anyone made it unscathed to Aachen, it would be the tough old lady and those she had under her wing.

As Emma handed the bundle to Sophie, her daughter said, "I heard what Agatha said. I'm not going anywhere without you!"

"Oh, sweetie. It may not happen at all, or it might be just for a few days."

"Nobody can guarantee that. I know full well what is happening here."

Her daughter definitely knew too much for a girl her age. Emma stroked her cheek. "It's too dangerous for you to stay here."

Her daughter's pouting face blanched, but she wouldn't relent. "If it's safe enough for you, it's safe enough for me."

"It's not safe for me either, but I *have* to find your brother."

"Agatha said you could leave him at the hospital and return

after the war," Sophie said, her words sending a stab through Emma's heart.

She would have to have a serious word with Agatha, just not now, because she was running out of time.

"We don't know how long the war will last. And you wouldn't want me to leave you either, if you were sick, right?"

Sophie began to bawl. "No..." sniff "...but..." sniff "... Agatha said he'll die if he comes with us. I don't want him to die. In the hospital they will take good care of him."

"We don't know that." Emma drew her daughter into an embrace. "Here's what I'll do: I'm going to fetch him right now and will be back in time to get on the train with you."

"Promise?" Sophie's eyes lit up with hope.

Emma sighed. How could she promise such a thing? She might not reach the hospital alive... and she might not find Jacob. "I will do everything I can, and the rest is up to God. You, be a good little girl and do everything Agatha and Luise say, will you?"

Sobbing, Sophie threw herself tighter into Emma's arms. "Don't go, Mami."

"I must. Just imagine, how much more afraid Jacob must be all alone, while you have our friends around." She extricated herself from Sophie's embrace, put the bundle with her own and Jacob's things on her back and turned around to Agatha. "I'm sneaking out. If I'm not back in time, will you take good care of Sophie?"

"I certainly will. Godspeed."

18

The sound of metal scraping against tiles woke Jacob from his nap. It took several seconds until he remembered that he was in the hospital. He sat up expectantly, Affie in his arms. Erich had told him his mother had been here, but couldn't wait until he returned from the examination room. Which was peculiar, to say the least, since his mami wouldn't just leave. He shrugged. At least Affie was with him, and that had to count for something.

All around him, people milled about the large room, searching for some thing or the other. Nobody took any notice of him. A beautiful blonde woman came up to his bed with a bright smile on her face, spreading out her arms. For a moment he wondered, what she wanted.

"Erich, get up, we need to leave," she said, embracing the boy next to him.

"Where's my mami?" he asked the lady after she'd hugged Erich so hard, Jacob feared his bedmate would be crushed.

She glanced over, her smile faltering. "I'm sure your mother will be here soon. There's quite the turmoil downstairs."

Jacob wasn't happy with her answer. She proceeded to help

Erich to put on his shoes and coat in a hurry, before she took him into her arms. "We have to hurry to get onto the train."

"What train?" Jacob asked.

She didn't answer, and all his new friend could do was wave him goodbye.

More and more grown-ups came, grabbed a child and hurried out with them. The more the ward emptied, the more fearful Jacob became. Whatever was happening wasn't good. He clearly recognized the carefully hidden tension on the faces of the adults—it was the same face Mami had made during most of their journey pretending everything was fine.

He wasn't a baby anymore and had known nothing was fine. What if his mami had forgotten him? Or if she didn't want him anymore, because he'd slowed them down too much? She might rather continue the trip to Agatha's cousin without him.

Fear constricted his heart, tears bubbled up. He clung to his mother's promise to come and visit. Feverishly scanning the room, he couldn't see anyone remotely resembling her. After a while he lost the fight against his tears.

Later a nurse with hair braided around her head like a crown came over. He faintly remembered her as the one who'd taken him into her arms, carrying him into the hospital and away from his mother. She'd been nice, nevertheless he hated her. If it weren't for her, he'd still be with his mother and wouldn't have to sit alone in this stupid hospital.

She said something he couldn't understand. Her voice was kind and soothing, so he forgot his hatred and stretched out his arms for her to pick him up. Rubbing her hand across his back, she murmured an unintelligible word again and again.

Although he didn't know what it meant, he liked the sound of it: soft and warm, reassuring. His sobs subsided until he even managed a small smile.

Again, she told him something before she put him back on his bed. Just as he wanted to cry again, she said, "Wait. Mami."

All around him, the children able to walk dressed themselves, while others were picked up by adults, probably their parents, and taken away. He sighed. If only he knew what to do.

What would Sophie do? As much as he hated the way she always teased him for being little, he full-heartedly adored his big sister who was as clever as any grown-up. Suddenly he could have sworn he heard her voice in his ear, saying, "Stop whining and get dressed. You better be ready when Mami comes to pick you up."

So he did just that. He fetched his things from under the bed and put on his jacket, shawl and hat. Last, he slipped into his shoes and bent down, completely focused on the ends of his shoelaces. Sticking out his tongue in concentration, he crossed them to a knot before he made a loop and tried to remember what exactly he was supposed to do after that.

Mami had been practicing with him to tie his laces, but with so much kerfuffle around him, he'd completely forgotten how to put the lace around the loop and where to pull it through. The first three attempts resulted in him having both ends in his hands without a bow, and he was close to tears, when a young woman with a baby on her arm came along and wordlessly helped him.

"Here you go. Where's your mother?"

He could barely prevent his tears from spilling over again. "I don't know."

She seemed to think, before she talked again. "This hospital is being evacuated. We must all leave."

Squinting his eyes, he looked around and indeed, one by one the other children left the room. Some older ones on their own, although most of them were carried. This had been going on for quite some time and he could barely breathe when the enormity of the realization sunk into his brain. "Me too? I have to leave?"

"Yes. Everyone. Do you know the way to your house?"

Jacob shook his head.

"The address maybe? I can bring you there, if your mom doesn't come to pick you up."

Jacob lost to his tears and sobbed, "My house is not here. We live in Lodz. What if my mami doesn't come?"

The woman patted his back. "Don't cry. I'm sure she'll come soon enough. The entire population is being evacuated." Her baby started crying and an SS soldier came to shoo her out of the ward.

"Sorry, can't stay. And I can't take you with me either. It won't be long before your mother arrives." Then she was gone and his tears were flowing down his cheeks like a river.

His vision was swimming and all he could see were blurred outlines. Furtively wiping away his tears, he looked around once more and found the room almost empty. Anxiety grabbed him like a furious dragon, shaking his entire body. What if his mami didn't come and he had to stay in the hospital all alone for the rest of his life? He jumped to his feet, screaming at the top of his lungs, "Mami! Mami!"

Finally someone noticed him and a blurry figure approached. He recognized her as the friendly nurse, telling him something he didn't understand.

"Where is my mami?" he asked her. "Or my sister?"

She looked at him, shaking her head, talking some more in her soothing voice. Despite not knowing her, he instinctively knew she was a good person and wouldn't harm him, unlike the scary-looking guard, who was waving his rifle and shouting something. Jacob, a baby and the nurse were the only ones left in the ward. An icy chill crept into his soul.

Moments later, a distraught couple rushed into the room and swept the baby up into their arms. They hugged her close and hurried from the ward, leaving Jacob alone with the nurse, who tried to explain something that didn't make sense. He couldn't understand what she was saying, except for a few German words here and there.

"Where is my mami? I want my mami," he cried.

The nurse gave a frustrated glance. She said something, turned and left the room, leaving him utterly, totally and completely alone.

He froze in fear, more tears rolling down his cheeks, until deep down in him a voice told him that he had to take his luck into his own hands and go searching for his mother.

Yes he would! Valiantly he left his bed, Affie pressed to his chest and walked on wobbly legs toward the hallway. Just as he arrived, gunshots rang from outside. In panic, he flopped to the floor and crawled beneath the closest bed.

Maybe leaving the hospital wasn't such a good idea after all. He crouched against the wall, peeked out into the empty hall-way. Nothing happened. No more gunshots, either.

Just when he gathered the courage to leave again, he remem-bered what his mother had taught him. "If you ever get lost, don't run away or try to find me. Stay where you are and wait, because I'll come looking for you. If you go someplace else, I may not find you, but if you simply sit down and wait, I'll always find you."

He gave a deep sigh, clinging to the hope she would keep her word. She would, wouldn't she?

After an endless time he noticed it was getting dark in the ward and it had been a while since he'd heard noises. No shout-ing, no footsteps, no nothing. Not even gunshots outside. A fear like he'd never known in all of his four years took hold of him and pressed so hard against his lungs that he could barely breathe. It was almost as bad as when he'd been so sick the constant coughing wouldn't let him inhale.

"Mami. Please don't leave me here. I promise I will be a good boy and always do what you say. I won't even fight with Sophie ever again. Please, Mami, come and get me!" He pleaded until the coughing returned and he lost his voice. Tears ran unchecked down his cheeks, his entire body shaking.

"Mami," he whispered brokenly, crawling from beneath the bed and lying on top of it, covering himself—coat, shoes and all—with the blanket.

"Please come back, Mami," he begged the empty room.

19

After finally having located the baby's parents, Irena went downstairs to the reception area in her quest to try and find Jacob's mother. She couldn't remember his last name, which had been wiped from the chalkboard on his bed during the kerfuffle, so she hoped there wouldn't be many boys called Jacob in the patient list at reception and she'd be able to locate his parents.

She pursed her lips. Some kind of parents! How come they didn't even care enough to pick him up when the entire German population in town was being evacuated? In this war she'd seen about everything, but parents leaving their children behind to save their own skin? That was a first.

Don't assume bad intent, she scolded herself. The mother could have been held up, or—Irena's soul chilled at the thought —she could be dead by now. With all the shooting going on, it was absolutely possible.

The reception area was empty, since the German hospital workers had fled as soon as the evacuation orders had been announced over the radio. The patients had been picked up by relatives, or walked out on their own feet and even the SS-guards had left.

She wondered what had been done with the patients who couldn't be transported. Would the SS be callous enough to leave them behind to be butchered by the Russians? Or did they secretly hope the Russians were better people than they themselves were and would take care of the wounded?

She doubted it. Being a German, sick or not, in a newly conquered town wasn't a fate she wished on even them—her worst enemies. Her hand slipped into her pocket to retrieve the red armband with the yellow hammer and sickle and put it on her arm. Since her grandmother had married a Russian, Irena spoke some rudimentary Russian. She hoped that the combination of wearing the armband, being Polish, and speaking their language would keep her safe.

For a moment she considered rushing back to the safety of her home, but her sense of duty wouldn't let her leave the young boy all alone. He must be frightened to death. It wasn't his fault that the Nazis were lawless criminals and his own mother had abandoned him.

With a sigh she entered the reception office to search for the book with the data of all incoming and outgoing patients that usually sat on the desk. Of course, tidy as the Germans were, they'd put it away, before fleeing. She probed the drawers, just to find out all of them were empty. Had the administrative employees taken the patient book with them? If so, for what reason?

Desperation washed over her. How on earth would she find Jacob's family without the book? Because of the language barrier, she couldn't even ask the boy himself. For the umpteenth time during the past weeks she regretted her decision not to learn German out of protest against the oppressors. With slumped shoulders she turned to go upstairs and find him.

"What are you still doing in here?" a doctor yelled at her, hurriedly putting on his coat while leaving the hospital.

"I'm trying to locate the parents of a boy."

"Forget about him and get yourself to safety. The Red Army is moving into this part of the city and there's fighting all over the streets," he said. Then he was gone, leaving Irena staring at his back with an open mouth.

It would be the reasonable thing to do, but how could she? She could not.

Turning on her heels, she raced up the stairs, still not entirely sure what she was supposed to do. She found Jacob crouched on the bed next to the door, wrapped tightly in a blanket and staring at her with the most frightened eyes she'd ever seen.

It shattered her heart.

The sound of grenades and artillery fire echoed in the distance, reminding her of the urgency. Without thinking it through, she picked him up and cradled him against her chest, murmuring words of comfort she knew he didn't understand.

It was getting late and she didn't have much time, if she wanted to return home before nightfall. Another mortar went off in the distance, reinforcing her resolve to take the boy with her.

"Jacob, that's your name, right?"

He nodded.

"I'm Irena." She pointed at her chest and he seemed to understand. Emboldened by his reaction, she said, "I'm going to take you home with me, because you can't stay here. Do you understand?"

Much to her chagrin he looked blankly, and she tried again. "Me and you. Go. Not hospital. Home."

His eyes squinted. She had the sensation that he wasn't quite on board with her plan, but she couldn't be considerate of his opinion. Therefore, she put him on the floor, tugged at his hand and said, "*Komm!*"

Despite his anguished look he followed her to the nurse's room, where she filled her bag with all the medicine she could find and then beckoned for him to follow her.

"Mami?" he asked.

Again, his pained expression broke her heart. Perhaps it was best to go along and pretend she was bringing him to his mother. "Yes. You and me. Mami. Come."

Afraid he'd run away, she took his hand and held it tight as she walked toward the exit. Once she stepped outside, the bitter cold made her shiver. Despite knowing he wouldn't understand, she said, "Don't be afraid. We can't stay here, because the hospital has been evacuated, but I'll take you home with me, where you'll be safe."

All the time she scanned the hospital yard for a woman, or anyone really, heading toward the entrance doors. Unfortunately she saw only nurses and doctors leaving, some helping invalids along. Briefly she wondered where these patients would be taken. She'd heard awful things about the Russians sweeping in and killing every patient left in the hospitals. Although she couldn't imagine anyone wanting to endanger themselves by harboring an invalid German. At least Jacob didn't present a danger, since no Red Army soldier would suspect a four-year-old of being an enemy spy.

Darkness settled over the town, while she hurried to arrive home before curfew, although there weren't any German soldiers roaming the streets who might enforce it. In fact, the streets were eerily empty. Most Germans were probably headed for the train station to be evacuated, while the Poles sheltered in place, waiting for the Red Army to liberate them. Luka would be worried sick about her.

The sound of gunfire erupted ahead. Several tanks drove down the street she had to cross to get into her borough. She could either rush for the other side or wait until the tanks had passed. Within a split second she decided to try her luck, picked up Jacob and raced across the street.

Her heart thumping hard against her ribs, she jumped across the ditch and disappeared into a narrow footpath between two rows of houses. Breathing hard, she set Jacob down, who immediately began to scream.

Afraid his cries would alert the soldiers, she put a hand across his mouth. "Shush. You must be quiet." She put the index finger of her other hand in front of her lips, indicating he had to be silent. "*Bitte. Ruhe.*"

He seemed to understand, because she felt how his mouth closed behind her hand. Ready to muffle his screams if needed, she slowly removed her hand from his face. Fortunately it wasn't necessary. "Soldiers coming. Russians. Be quiet." It was frustrating to talk to someone who didn't understand her language, but at last he seemed to grasp what she was trying to explain and nodded. "*Ich schreie nicht mehr.*"

Despite not understanding his words, she assumed he was on board with her and smiled. "Good boy. Now let's go." Emphasizing her words with a tug at his hand, she walked on, never letting go of his little hand until they reached her house.

There, she unlocked the door, pushed Jacob inside and immediately turned the deadbolt.

20

Emma lingered at the entrance to the refugee camp, where countless soldiers milled about, putting people into lines for evacuation. She couldn't risk getting stuck in one of those lines being marched to the train station.

Walking the perimeter of the camp she finally came upon a hole in the fence and crawled through. It took her some time to regain her orientation and find the street leading to the Catholic Hospital.

When she reached it, she realized it was impossible to get to the hospital. The street was crowded with masses of people coming in her direction. Scrambling, shoving, pushing in an effort to be the first ones to be evacuated.

Tears pooled in her eyes as she recognized the futility of trying to fight her way against the onslaught. She retraced her steps to a smaller street, trying to circumvent the masses, but it seemed that every damn road in the city lead to the main street.

Finally she approached one of the soldiers, organizing the exodus. "Excuse me."

"Ma'am, you have to stay on the main road."

"Please, I need to get to the Catholic Hospital."

He looked at her, stupefied. "There's no way to get there. Don't you see that everyone is walking away from it?"

"I do, but you must understand, my son is in the hospital."

He shook his head. "You must be mistaken. We evacuated the place an hour ago, there's nobody left."

"But my son..."

"I'm sure someone took care of him."

"But he's only—"

"You really must move, I have my orders."

Emma sighed with despair, since there was no way this soldier would help her. She nodded and joined the stream of evacuees, walking away from the city center where the hospital and Jacob were. Carefully weaving her way through the crowd, she finally reached the other side of the street and jumped into the ditch.

Without local knowledge it would be close to impossible to find an alternative route to the hospital. Since she remembered the church next to it, she looked around for the bell tower to give her guidance.

Her undertaking was fraught with danger, both from the Red Army and the mass of refugees, yet nothing could deter her from finding Jacob. No mother worth her salt would abandon her baby to a bunch of strangers in a critical situation like this one. Definitely not her! Emma was still angry at Agatha for even suggesting she'd commit such a heinous deed.

Always keeping to the shadows, she moved around the main street in a wide arc, taking her far away from her target, before she finally turned back toward the hospital's location.

It took Emma several hours until she reached the hospital after dark. An eerie silence hung inside the walls surrounding the old building with the huge gardens. She imagined how nice it must look in summer, as opposed to right now, when the plants were hidden by trampled snow. Even in the dim moonlight, it looked as if a horde of cattle had stampeded through here, leaving dirty marks in the snow.

Black smoke rose from the building in several locations, not a single soul was going in or out. Her heart missed a beat when she heard the caw of a crow. These birds were the true winners of the war, since there was never a shortage of carrion to feed on.

Gathering her skirts, she sped up the steps until she reached the entrance door. Unlike the day before, no soldiers guarded it. Her heart beating wildly in her throat, she turned the door handle and it sprung open.

She peeked inside, greeted by more emptiness. Nobody and nothing moved in the long hallway that had been bursting at the seams not long ago. Panic surged through her veins as she set a probing foot into the building, half-expecting someone to jump out from the darkness and scold her for trespassing.

But nothing happened.

The inside was as deserted as the outside. Fighting against the urge to run away and hide, she tentatively walked deeper into the hallway, opening every door to look behind. What she found was more emptiness. Overthrown chairs, broken mugs, a scene of frantic escape. It seemed the hospital had been evacuated in a hurry.

She went upstairs. The first ward she came upon was filled with occupied beds, but no sounds came from there. Wondering, she inched nearer to the first patient and gasped in horror as she noticed a huge red hole in his chest.

Fighting down the urge to vomit, she crossed the entire ward, finding the same scene in every bed. She bit on her lips to keep herself from screaming as reality of what the Red Army had done after conquering the hospital trickled into her brain.

Her heart thumping frenetically, she forced herself to continue on, hoping that by some miracle Jacob had survived the massacre. Even if he hadn't she wanted to hold him in her arms one last time. Soon she entered the ward where he'd been, found empty cribs, soiled diapers, and a lone shirt hanging from the clothesline crossing the room from wall to wall.

"Jacob!" she yelled. "Jacob! Jacob! Where are you? Are you here?"

No answer came.

When her voice became hoarse, she stopped screaming, unable to accept what she knew was true: her beloved son wasn't here. She'd come too late.

Tears fell down her cheeks. The empty bed where he'd lain called out to her, tempting her to lie down and stay, never to move again, never having to face a life without him.

Just as she was about to give in to her desperation, Sophie's darling face showed up in her mind, forcing her to compose herself. As much as she ached for Jacob, she had another child to take care of. Sophie needed her, now more than ever.

Emma swiped away her tears and forced herself to return to the refugee camp, determined not to lose two children in a single day. She clung to the hope that Jacob had been evacuated together with the hospital employees and somehow, somewhere, she'd find him again.

The way back was fast, effortless even, because all she had to do was to drift with the masses until she reached the side street leading to the hole in the fence.

"Mami!" Sophie rushed into her arms, the very moment she stepped into the tent, where Agatha was arguing with a soldier.

Emma felt the warmth emanating from her daughter, and the immeasurable love for her children tied her stomach into a knot. At least she had returned in time to find her daughter.

"My sweet darling!" Emma buried her face in Sophie's hair, in equal parts happy and sad.

"You have to leave now. We can't wait any longer," the soldier said, just as Agatha, alerted from Sophie's cry, turned around to look at Emma.

"She's just arrived, officer. We're ready to be evacuated. Thank you so much for your patience." Agatha picked up her bundle and said in a voice that brooked no argument, "Luise, Sophie, Hans, get your belongings. We're leaving." Sidling up to Emma, she added, "It's about time. We almost had to leave without you, since this soldier was threatening to force us at gunpoint."

Emma automatically fell in step beside her and Luise, but couldn't find the strength to utter a single word.

As they left the tent, Agatha looked at her again. "Where's Jacob?"

It took all Emma's strength to keep the overwhelming emotions at bay, and her voice was a hoarse whisper when she answered, "I have no idea. By the time I arrived, the hospital was completely empty."

"I'm sure he's been evacuated with everyone else. They wouldn't have left a child behind," Agatha said.

"I guess you're right." Emma had been clinging to the exact same thought ever since she'd left the deserted hospital. But how would she ever find him again? He was only four and didn't even have papers with him, unlike Sophie who wore hers day and night in a bag around her neck.

Then she felt Luise reach for her hand. "You must have faith."

"Faith in what?"

"That your son is still alive."

Sympathy for her friend poured out of Emma. Luise had just been forced to bury her newborn, while Emma had every reason to believe Jacob was still alive. "I'm so sorry for your loss. I can't imagine—"

"Don't." Luise stopped her. "My soul is crushed, that's true. Yet, I keep telling myself that I still have Hans who needs me so much. Watching him is what keeps me from falling apart. Without him, I might have simply stayed in that tent, not caring what happens to me, even looking forward to soon joining my darling daughter."

Emma felt a lump forming in her throat. There was nothing comforting, wise or otherwise helpful for her to say.

"For now, you need to focus on Sophie. Make sure she survives this journey without major damage. Once we've reached safety, you can put all your efforts into finding Jacob again."

Slowly nodding, Emma finally responded. "You're right. For now all I can to is to look after the child that is with me, praying to God that someone will have taken Jacob under their wing."

21

Irena removed Jacob's shoes and coat, before she beckoned for him to sit on the bench by the tiled stove. The poor boy was tired to the bone and could barely keep his eyes open. She took the medicine from her bag and walked into the kitchen to grab a spoon and a glass of water, by the time she returned to the living room, he was fast asleep, flopped against the tiles.

Watching him warmed her heart, making her smile. She had done the right thing by the boy. It didn't bear contemplating what the Red Army might have done to him, and even if they had done nothing to him, he'd probably not have survived the night in the unheated, deserted hospital.

She woke him up just long enough to make him swallow the medicine, then she picked him up and carried him upstairs to her bedroom.

The bedside lamp was still on, because Luka had fallen asleep reading in bed, the book lying atop his face. As quietly as she could, she lowered Jacob into the empty crib and tucked him in. She smoothed his damp hair off his face and leaned down to kiss his forehead. "Sleep now, little Jacob. Tomorrow we will figure out what to do next."

As she stood there, admiring his lovely little face, she heard Luka's voice. "What are you doing?"

How should she explain? She had acted on impulse, not thinking her actions through. Irena lifted a hand to her lips and whispered, "Come downstairs with me and I'll explain everything."

Together they exited the bedroom, leaving the door open a crack so that she could hear if Jacob cried. After settling downstairs next to the tiled oven that would give off heat for the entire night, Luka took her hand and asked, "Irena what have you done?"

She looked at the man she loved with all her soul, begging him with her eyes not to get upset, and explained. "They evacuated the entire hospital. Relatives came to get the children, but no one came for little Jacob. I was told to leave him there together with the patients who couldn't be transported. But I couldn't do that."

"Is this Jakub a Pole?" Luka asked with a raised brow, pronouncing the boy's name the Polish way.

"No, he's German." She shrugged in a helpless gesture.

"You should have left him at the hospital, I'm sure the German doctors would have taken him with them."

She shook her head. "No, Luka, I was the last one to leave, all the Germans had already fled."

"What if his mother comes looking for him?"

"I don't think she will. She's probably dead by now, or fleeing to Germany." Irena furrowed her brows. "It had been hours since the population was alerted to come and get their relatives."

Luka gave her a stern look. "What if his mother is one of the refugees sheltering in the camp? You know it's too far out to hear the loudspeaker announcements in the streets."

Now that he mentioned it, she vaguely remembered a young woman, desperately begging to admit her son to the hospital. With the number of people she met each day, she couldn't be sure that her memory served her right. But if there was even the slightest chance she could find Jacob's mother, she had to grab it. "Should I go to the refugee camp?"

"Not now. Curfew starts in a few minutes and the Russians are everywhere. You'd probably be shot on the way."

Suddenly she felt insecure. Slumping forward she murmured, "What will we do?" When Luka didn't respond, she added, "I couldn't leave him there. He's very sick and wouldn't have made it through the night on his own. Do you have any idea how scared he must have been? With everyone gone and nobody talking to him? What do you think the Red Army would have done to him? To a child of the enemy? I didn't want to take that risk. Would you?"

Luka leaned over and put his arms around her. "You know I wouldn't. Nonetheless what are we to do with this child? He must have parents, or at least relatives, out there looking for him, even if his mother is dead. We can't just take him."

"I didn't take him, I rescued him from certain death."

"In any case, you need to return him to the hospital, or at least alert the authorities about his existence."

"You're right. First thing in the morning I'll walk to the hospital and the refugee camp to search for his mother."

Luka pulled her onto his lap and she soaked up the warmth emanating from him, feeling the tension seep from her body. With him by her side, she'd be able to withstand anything fate had in store for her. After several minutes, the doctor in him took over and he released her. "So, what is young Jakub suffering from?"

"Besides being severely malnourished, he was dehydrated, feverish and has a severe case of bronchitis."

"Well, at least that's something curable. If only we had the medicine for it," Luka surmised.

Irena pushed away to look at him. "We have. I grabbed everything I could find and put it into my bag."

"You stole medicine from the hospital?"

"The abandoned hospital. How much do you think the Red Army will leave intact? Better I take it to care for a sick boy, then let them destroy the valuable medicine."

He shook his head, but she could see that he was only pretending to be angry about her actions. "I guess, in this particular instance, you might be right. Let's see what you have got." With those words he gave her a heartwarming smile along with a little nudge and she walked into the kitchen to retrieve her bag.

"Here you go," she said as she handed it to him.

His jaw dropped when he opened it. "Well, that's quite some haul. I can surely use some of this for my patients."

"Lucky for you and them that I grabbed as much as my bag would hold," she said with a teasing smile.

"I suppose under the current conditions it was the best course of action you could have taken, although you'll still have to confess the theft."

She didn't comment. Their priest would surely think the same way and let her get off saying a few Ave Marias and an Our Father. "Thank you for supporting me always."

This time, it was him who issued a teasing smile, while his eyes got dark with desire. "It seems we both have lost our jobs at the hospital and can sleep in tomorrow." He pulled her back onto his lap and began to unbutton her blouse, his hands moving over her bare skin, leaving delicious tingles in their wake.

"What about the boy?" she murmured beneath her breath, even as he freed her breast from the chemise.

"We'll be very quiet not to wake him," he whispered and carried her upstairs to their bed.

Much later, she snuggled in Luka's arms, listening to his

breathing, when suddenly Jakub coughed in his crib. Worry attacked her and she was about to jump from the bed, but Luka held her back. "He's fine."

"I just wanted to check on him."

"I thought as a nurse you should know there's no reason to check up on every single cough."

She smiled into the darkness. His words were true, but Jakub wasn't just another patient, he felt like so much more, and she was unreasonably worried about him. "I couldn't find out his last name."

"How come?" His voice carried a trace of alarm.

"The blackboard on his bed was wiped in the kerfuffle. I even went to the reception desk to search for the registration book, but it wasn't there."

If he was appalled that she had rummaged in a desk that wasn't hers, he didn't let it show. Instead he pressed her tighter against himself.

"What if I can't find his mother?"

"Let's cross that bridge when we come to it. Take him back to the hospital tomorrow. If his mother is looking for him, that's where she'll be."

Irena yawned and nodded. "I'll do that. Tomorrow we'll go back to find his family."

22

Jacob woke with a start, instinctively fumbling for Affie and grabbing him tight. A coughing fit shook his body, yet somehow the cough felt different, softer. It didn't end in a burning sensation starting in his throat and spreading across his entire core.

Another thing was different, too. He wore a soft, oversized flannel shirt and was tucked in beneath a fluffy eiderdown much like the one he used to have at home. Before he even opened his eyes, he remembered the nurse taking him to what he assumed was her home.

A frightening worry crept up his spine and he squeezed his eyes shut, hoping he'd hear his mother tell him the entire hellish journey had been nothing but a bad dream. Next, he heard steps crossing the floor to his bed, still not daring to open his eyes, wishing so hard his mami would rub his head the way she did every morning.

"Jakub, nic ci nie jest?"

He slammed his eyes open with shock, just to see the nurse from the day before. His most fervent wish was shattered, so he started crying. "Mami! Where are you? Mami!"

The nurse heaved him out of the bed and into her arms.

Despite her not being his mother, it still felt good to be held. Despite not understanding a single word she said, he found her tone of voice soothing. After a while he stopped crying and hesitantly opened his eyes to look at her more closely.

She wore a nightgown, and her long dark hair fell down almost to her waist, which made her look kinder than at the hospital where she'd had her hair in braids around her head and a white hat on top. Her brown eyes twinkled with kindness and concern, similar to the way his mother used to look at him when she was worried. As soon as he stopped crying, she talked again, but he couldn't understand, which caused a new slew of tears rushing down his cheeks.

"Shush. No cry," she soothed him, walking around and rubbing his back until he calmed again. He was so awfully scared. A million questions at once attacked him. *Where am I? And why? Where's my mami? Why has she abandoned me?*

Looking around the room, he noticed the marital bed, where she must have slept, since it was unmade. There was no other person present, so he assumed her husband must be at war like his own father.

The room looked pretty much like his parents' bedroom, although worse for wear, a shabby wallpaper hanging loose in several places. The big bed stood against one wall, a small nightstand to either side, a wooden cross watching over the couple from the wall, and a crib standing in the opposite corner. This must be where he'd slept the night. Righteous indignation filled his chest, since he was much too old to be sleeping in a crib. He'd have to tell her that under no circumstances would he be treated like a baby for another night.

The alarming thought of spending a second night in this house sent fresh tears to his eyes, but he valiantly swallowed them down. The nurse walked to the big bed, sat him down and settled next to him. She pointed at him and said, "Jakub?"

His brow scrunched up at the peculiar pronunciation of his name, but he nodded. "Jacob. My name is Jacob."

"*Tak*. Jakub," she said with a smile.

"No, Jacob," he tried to correct her.

She frowned, seemingly confused. "Jakub."

For whatever reason she didn't seem to notice that Jacob and Jakub were two completely different names. The first was his name, and the latter was some Polish name... A shiver raced down his spine. She didn't think he was Polish, now did she? Was that the reason she refused to speak German with him?

Everyone had warned him that Poles were malicious people, who couldn't be trusted. They were not as intelligent as Germans and therefore couldn't do more than the most menial work.

He hadn't been allowed to play with Polish children, because good Germans didn't do that. Nevertheless, they'd had a Polish maid and a nanny for a while. As far as Jacob remembered, both of them had always been kind to him and Sophie. Until one day, his father had explained that it wasn't good for Jacob to pick up language and behavior from a woman belonging to an inferior race. The next day the nanny was gone and the maid had received strict orders not to talk to the children and to address them as "Fräulein Sophie" and "Herr Jacob" when asking about their breakfast wishes.

The nurse pointed at herself, saying, "Irena."

Jacob repeated the word, pointing at her. "Irena?"

She beamed at smile and nodded. "*Tak*."

That was easy enough, since he knew *tak* meant yes, so he smiled as well. The next moment his stomach grumbled, making him look away, embarrassed.

Irena didn't seem to be fazed and stretched out her hand. "*Chodź*."

Unsure what she meant, he opted to take her hand and let her pull him out of the room and down the stairs into a cozy

living room. Once again, tears pooled in his eyes, as he was
reminded of his home. Her house was smaller and less well
kept, but it emanated the same homey atmosphere. Instinctively
he realized that he was safe with this Irena woman.

She motioned for him to sit at the table and left for another
room, which he assumed to be the kitchen. And just minutes
later, she returned with a bowl of porridge and a glass of water.

"*Jedz!*" she said, putting the food in front of him. This time
he had no doubt what she meant and greedily shoveled the
porridge into his mouth. She smiled before she left again, only
to return with a small brown bottle in her hand, which he recognized as the horrid tasting medicine.

He wanted to throw a tantrum, but one look at her face with
the stern expression told him he'd have no choice but to swallow
the awful stuff. With all the contempt he could muster he
opened his mouth for the spoonful of medicine. The bitter,
slimy liquid entered his mouth, making not only his tongue and
gums convulse, but his entire face. He scrunched up his nose
and shook his shoulders, before grabbing the glass of water and
downing it.

Still, the disgusting, acidy, yet furry feeling lingered in his
mouth until he ate a spoonful of porridge, carefully sloshing the
mush from one cheek into the other to sweep away any trace of
the horrid taste.

Why did medicine always have to taste so bad? *Because
otherwise it would be a treat and wouldn't help.* That was what
his mother had always said. The thought of her saddened him
incredibly. He looked up at Irena. "Where is my mami?"

She sighed and answered something he didn't understand.
Observing the sad look in her eyes he got the distinct feeling
that either she didn't know, or she was hiding something from
him. That realization was more than a bit troubling, yet he
determined he would be brave and put his entire focus on
munching the porridge. Irena took his empty bowl and walked

into the kitchen, returning with two bowls this time; a small second serving for him and about the same amount for her.

Having been up for what seemed all morning had exhausted him and he yawned.

"*Śpij!*," she said.

He gave her an inquiring look, hoping to get some clue what he was supposed to do.

She put her hands together and inclined her head to the side, coming to lie atop her hands, while she closed her eyes.

He nodded. Normally, he'd protest the order to go to sleep, but right now he felt so very tired and was actually thankful for being allowed to go to bed. Like a good child he followed her upstairs and let her help him into the crib, where she tucked him beneath the covers. His eyes closed immediately and he drifted back to sleep, even before he could ask about his mother again.

In his dream, he saw Mami's lovely face as she whispered, "I love you, Jacob, I love you so much."

23

Emma's heart was bleeding, as she put one foot in front of the other toward the train station.

"Do you want to go back to the hospital one more time?" Luise asked as they made their way out of the refugee camp and toward the train station.

"I'd like to," Emma murmured and looked at Sophie walking by her other side. She couldn't stay here and risk her daughter falling into the hands of the Russians. As much as she yearned for Jacob, she had to consider Sophie too, and needed to make the best decision for everyone involved.

Even if she wanted to though, there was no way to return to the abandoned hospital, since SS soldiers urged the refugees forward. Those who couldn't keep up were told to wait for the *Lumpensammler*, the truck driving behind and picking everyone up.

Meticulous as always, the Nazis who had forbidden the civilians to flee for such a long time, would now make sure not a single person was left behind. Surprisingly that knowledge gave her some reprieve, because surely they had registered Jacob in their lists and would make sure he was put on one of the trains.

Once they arrived—wherever that would be—it was simply a matter of time and patience, until she found her little darling again. She just hoped he wouldn't be too afraid and had a kind woman taking care of him meanwhile.

Sophie's hand sneaked into hers. "Do you think Jacob will be alright?"

"I'm sure he is. The entire hospital was evacuated, so don't you worry."

Sophie didn't seem convinced, but the quick pace of the crowd didn't let her catch her breath to engage in a discussion, for which Emma was grateful. She was worried enough as it was, without having to explain how exactly they'd manage to find Jacob again.

Luise walked by her other side, holding Hans tightly by the hand. "We'll find him."

"Thank you." Emma was genuinely grateful for the support of her friend, who must be out of her mind with grief over the loss of her baby.

As they reached a small rise just ahead of the train station, she looked back one last time. The reddish-orange glow from buildings on fire rose into the sky, mixing with dark black smoke. It felt as if someone was ripping her heart out of her chest, throwing it to the ground and trampling all over it. How would she ever be able to be happy again if she didn't find Jacob?

The spire of the church next to the Catholic Hospital stood erect, calling out to her. Luring her. Promising her. Shaming her. She should have insisted on staying with him, should have slept in the hospital yard, should have...

"I'm not leaving my son!" she said and turned on her heel, suddenly intent on doing whatever it took to find him.

But she hadn't taken more than a few steps, when a soldier stepped in her way. "What the hell are you doing, woman?"

"I have to go and find my son."

"You can't. Nobody can return into town, or the Russians will kill you."

"I'd rather be dead than abandon my child," she whimpered.

"Please, I have orders to force everyone to evacuate, at gunpoint if needed," he pleaded with her.

A hand landed on her shoulder and she turned to look into Agatha's stern eyes.

"Officer, I'll make sure she doesn't do anything stupid."

He nodded, apparently relieved that someone had taken the frantic woman off his hands.

For better or worse, Emma had to follow the crowd. She gazed over her shoulder, begging God: *Please let my boy be safe. And let me find him again. Please!* Every time they passed a woman with a small child, she looked down into the little one's face, hoping against hope, it would be Jacob. It never was.

When they arrived at the train station, they were distributed into the railcars. Once more, Agatha assumed command, and kept their small group together as she herded them into a compartment, where the women were assigned three of the six available seats and told to take the children on their laps.

As the train departed, Emma peered out of the window into the gray faces of those waiting for the next opportunity to evacuate, while every cell in her body yearned to return to Posen and search for Jacob.

With every yard the moving locomotive laid between her and the place she'd last seen her son, her heart broke a bit more, until it felt as if her entire being—body, heart and soul—had been torn in half. How could she survive this? How could she ever live with the knowledge that she hadn't fought hard enough for Jacob? That she had abandoned what she loved most in this world?

When the silhouette of the city faded into the clouded sky,

she buried her face in Sophie's hair, attempting to hide her tears from the others.

"Mami. Please don't cry," Sophie whispered, pressing her thin body against Emma's chest. "You said Jacob will be fine."

"Yes."

"Why are you so sad then?" Sophie's voice turned into a high-pitched shriek and Emma sensed her daughter was about to break down. Emma had to stay strong for her sake, had to pretend there was nothing to worry about.

"It's just because I've never been apart from him." She furtively swiped her tears away, took a deep breath and tried a tentative smile. Her gaze fell on Agatha, sitting opposite her, whose face was suddenly a picture of misery.

Agatha looked decades older than she had just an hour ago. The determination with which she'd fought for her little group all the way from Lodz to the railcar was gone. Instead, she slumped in her seat, her lips quivering. Even her immaculate bun of dark hair had come undone, revealing a disturbing number of gray streaks that hadn't been there even a week ago.

Emma leaned over and touched Agatha's hand. "We are safe. Thanks to you."

"This was my home. I've never known any other place than Lodz." Agatha shook her head. "You shouldn't uproot an old tree like me."

Luise, who was rocking Hans on her lap, while she silently wept over the loss of her newborn, didn't even open her eyes, as she accused her mother-in-law, "It was your idea. You wanted to go to Aachen to those cousins of yours. If we had stayed, my baby would still be alive."

"Shush, you can't be sure," Emma said, although she understood her friend. If they had stayed, Jacob would still be with her, too.

Luise put Hans aside, got up and yelled, "I am sure. I'd be lying in my warm and cozy bed, nursing my sweet little daughter instead of sitting half-dead in this cursed train to God knows where! It's all your fault!"

Agatha crouched deeper into her seat, all strength sucked from her person, muttering, "I did what was best. We couldn't stay."

"We could! Who knows whether the Russians are really as bad as we're told? We've been fed lies from the propaganda ministry for years. 'Strategic straightening of the front line' this, 'reinforcement by regrouping' that. You know what? All sham and lies! This war is lost and we'll all pay for it dearly." She slumped back into her seat, leaving the other passengers speechless with their mouths hanging agape. "I already sacrificed my baby on Hitler's altar. What else does he want?"

"Shush." Despite her own turmoil, Emma wrapped her arms around Luise, rocking her like a small child. "Please excuse my friend, she doesn't mean it. She just gave birth and the newborn died the same day. It's been too much for her."

The other women in the compartment nodded. It'd been too much for each one of them, at one time or another. Every single one of them had experienced the loss of relatives and so were willing to ignore her outburst against the Führer, chalking it up to the horrible grief a mother felt when losing one of her children.

"We'll get over this," Emma whispered the words into Luise's ear, although she wasn't sure she herself believed in them.

It wasn't only the worry about Jacob that had her anxious to her core, but also the fact that she and Sophie depended solely on the kindness of Agatha's relatives to take them in. What would she do, if they refused? Where would they live? And how would Herbert find her then?

Thoughts of her husband didn't help to alleviate her worries. It had been months since his last letter and she had no idea where he was, or if he was even alive. He could have fallen and since the authorities didn't have a forwarding address, she'd never received the dreaded telegram.

Renewed grief shot hot and cold shivers down her spine. The emotion was too powerful to fight, so she closed her eyes and bit her lips, holding to her last shred of composure. *I must stay strong. I must stay strong. For Sophie. For Luise. For Hans. For Agatha. They all need me now.*

She tried to find the positive in her situation, tried to be grateful that her daughter and her friends were with her, but it wouldn't dissipate the sorrow for Jacob and Herbert. It didn't take long before the monotonous rattle sent everyone else to sleep, but she sat there, wide awake, reliving every moment of Jacob's young life.

The day he was born. The first time he walked. His first haircut. The first word he said. "Mami."

Please God. Please, keep him safe. I beg you.

24

After tucking Jakub into bed, Irena retreated into the kitchen to clean their breakfast dishes and prepare lunch. She hadn't thought about this before, but feeding an extra mouth on their ration cards wouldn't work for long.

Luka was right, she had to return to the hospital and find Jakub's mother as soon as possible. She pondered going right now, but didn't dare leave the boy alone in her home. He'd be frightened to death if he woke and nobody was there. He might even crawl out of the crib and run away, to freeze to death before the day was over.

Sighing, she put the clean dishes onto the shelves. It had to wait until he woke up. Then the two of them would go to the hospital together and see if they could find his mother.

It wasn't until noon that Jakub woke, crying. She rushed upstairs to console him and her soul lit up at the bright smile he cast her, thrusting his arms toward her. This was exactly how she'd imagined life with a child of her own. She picked him up, brushing a damp curl from his forehead.

"Jakub, we'll get you dressed, because we are going to the

hospital to find your mami," she told him in a cheery voice. As usual, he didn't understand, although his smile became brighter when she said 'Mami' and he nodded fervently.

With little food to spare, she made them both a cup of hot tea. While it brewed, she measured a spoonful of the cough medicine and handed him a glass of water to swallow it down. His disgusted-but-brave face was hilarious.

"Good boy," she murmured, patting him on the back. "Taking the medicine and staying in the warm bed, you'll get better in no time at all." The experienced nurse in her raised a warning finger, whispering, "You know he shouldn't be outside in his condition."

From a medical point of view her endeavor was reckless, but what else was she to do if she wanted to find his mother?

She removed Jakub's shoes from atop the tiled stove and said, "Put them on."

Her heart swelled with warmth when the intelligent boy immediately understood and went to work. As she bent down to tie his shoelaces, he already was on it, albeit clumsy and slow.

"Well done. Come, Jakub. Let's go find your mami."

"*Ja,*" he answered, his pale face shining brighter than the sun itself.

She almost regretted having to return him to his mother, since he was such a delightful child. Putting on a hat, scarf and gloves, she motioned for him to wait while she rushed upstairs to get him a sweater of Luka's.

Wrapped in her husband's oversized sweater, Jakub looked hilarious. At least it would keep him warm. She wrapped a scarf around his head and opened the door for them to leave.

The chill outside was a shock, biting deep into her exposed cheeks. She readjusted first Jakub's scarf and then her own to cover most of their faces, barely leaving squints for their eyes.

Taking his hand into hers, she set out to walk toward the

hospital. Today the streets were all but deserted, save for a few Wehrmacht stragglers making their way to the train station in a last-ditch attempt to avoid being captured by the Red Army.

As much as she hated the German oppressors, empathy tucked at her heartstrings looking into the defeated faces of the young men—only boys really. How lucky she was that her Luka had never been drafted into the Polish army, or sent to work in the Reich, because his services as a doctor were very much in demand by the new administration.

Despite knowing that Jakub didn't understand her, she kept talking to him. It seemed listening to her voice calmed him. In that respect he was like any other baby, who needed the human voice to flourish. But mostly she talked to reassure herself.

"We're going to search for your mother. I probably shouldn't have taken you home last night. But then, everyone else had been evacuated and I was afraid you wouldn't survive the night on your own. The Red Army was about to conquer the hospital and who knows what they would have done to you... I mean they are not bad, but they are rightfully angry at the Germans, and since you are German..." She was babbling and she knew it. She couldn't stop though, because it helped to sort through her thoughts, to clear her mind and, most importantly, to assuage her guilt.

The moment they arrived at the wall surrounding the hospital grounds, she gasped in shock. It was a sight of utter destruction, looking even more devastating than when she'd left the day before.

"It's destroyed," she murmured aloud. Smoke rose from the building and the blackened stones spoke of there having been a raging fire.

"The Russians..." she stammered, not noticing the small group of people standing next to her.

"The Russians didn't do this," a man spat out. "The

Germans did this themselves. They didn't want their enemy to be able to set up a field hospital here."

She looked at him and shook her head. "They wouldn't do that, would they?"

"Sure they did. Or have you forgotten how evil they are? Capable of anything?"

"But why would they do that?" Irena asked.

"They know they're losing this war, and want to leave their enemy nothing but scorched earth," another man murmured.

"What about us? This is our city," another nurse asked.

"When have the Nazis ever cared about us? To them, we are expendable, in every way," Irena murmured. Suddenly she felt incredibly glad about her rash decision to take Jakub home with her. It didn't bear contemplating what would have happened if he'd been in there during the fire.

Grabbing his hand tighter, she ventured beyond the walls into the huge hospital yard, and then wished she hadn't. There were not only crushed pieces of furniture and broken glass lying scattered on the trampled snow, but also bloodied corpses.

Dear God! Her first reaction was to shield Jakub's eyes so he wouldn't have to see this. Though, this might only alert his curiosity, so she decided to behave as normally as possible. With him by her side, she didn't dare go further inside, for fear of what else she might find.

She wiped the snow from a bench and sat down, propping Jakub on her lap and contemplated her next steps, when the matron stepped out of the building. The veteran nurse was pale as a bedsheet, swaying as she walked down the steps.

"Matron!" Irena jumped up and rushed toward her, Jakub in her wake. "Are you alright?"

"It was a massacre. They killed each and every remaining patient in the building."

"Oh," was all Irena could answer. Too outrageous were the

matron's words. For once she was glad Jakub didn't understand Polish.

"God knows, I'm not fond of the Germans, but this... these were the sickest patients, those who couldn't be transported. Each and every one executed with a bullet to their heart."

Irena felt the vomit rising in her throat. It didn't matter whether the Germans had done it themselves, or the Russians when they arrived. It was an awful, unspeakably gruesome crime either way.

Matron's gaze fell on Jakub. "Who is that boy?"

Unsure how to explain, Irena hesitated. Thankfully another nurse approached them and relieved her of having to give an answer. "Matron! I'm so glad you're unharmed."

Jakub tugged on Irena's coat with a hopeful smile. "Mami?"

"I don't know where she is, little one. We'll wait right here for a while and see if your mami shows up," she said, leading him back to the bench, sitting down and cradling him on her lap.

As time passed, her doubts intensified. If the Germans had evacuated the walking patients and the Russians had shot the rest, there was little chance Jakub's mother would return to the hospital grounds on the off chance that some rogue nurse had taken Jakub with her for the night. She snorted at the ridiculousness of her thought.

Still, she determined to sit and wait for another half hour, before making their way to the refugee camp. Knowing how well-organized the Germans were, there must be some kind of registration desk where people could inquire about their loved ones.

Inside the outer wall, they were protected from the worst gushes of wind, yet after a while the cold seeped into her bones and Jakub began coughing. She got up from time to time and walked around with him, praying for his mother to arrive. But the only people showing up were employees who'd come to see whether their services were still needed.

They invariably left after a glance at the utter destruction. Just as she decided to tackle the march to the refugee camp, she heard loud shouting in Russian. Seconds later a group of soldiers strode into the yard.

She frantically searched for a way out, but there was none. The only exit was through the very door the soldiers had come through. To make things worse, they had spotted her and walked directly toward her. She jumped up, shielding Jakub behind her body.

"Hey, you!" one of them shouted in a mish-mash of Russian and German. "No loitering. Go home."

Panic constricted her throat. They mistook her for a German and who knew what they would do next. Gathering up all her courage, she swallowed down the lump and answered them in their own language. "I'm a nurse. I work here."

"You speak Russian?" the tallest said, slightly less hostile.

"Yes, sir. I'm a Pole." She thought for a moment. It wouldn't do any harm to lay it on thick. "I love the Red Army and am so glad you came to liberate us from the Nazis."

A genuine smile broke out on his face. "Our great Soviet Union will prevail and fight all evil in this world. The Polish nation can be proud to be a Socialist brother nation, because we are all in this together."

She understood only half of the political propaganda he spewed, nevertheless she put a good face on the matter and even allowed him to enthusiastically shake her hand and praise her for the heroic work she was doing as a nurse.

"We do need courageous locals to help us rebuild this country," the shorter one said.

"Only those who never collaborated with the enemy," the first one added.

A cold shiver ran down her spine, as she considered his

words. Technically, she'd been a collaborator from the day the
Nazis had evicted all Polish patients in the Catholic Hospital
and forced the employees to cater for German patients from
then on.

Jakub's tight grip on her leg, as he was hiding behind her,
added to her predicament. What would they do if they found
out she was harboring a German boy? Would they see the
enemy in him despite his tender age? With trembling lips she
pressed out, "I'm most willing to do my bit helping the great
Soviet Union to rebuild my country."

"We'll need a few days, but as soon as the new administration is set up, go and offer your services. Tell them Lieutenant
Samarov sent you."

"I will certainly do that." Despite their friendliness, she
itched to get away from them. Just then, Jakub peeked out his
head from behind her skirts.

"Is this your son?"

Panic left her speechless, so she nodded, praying Jakub
wouldn't betray them by speaking German.

"What's his name?"

"Ja...kub."

"I had a friend with the name of Jakov," the taller soldier
said. Before he could launch into a lengthy reminiscence, the
other one pointed his head toward the hospital. "We have to
search for surviving Nazis." Then he moved his flat hand across
his throat and laughed.

"It was nice chatting with you, miss," the first one said. "You
and your boy should better leave now. What we have to do is
nothing for a woman to witness."

"Yes... thank you..." Shaken by their callous lust to kill, she
took Jakub into her arms and fled from the hospital grounds
with lightning speed. Huffing and puffing like a locomotive, she
didn't stop to set the boy down before she'd put two blocks
between them and the hospital.

"Die Russen sind böse," Jakub said, gazing at her with his big blue eyes.

For once she had no difficulties understanding him. The Russians are mean. Those two might have been kind to her, but she wouldn't want to be in a German's shoes during the weeks to come.

And neither should Jakub.

25

Luka was waiting for her when she arrived home in the afternoon.

"Where have you been? I was worried sick..." His gaze fell on Jakub, so he didn't finish his sentence.

"We were at the hospital. It's completely destroyed. Matron was there and said all the remaining patients had been killed in their beds." She was close to breaking down in tears.

"Why did you bring him back?"

"We waited for quite a while at the hospital, but nobody came, except some other nurses, and then two Russian soldiers who urged me to go home. Then we walked all the way to the refugee camp, just to find it had been evacuated. There was nothing but trampled snow, not even the tents. Nothing." She gave a deep sigh. "I couldn't well leave him out there, now could I?"

Luka shook his head, as he helped her out of her winter coat, hanging it next to the door, while she peeled Jakub's clothes off him.

"What do you propose we do now?"

Irena looked back and forth between the little boy and her

husband. "I'll go to the administration first thing in the morning to register him."

"The Russians have taken over already. I don't think it's wise to tell them we have a German boy in our custody. They weren't exactly friendly toward the Nazis."

"Then... what?" Irena settled on the bench beside the tiled stove to warm her chilled bones, cradling Jakub on her lap.

Luka settled beside them, hugging them close. "We'll make inquiries as soon as the chaos has settled. For now, he'll stay with us, at least until he completely recovers from his illness."

As if to emphasize Luka's words, Jakub broke out into a violent coughing fit.

"I'll get his medicine," she said, settled Jakub on the bench and walked into the kitchen.

Luka followed her, helping her to measure the cough syrup while she poured a glass of water from the tap.

"We do need to find his parents," she murmured.

"And we will. Once the new structures are in place, we'll register him as a missing child with the Red Cross. They'll find his relatives, I'm sure."

As they left the kitchen, they saw that Jakub had walked toward the table and was climbing on the chair. Once settled, he said, "*Ich habe Hunger.*"

"Do you know what he wants?" Luka asked.

Irena's heart warmed. Jakub was such an intelligent, well-behaved little boy. "Isn't it quite obvious? He wants something to eat."

"Oh." Luka, like so many men, was better equipped for technical problems than divining the needs of small children.

"We haven't eaten since we left the house around noon. I'll go and prepare dinner, you give him the medicine."

She was washing potatoes, when Luka's panic-stricken voice caused her to rush into the living room with dripping wet hands.

"What am I supposed to do with him now?"

She barely contained her laughter. "You could teach him to set the table for starters."

A panicked gleam appeared in Luka's eyes. "But he doesn't speak Polish!"

"Well, then show him, he's a bright little guy." She returned to the kitchen, feeling lighter than in a very long time as she cut the potatoes into pieces and dropped them into a broth. They had no meat, but she added two carrots, to provide some needed vitamins for Jakub's speedy recovery.

When she called them to dinner half an hour later, Luka and Jakub were sitting on the bench next to the tiled oven, leafing through a photo album. She broke out into a smile seeing the two of them together in such peace and happiness.

"Dinner is ready," she announced, putting the pot on the table. She ladled soup into three bowls and gave one slice of bread to each.

Jakub looked at her with expectant eyes. Then he held up his hands, making a wringing gesture as he said, "*Hände waschen.*"

"Oh, yes, wash your hands." She led him to the kitchen sink and held him up so he reached the faucet. Then she handed him a towel to dry his hands.

Luka was waiting for them at the table, his hands folded for prayer. Even in their darkest times, they'd never renounced the custom to say a prayer before meals, thanking God for the food and asking for the war to end.

Jakub attentively observed Luka, as if he understood something important was happening and ate his soup only when Luka wished them a good meal and took his own spoon.

"We need to find someone who speaks German to help us communicate with him," Luka said after a while.

"The poor boy must be out of his mind, not knowing where his mother is and why he's with us. It'll be easier for him if he understands the reasons." Irena nibbled on her bread. What had been planned for two people would now have to suffice for three. "At the hospital today he seemed to recognize the soldiers were Russians and was hiding behind my back when they spoke to me." A disturbing thought occurred to her. "Do you think he believes they killed his mother?"

Luka spooned his soup. "It's quite probable, or she would have come to fetch him. Although, as long as we don't have confirmation of that, we should let him believe his mother is alive and searching for him. We might have to come up with some story why she can't be here with him."

"I know." Irena worried her lip. Children had the habit of questioning anything and everything, and kept on asking for answers until they finally got one that satisfied their curiosity and made sense to them. She'd experienced it many times at work. Children were amazingly adaptive to new situations, but they needed a meaningful explanation. "Who do you think we could ask?"

"Ask about what?" From the frown on his face, she realized that Luka had mentally moved on to the next problem, probably some patient whose illness and treatment he had yet to figure out. It was a habit she'd found rather annoying in their first years of marriage, but had come to accept as being the way he was.

"To speak German with Jakub."

"Oh... right. That won't be easy. I assume everyone with German roots has been evacuated and most others won't dare to admit they speak the language." He must have seen her dejected face, because he added, "But I'm sure we'll find some-one. Let me think about it."

26

Jacob was woken in the early hours of the night from loud snoring. He gazed into the other corner of the room, where Irena was sleeping with her husband Luka.

Luka had been nothing but friendly the previous day, but he too hadn't been able to tell him what was going on. It was so frustrating having to deal with people who couldn't speak German.

You'd think everyone should be able to, if even *he* had learned it and he was only four years old. He remembered his father saying the Poles belonged to an inferior race and weren't very bright. Was that the reason why these two grown-ups hadn't mastered the German language?

Yet, he liked then. Irena had rescued him from spending the night all alone in that awful hospital and brought him to her house, given him food, dry clothes and a bed to sleep in.

Of course, the bed was much too small. At home he'd moved from his crib to sharing a big bed with Sophie years ago. Thoughts of his sister saddened him and he quietly began to cry. His mami had promised to come back for him, so where was she?

A cough erupted and he put the blanket over his head, so he wouldn't wake Irena and Luka. Then it struck him with disturbing clarity. His mother had not returned because he was sick. She was angry at him for slowing them down on the trek.

Sophie's spiteful words echoed in his head. "Because of you we're so far behind the others. You'll get us all killed."

He lay under the blanket stiff as a poker, trying to get to grips with the notion that his mami was punishing him for slowing them down. He was a danger to the rest of the group. That's why she'd abandoned him!

His sobs soon became uncontrollable and he whimpered, "I didn't mean it! I didn't get sick on purpose. You must believe me, Mami, I never wanted to get you killed. Please, if you come back for me, I'll always behave. Big promise!"

A hand stroked over his head and murmured soothing words. Moments later, two arms grabbed him and heaved him out of the crib.

"Jakub, shush," Irena whispered, rocking him back and forth on her lap. It was such a comfort to feel her presence, her soapy scent. Automatically, he wrapped his arms around her, burying his face in her soft bosom.

She might not understand his language, but she certainly cared for him when the rest of the world, including his mami, had abandoned him. New tears flooded his eyes and streamed down his face, wetting her nightgown.

He shrunk back, afraid she'd deride him, but she only held him tighter against her. "Shush, Jakub, shush." The warmth of her skin was so comforting he leaned into her once more, slowly relaxing as the sobbing eased off. Finally he managed to breathe properly again.

In the morning, he woke by a tickle in his nose. Gazing around, he noticed that he was lying in the big bed cuddled against Irena, who had her arm wrapped around his midriff, making him feel protected.

His eyes were drawn to the crib, where he'd been sleeping the last two nights. *Why isn't their child sleeping in there?* And, more importantly, would she send him away, once her own child returned? He held his breath with fear, until he couldn't anymore.

A sudden nervousness took possession of him and he fidgeted to get away from under Irena's heavy arm. He needed to get to the hospital right now and make sure his mother knew he was with Irena and Luka.

Once he'd freed himself, he slipped out of the bed and climbed downstairs with the plan to return to the hospital grounds and leave a note for his mother. He found a piece of paper and a pencil next to the door and laid on his stomach in front of the tiled oven to put in scribbly letters the only word he knew to write: JACOB.

That would have to suffice. With this, his mother would know what to do. The note in one hand, he had just located his shoes and coat, when Irena came down the stairs.

"*Jakub, co robisz?*" she asked.

"Nothing," he said, flushing, because she'd caught him in the act. Like any adult, she wouldn't approve of him going out on his own, therefore he hid the note behind his back.

She took his hand and led him to the table, motioning for him to sit down. Then she sat beside him and explained something in a very serious tone. Even though he didn't understand the words, he knew exactly what she was saying: "You can't go out on your own, it's too dangerous. It's not even light out yet. And it's too far to go to the hospital. I'll go with you later. Don't you worry." Well, at least that's what his mother would have said and Irena had been acting very much like her these past few days.

Jakub went back to sleep for another couple of hours. When he woke again, it was light outside. After breakfast, Irena and Luka took him between them and walked back to the hospital.

It wasn't different from the day before, there was still broken furniture on the ground, and there were still people sleeping in the snow. He wondered whether they didn't feel cold out there. He was certainly cold, despite being wrapped in an oversized sweater that reached down to his ankles and a woolen scarf on top.

His mami wasn't there again though. Secretly he doubted she would ever return for him. He remembered all too well the urgency with which Hans' grandma had pushed them on throughout their journey, always insisting they had to hurry up to reach central Germany before the Russians caught up with them.

The Russians obviously had arrived in this town, because the streets were full with their soldiers, so his family must be either dead or gone. He hoped the latter was true and they had managed to flee in time to reach safety with Hans' relatives. If only he knew where they lived, then he could go there by himself.

Deep in his thoughts, he didn't pay any notice to Irena and Luka who were talking with everyone that passed, until he suddenly heard someone speak German.

His head popped up and he looked around until he found an older man standing a few feet away, muttering to himself. Jacob jumped up and rushed toward him, ignoring Irena's exasperated yelp.

He reached the man in no time at all and tugged on his coat to gain his attention. "Can you help me find my mami?"

The man looked at Jacob with a shocked expression. "Where did you lose her?"

Jacob started talking quickly, backing away from Irena, who'd sidled up to them. She said something to the man in Polish. Afraid, he would leave without helping him, Jacob tugged on his coat once more.

"Where is my mami?"

The man smiled and answered, "My name is Karol and this woman here, Irena, would like me to translate for you. Your name is Jakub, isn't it?"

Jacob nodded. He'd given up correcting their mispronunciation of his name. In any case he had more important questions to ask.

"Does she know where my mami is?"

"Irena and her husband have been trying find her for you, but haven't been successful yet. They suggest you live with them for a while, just until things settle down and they can find a way to contact your mami. Would you like to do that? Live with Irena?"

Jacob slowly nodded. Karol smiled before speaking to Irena once more. She answered him and hugged Jacob close.

"Where is Sophie? Can I see her?" Jacob asked.

"Who is Sophie?" Karol asked.

"My sister. We fight all the time, because she's so bossy. But now I really miss her and want her back."

More words were exchanged between the grown-ups. Jacob felt the urgent need to clarify one more thing, "I'm so sorry. It was always so cold and I was so hungry. Can you tell her I didn't do it on purpose?"

"What?" Karol seemed confused by Jacob's explanation, so he tried once more.

"I was too slow, so they always had to wait for me. Sophie was mad and said I'd get them all killed. And then I got sick. Do you think she convinced Mami to leave me here?"

"I'm sure that's not the case. Your mami loves you. That's why she brought you to the hospital so that you could recover."

"Mami was always crying when she thought I didn't see. She told Luise that she wished they'd never gone on that trek. It's all my fault." Jacob looked down at his feet.

Karol was getting visibly impatient. "It's not your fault, so stop saying that. For the time being you'll stay with Irena and Luka, and they'll help you to find your family."

Irena talked to Karol for a while, before he turned to Jacob again and asked, "What is your last name?"

"Jacob Opaman." He smiled with pride. Back at home his mother had drilled this and his address into him in case he got lost. Valiantly fighting against his tears, he also told Karol that his hometown was Lodz and that they'd been fleeing to some relatives of his best friend's grandma.

"This is very good. It will be useful finding your mami. But you have to be patient. Nothing can be done before the war has ended."

Jacob tore his eyes wide open. During his lifetime there had never been a time without war. It was as normal as the snow in winter and sunshine in summer. Why should the war suddenly end? And when? His voice was but a whisper when he asked, "How long is that?"

Finally, Karol smiled. "Not long now. The Russians have already liberated half of our country."

Now, Jacob genuinely doubted Karol's sanity. The Russians were the enemies. Everyone he knew was deathly afraid of them. So, how could Karol pretend they were friends? But before he could formulate his thoughts, Karol asked, "What about your father. Where is he?"

"Papa is a soldier. He's keeping us safe by fighting the Russians."

Karol didn't acknowledge his words, instead he spoke to Irena for what seemed an eternity. "You need to learn Polish while you're living with Irena. I have agreed to visit every week and help, but you must also do your best to learn from her."

Jacob didn't understand the world anymore. Back at home, he hadn't been allowed to play with the Polish children, his father even insisted the maid speak German with him, because theirs was an inferior language. When had all of this suddenly changed?

He squinted his eyes at Irena, wondering whether the nurse was simply not intelligent enough to learn German, a superior language. Well, if it helped to communicate with her while she searched for his mami, he could certainly do this. It might even prove to be fun.

"Agreed." He nodded and shook Karol's hand the way he'd seen his father do when conducting business.

"Now be a good boy and obey Irena. I'm sure she'll find your mami." With these words, Karol waved and walked away, leaving Jacob feeling bereft.

"Jakub?" Irena's soft voice said.

He turned and gave the woman a smile as she reached for his hand. She explained something to him he didn't understand. Just as despair was filling his lungs, Luka reached for his other hand and they returned to their home.

My home too, he thought. *At least for the time being.* He'd experienced worse during the trek, so perhaps all wasn't bad? Wherever his mami was, he'd just have to wait until the war ended—hopefully soon—then Irena would find her for him. He pushed the doubts away that whispered into his mind, claiming the war would never end. It had been there before Jacob was born, why should it suddenly go away? Things were so confusing and he wished he'd had more time to talk with Karol. He would have asked him, why he was so sure the Russians would stop fighting when they hadn't all these years?

And hadn't his father always told them the Wehrmacht was invincible, and would protect them from the Russians? Had all of this changed? Why? And how?

27

MAY 1945

What Irena hadn't dared to hope anymore had finally come true. The war was over. Not only in Posen, which had been liberated already by the end of February, but everywhere in Europe.

After the brutal month-long battle of Poznán, as the city was now called, more than three quarters of the of old town was destroyed, along with at least half of the houses in the entire city.

Irena and Luka had been luckier than many. Their house had remained intact, apart from a few shell splinter holes in the wall facing the street. After the liberation, or perhaps occupation, by the Red Army, there had been mayhem in the streets for several days, until the new administration, Polish Communists, backed by Stalin, had provided law and order once more. Slowly, life returned to something close to normal in the city.

Luka had immediately returned to his former job in the hospital under the new administration, while Irena split her time between working as a nurse and caring for Jakub.

One day, about a week after the end of the war, Luka came

home from the hospital and said, "There's a new Red Cross station next to the town hall."

She had known that this day would come, though with every passing day she'd dreaded it more. Little Jakub had burrowed himself deep into her heart, making her feel happier than she'd been since she'd lost her own child.

"I guess the time has come," she said.

"Yes." Luka paused. She knew he had come to love the boy as well, and both of them hadn't exactly bent over backwards to get him registered with the authorities. First due to fear of retaliations for harboring a German boy, then because he'd become a beloved part of their family.

"His mother will be looking for him." Irena sighed. "We'll go first thing in the morning to register him with the search service for missing persons."

"It's the right thing to do." Luka put his hand on hers.

"I know." She turned her head to look out the window, where Jakub was playing with a friend on the street. As always she was amazed by his ability to adapt.

The first weeks had been incredibly hard and he'd cried himself to sleep every single night, waking up several times and screaming for his mami and his sister Sophie. Sometimes he asked about Hans, who Irena assumed must be his father.

Her heart squeezed painfully with the knowledge that once she registered Jakub with the Red Cross, he could be taken away from her and returned to his real parents at any time. She shut her eyes, thinking about her hopes and dreams for the future, back when she'd been pregnant with their first child.

How much worse must it be to lose a child you had loved and nurtured for years? Not even knowing whether he was dead or alive? She willed her sadness away. It was her duty to try and find his parents. For them. For Jakub. Even for herself, because how could she look into the mirror every morning if she had deliberately stolen a child?

The next morning, Luka left for work, and half an hour later, Irena and Jakub headed for the Red Cross station in the main square. During the past months he had learned enough Polish to understand and answer easy questions. She couldn't have been prouder of him if he'd been her own flesh and blood.

She had enrolled him to start pre-school after summer, when the new school year started, hoping that would further improve his Polish and help him find friends. Sadness engulfed her. Perhaps by then he wouldn't be with her anymore.

"We are going to the Red Cross. They might know where your mother is," she explained, as they walked hand in hand down the street.

"Really?" Jakub asked in Polish.

"It's not for sure. But they will fill out a missing person request for you and if your mother did the same, it's only a matter of time." *If she's still alive.* Irena half-hoped his mother had perished during her escape to Germany.

It wasn't improbable, since they had heard so many awful stories in the news. The Polish people didn't behave exactly kindheartedly toward their former oppressors. She didn't condone the atrocities that had been committed, but deep in her heart she understood the rage and how it could erupt with such violent brutality. Jakub's mother and sister might never have made it into safety.

There'll be other relatives, her inner voice warned her. *They would have enough problems of their own and might not even be looking for the boy, or they might assume he died along with his mother*, she answered her conscience.

Her steps grew slower as they drew near the Red Cross station. For a moment she was tempted to turn on her heel, never to come here again. But Luka would be so angry with her, and rightfully so. There was no way around it. She had to register Jakub. It was the right thing to do.

She grabbed his small hand tighter and climbed the stairs

into the dilapidated house. The receptionist wore a white armband with a red cross and greeted them with a friendly voice.

"Good day, my name is Irena Pawlak. We want to register a missing person," Irena said.

"Are you looking for your father?" the Red Cross worker asked, looking at Jakub.

"My mother," he answered.

"Actually, he's the missing person," Irena explained. "I found him at the hospital where I worked after everyone else had been evacuated. To protect him from the soldiers I took him home with me."

The woman wrinkled her nose. "Have you registered him with the authorities, *Pani* Pawlak?"

"Not yet." Irena hesitated. "I... I was afraid... See... he's German and we didn't want to be punished for harboring an enemy."

"He's German?" the woman said with some disbelief. "I would have sworn he's your son when the two of you came inside."

Her affirmation warmed Irena's heart, but at the same time sent a searing stab through her entire body. The woman had spoken out loud what Irena had felt inside for a long time.

"We'll fill a 'seekers card' for him." The Red Cross worker produced a file card and handed it to Irena, who quickly scanned the questions.

"I'm sorry, but I can't answer most of them. Is there anyone who can speak German?"

The woman's face fell. "I guess... Can you return tomorrow? I'll make sure we have a German speaker here."

Irena nodded. "We'll be here."

The next day the two of them returned, and as the young woman had promised, there was an elderly man who introduced himself as *Pan* Wozniak. Together with him, they interviewed Jakub to get as many details from him as possible.

"What is your name?" *Pan* Wozniak asked.

"Jakub."

"And your last name?"

"Opaman."

Pan Wozniak wrote it down, looking slightly unsure whether that was the correct spelling. Irena gave him a helpless shrug, indicating she had no idea. He apparently decided it didn't make sense to ask the boy about it. Then he continued his questions.

Jakub remembered his age and that his birthday had been way before fleeing, but neither the month nor the day. The same was true for his last known address. He could tell them it was in Lodz and even the borough, but didn't remember the name of the street.

Instead he gave a vivid description of the house, the garden and the sledding hill nearby. Irena doubted any of that would actually help.

"What is the name of your mother?" *Pan* Wozniak asked.

"Mami."

Pan Wozniak groaned. "Your father?"

"Papi. He's a soldier in the Wehrmacht."

Another sigh. "Do you have sisters or brothers?"

"Yes. Sophie. She's seven."

"Is there anything else you remember about your family? Perhaps where they were headed? Or other relatives you have? Friends?"

Jakub scrunched up his nose in heavy thought, before he burst out, "We were traveling with friends. My best friend is Hans, he is the same age as I am."

"Do you happen to know his last name?"

Again, strained thought showed on Jakub's face, before he shook his head. "No. But his mami's name is Luise and then there's his grandma Agatha. She's a very strict woman who always scolded us for being misbehaved. I was quite afraid of her."

Pan Wozniak wrote down every little detail onto the blank back of the file card and then addressed Irena. "Is there anything you can add, *Pani* Pawlak?"

Irena repeated how Jakub had been admitted to the hospital and how she'd found him after everyone else had been evacuated. She even added that she'd tried in vain to find the patient register to locate his relatives.

"Well then." He handed the card to the Red Cross woman who explained, "We'll do everything we can, but it might take longer than you expect."

Irena's heart jumped for joy. "How long?"

"I really cannot say. It seems there are hundreds of thousands of missing children registered with the German Red Cross and every day they receive more requests. Cross-border searches are a lot more difficult and time consuming, so I'd say at least a few months. Perhaps even a year?"

"That long?"

The woman must have mistaken her elation for shock and said, "We understand this is a burden on you and if you cannot cope with caring for the boy anymore, we can always place him in an orphanage."

"Oh no! Not at all. We will definitely give him a home until his family is found." Deep down in her soul though, she hoped that day would never come.

28

FRIEDLAND, NEAR GÖTTINGEN. FOUR MONTHS LATER

Emma dropped to her knees, picking up a piece of earth and giving thanks that they had finally arrived at the Friedland transit camp, roughly three hundred and seventy miles west of Posen. At last she felt secure.

After months of traveling on foot and by train, being held up by battles, deviated north and south, shoved from one temporary holding place to another, they had reached the British occupied zone. Friedland camp was the place where all refugees coming from the East were registered and processed.

With nothing but the bundles they'd strung together in Posen on their backs, she along with Agatha, Luise, Hans and Sophie had finally made it. After leaving Posen their journey had been fraught with mishaps, including Luise getting a puerperal infection, meaning they had to stay in yet another refugee camp.

Agatha had urged Emma to continue alone with her daughter, but how could she abandon the two women who'd done so much for her? Luise was in dire need of a friend and Agatha too. She might not be able to admit it, but the old woman had been at her wits' end, lacking energy and hope. Therefore it hadn't taken much on Emma's side to convince them to stick together.

Inevitably, the front had caught up with them and her encounters with the Russian soldiers were something she never wanted to think back to again in all of her life. An uncontrollable shivering took hold of her, and she swayed, despite lying on her knees on safe ground in the British zone. Taking a labored breath, she forcefully shoved aside the memories of how she'd sacrificed herself to save Sophie.

Back then she'd made a pact with herself, never to talk about *that*, and never admit to anyone, even herself, how much trauma it had caused. As far as she was concerned, this *incident* would forever stay in the past, far away from her current life, almost as if had happened to a completely different person, who wasn't actually her.

Then they'd been assigned to yet another refugee camp, where they hadn't been allowed to leave the village, although that hadn't been possible anyway, while Luise still fought for her life in the camp hospital. The moment she'd been released, Emma had made her decision.

Throughout the past weeks, time and again, young, able-bodied girls had been taken by the Russians on work details. Most of them never returned to the camp. The gossip factory was working overtime, and sadly, some of the rumors became certainty: those fetched to work were often placed on trains and shipped to Russia where they were earmarked to pay for Germany's collective guilt with their labor, sweat, blood and ultimately their lives.

Emma had no intention of ending up like them. As soon as Luise was able to walk, she stepped in front of Agatha and said, "We need to leave this place sooner rather than later if we don't want to end up in a Soviet labor camp."

Agatha nodded. "They won't take me, but you and Luise..."

Emma gazed at her friend who was still weak on her legs

and wouldn't survive a single day of hard work. "Then it's decided. We're leaving tonight."

Not having been idle during the past weeks, she had explored the area surrounding the camp, and found a way to pass by the soldiers guarding the main streets leading in and out of the village.

This last leg of their journey had been equally arduous as the first one in January, with the difference that this time they suffered from scorching heat and thirst, as opposed to biting cold and hunger.

The war had ended months ago, brutally shattering her secret hope to be able to return to Lodz one day. The Russians had claimed all parts of Germany east of the Oder River as bounty of war and given it to the Poles. To the Poles of all people! Knowing their lackadaisical work ethics, it was only a matter of time until they ran the formerly fertile and productive region into the ground.

Emma didn't have time for self-pity though, because she'd been too occupied to ensure her little group reached safety. From the moment the train had departed Posen, Agatha had lost her verve and had retreated into herself evermore. Luise was too occupied grieving for her daughter to be of any use either, so the role of group leader had fallen on Emma, whether she wanted it or not.

In fact, she had often wished to curl up into a ball and cry for Jacob. She had given all his things to Hans and had only kept his favorite tin soldier that she kept in her pocket at all times.

"Let's go and register." She took Sophie by the hand and searched for the end of the long queue of refugees waiting to receive their paperwork.

Emma had never seen so many displaced people in her life, not even during their long trek. The moment she and Sophie took up their place in the line to register, she realized that life as she'd known it before the war was never going to return. She'd never return to Lodz either... and God beware, she shook her head to keep the disquieting thought away. She'd not give up on Jacob, ever. As soon as she got her bearings, she'd begin searching for him.

"Papers," a woman wearing the uniform of the British Salvation Army asked with a smile.

Emma handed over her and Sophie's identification.

"Do you have any relatives in Germany that we can inform?"

"Only in the Wartheland." Unfortunately, the region where she and her relatives had lived now belonged to Poland.

"Welcome to Camp Friedland." The young woman wrote some information in a ledger and returned the papers, plus a slip with a number on it. "The number indicates your hut. Go there and ask the person at the entrance to assign you bunks. But first you'll need to follow the line and register with all the other desks, where they'll give you the required stamps for ration books, clothing, search for lost relatives, et cetera."

Despite her friendliness, the British official had made it clear that Emma and Sophie were just another pair of refugees flocking in from all over Europe to what would be the new, dismembered Germany.

"Thank you." Emma nodded, took Sophie's hand and stepped away from the registration desk. Behind them Agatha, Louise and Hans handed over their papers. She hoped they'd end up in the same hut with them.

"Mami, do we have to stay here?" Sophie asked.

"For a little while. But first we have to register with all the other desks, like that woman said." She looked down the main street of the camp with several different queues, all leading to a desk positioned in front of a building shaped like a half-circle, with a green metallic roof and a brown wooden front, a structure known as a Nissen hut.

She sighed and queued up at the nearest one. Hours later, they'd finally finished what other refugees jokingly called running the gauntlet and were ready to wait in front of yet another Nissen hut, where people from the International Voluntary Service for Peace handed out hot chocolate and pieces of bread, with the promise of a meal when dinnertime came around.

Luise and Agatha joined them shortly after and it turned out they had been assigned to a hut on the opposite end of the camp.

"Within the next days, we'll be put on a train to Aachen to stay with my cousins," Agatha said and gave a sad smile. "You'll have to stay here until I can get confirmation from my cousins that they are willing to host you as well."

Emma's heart fell. The British might be kind and eager to help, but a refugee camp was still a refugee camp. Sophie hated them with a passion, especially because she couldn't go to school and every time she found a friend, they were gone a short time later or she herself had to move on. This wasn't a way of life for a child.

Again, her heart grew weary as she thought of Jacob. In her mother's heart, she knew he wasn't dead. But was he alright? Had some kind woman taken him under her wing?

"We'll see you later at the kitchen tent then?" Emma said, before she took Sophie by the hand to search for the hut with their number on it. There, they were assigned two neighboring bunks.

Compared to the Russian camps, and even the German ones during the end of the war, this was exceedingly well organized, though it was still a camp.

She left Sophie in the hut to put on the new clothing she'd received, since she'd outgrown her own ones. The poor mite looked exhausted, so Emma said, "Stay here and relax. I'll do the rest of the check-ins on my own."

Sophie nodded wordlessly and Emma left her to walk over to the hut with the banner *German Red Cross – Search Service*.

A female Red Cross worker greeted her. "*Guten Tag*, you must register yourself first."

"Again?" Emma groaned.

"Yes, this is for our search index. You need to fill out a 'seeker' card for yourself and a 'searching for' card for every missing relative or friend. These will then be sorted by last names in one central location. We constantly have volunteers going through the register entries trying to find matches."

"Oh well." She filled out her personal data, her address prior to the war and hesitated when she came across the current address. "What am I supposed to write here?"

"Do you already have a known destination, perhaps with family?"

"No."

"Then you write 'Camp Friedland' and your hut number. As soon as you know where you're going from here, you can return and we'll change the address on the card."

"Thank you." While writing down her current location, the awareness of being homeless hit her with force. Of course, they'd been without a home for quite a while, but writing it down on this filing card made it official.

She added Sophie to the family members under her care and then proceeded to fill out 'searching for' cards for her husband, giving his *Feldpostnummer*, that included his rank and regiment.

The Red Cross worker took the card and put it into a file cabinet. "The Wehrmacht records are much better than those for civilians, so I hope we'll get a result within the week."

"And for my son?"

"How old is he?"

"Four."

"You fill the same card with every detail you can think of. If you have a photograph, that would help a lot."

"The only one I have was taken on his first birthday."

"It's not ideal, but better than nothing. In any case, write a description of him onto the card, color of hair and eyes, approximate height, anything that could help to identify him."

Emma did as requested. Finally she reached into her pocket to take out the only visual memory of her son. He looked so cute with his chubby cheeks and the shock of white blond hair. Just before she handed it over together with the card, she shrunk back. "Will I get the photo back?"

The woman shook her head. "No. But you could go to the photographer. Return here when he has made a copy of it. With children a photo really helps, because they don't carry papers and some don't even remember their last names or their home address."

At least this offered a modicum of solace, since Emma had drilled into her children, and especially into Jacob, the ability to recite their full names and address in Lodz.

A horrific thought crossed her mind. "But who will fill out his seeker card?"

"Red Cross workers in the Eastern regions, Polish government officials, Red Army soldiers, civilians. We get file cards for lost children all the time and have reunited many of them already. I'm confident we'll find your son, too." The woman gave her an uplifting gaze. "Although it might take a while."

"How long?" Panic croaked Emma's voice.

"I really cannot say. It may take weeks or months..."

"He was in the hospital and they wouldn't let me leave the camp to fetch him." Emma felt the need to defend herself, lest the Red Cross worker would assume she was a horrible mother.

"I'm sure you did the best you could. With some luck, his matching card is already in the central location."

"Thank you." Emma left the hut to search for the photographer. There was a long line of volunteers with unaccompanied children waiting to have their photo taken. When it was Emma's turn, she felt slightly more hopeful, seeing how all these children had made it into the camp despite having lost contact with their families at some point during their flight.

"Please sit," the photographer said, pointing at the chair opposite his camera.

"It's not for me," she explained and handed him Jacob's photo. "Can you make a copy of this? He's my missing son."

The man rubbed his chin, scrutinizing the hackneyed paper. "The quality won't come out very well, but yes. I can make a photo of it."

"Thank you so much."

He clicked his camera and handed her a slip of paper with a number. "Return tomorrow to fetch it."

Mentally and physically exhausted she returned to her sleeping hut, where Sophie lay curled up in a ball on her bunk. Her heart flowed over with love for her daughter, even as sad tears pooled in her eyes because of Jacob.

She walked over, arranged their few things in the assigned locker and then settled on her bunk. She fingered Jacob's photograph. How long would it be before she could wrap him into her arms again? Was he scared? Alone? Sick? Hungry? Dead?

A tear fell on her hand. She wiped it away, swallowing down her distress. For Sophie she had to stay strong, since it seemed the two of them would have to spend some time in the camp, at least until Agatha's cousin sent word that they were welcome in her house. It didn't bear contemplating if she refused... Emma shook her head. The worst part of the journey lay behind. They'd managed to arrive in what was left of Germany. They had food, shelter and each other.

Friedland was a safe harbor in a riotous sea of uncertainty. It might not be such a bad thing to stay here a few weeks, since Emma dearly needed a break to renew her energies and decide how and where to pick up the pieces of her life. Deep in her heart she feared Herbert was dead, though she clung to the hope he might somehow still be alive.

In almost a year, she hadn't received a letter from him, yet she hadn't received the dreaded telegram announcing his death, either. As long as it wasn't written in black ink on white paper, she would cling to the hope.

Three days later she and Sophie said goodbye to their dearest friends, who were earmarked to board a train to Aachen to stay with Agatha's cousin. Luise promised to write as soon as they arrived, and Agatha was certain she'd soon send the good news that Emma and Sophie could join them there.

Emma hugged Luise, barely able to keep her tears at bay. As much as she envied her friend for being able to move on to a new home, she also pitied her for losing her second child. At least she herself could hope for Jacob's return.

Sophie hugged Hans, who'd become almost like a brother to her and for many weeks her only playmate. She would miss him. Emma hoped it would only be for a short time, before her daughter found a new friend.

About a week later, during one of her regular visits to the Red Cross station, she got the news that her beloved husband of ten years had been killed in action during the very last days of the war.

"I'm so sorry," offered the worker.

Emma stared in disbelief at the "searched for" card that had a big red stamp on it, indicating the person was dead. Her worst fears had come true. She felt as if someone had thrown her into a giant dark hole with no way out. How was she supposed to continue without him? To raise her children alone? To start a new life in an unknown place? To find a job and support her family? How was she supposed to do all of this without Herbert by her side?

Since she didn't want to burden Sophie with her grief, she

went for a long walk around the camp, cursing God and the world, while bawling her eyes out. When she was done, she took a deep breath and brushed the grief away, locking it deep down in her soul, determined to never let it surface again, just as she had done with the crippling emotions she'd experienced after being raped by the Russians.

She had a daughter to care for. She had no time for pain.

29

POZNÁN

After their visit to the Red Cross station, Jakub had been filled with hope. Surely, now, they'd find his mother and she'd come to pick him up.

But day after day passed and nothing happened. Despite missing her awfully, he grew fond of Irena and Luka who cared for him as if he were their own child. One day, Irena took him by the hand and said, "We're going to register you for pre-school."

"School?" He was elated, since he'd been so jealous when Sophie had had her first day of school back home. True to a beloved German tradition, she'd been given a huge school cone filled with gifts and had looked so smart in her dark-blue skirt and starched-white blouse. She'd even received new shoes to go with her outfit.

Finally it would be his turn to become a schoolboy. His elation didn't last long, because thoughts of Sophie always saddened him. He'd never thought it possible that he could miss his annoying, bossy sister so much.

"It's pre-school. They're just now opening up," Irena answered. Throughout the past months he'd picked up more and more words in her language. Even though he still thought in German, it frequently happened that he only knew the Polish word for a certain thing. He never dwelled on this, as long as he understood what people said to him, he was fine.

He and his best friend Alek, who lived a few houses down the street, understood each other without words anyway. There wasn't much need to talk when they went out on an adventure, scouring the ruins for shrapnel, artillery bullets or other treasures they could find.

He knew Irena didn't want him to collect these things although he never understood why. Since Alek's mother shared the same opinion, the two boys had found a safe hideout to stash their bounty and play war.

"Will Alek go to school as well?" he asked, suddenly hesitant to meet a classroom full of strange children.

"Yes. He'll attend the same class as you do."

"Great!" Together with Alek there was nothing he feared. His best friend was always full of fun ideas and never stumped for an answer. He also fiercely defended Jakub whenever someone called him stupid for not understanding a question or being slow in giving his answer.

"We'll have to get you new clothes before school starts," Irena said, with a gaze at his shorts and the shirt that barely covered his stomach.

Personally he didn't think that was necessary, since it was too hot anyway. But he wouldn't have minded a new pair of shoes, because his toes were painfully pinched together in his old ones.

When they went to the school building to register him, Jakub was quite disappointed to learn that he wouldn't actually attend class until after summer. Anyhow, he saw about a dozen other boys and girls his age waiting in line in front of the principal's office, all of them eager to turn another page in their lives and become schoolchildren. Most of all he relished meeting Alek and his parents there.

In the principal's office, an old gray-haired woman sat behind a huge desk, looking down at him and asking for his name.

"Jakub Opaman," he said.

The principal furrowed her brows and spoke in rapid-fire to Irena. He understood only fragments of their conversation, and focused his attention on the colorful paintings behind her back, until the principal stated, "Jakub Pawlak it is then."

Irena's glaring gaze kept him from protesting, so he waited anxiously until they'd left the school building, tugged at her hand and asked, "Why didn't she like my name?"

"Oh, Jakub." Irena stroked his hair. "It's not that she doesn't like it, but... See, during the war, the Polish people suffered a lot under the German rulers. And now that we're free again, many people have prejudices. The principal was afraid other pupils might treat you badly if they knew you are German. Their parents might even protest and have you expelled from school."

"But I want to go to school!" Jakub didn't understand what this principal was afraid of. He played with Alek every day, didn't he? Why should the other children have something against him?

"And you will. It's just... to make it easier for everyone, most importantly for you, we'll pretend you're our relative. A Pole called Jakub Pawlak."

"A Pole?" he hissed, shocked to the core. Hadn't his father always told him the Poles were inferior people, too stupid to run their own country, useful only for menial tasks and services?

"Just for the school. It's better this way."

If Irena thought so, who was he to argue? The Polish children might like him better if he was one of them, and that was all that mattered. He surely had no desire to sit alone in class without friends.

30

Summer had come and gone and Jakub had started pre-school. She and Luka had been as proud as any of the parents celebrating their child's big day. It had been a stretch, but they'd been able to afford a new set of clothes and even shoes for him.

Jakub had been beaming like a Christmas tree and she couldn't help but furtively shed a few tears. Her baby was growing up.

Day after day, she waited for the elusive sound of a person knocking on her door with the news that Jakub's real parents had been found. Her breath hitched each time someone came calling, but as autumn turned into winter, and winter into spring, the anxiety gradually eased.

She and Luka never talked about the looming threat over their heads, since they had decided to enjoy every day God allowed them to spend with Jakub to the fullest. He had become fluent in Polish, without even the trace of an accent that might distinguish him from the other children.

After the discussion with the school principal, they had taken precautions and introduced him at school as the orphaned child of a distant cousin, Polish by all means and matters, so as not to raise any dormant anti-German sentiments.

Following the end of the war, the Polish government had introduced several anti-German laws that culminated in expelling every citizen with German roots, no matter how many years, decades or generations their family had lived in what was now Poland.

One day, Luka came home with a serious face and said, "They're rounding up anyone German and putting them on trains westward."

"Will they take our Jakub?" Irena hissed, pressing a hand on her chest.

"They might. Or they might not." He was visibly agitated, which was quite unusual for him.

"What aren't you telling me?"

He climbed upstairs to make sure the door to Jakub's room was firmly closed, before he returned to settle at the table and tell her. "It's not safe for him. I heard, the able-bodied, men and women alike, are sent to labor camps, while the rest are robbed of all their possessions and pressed into cattle wagons like sardines into a tin."

Much like they did with the Jews. But now it's them getting a bitter taste of their own medicine. Irena paled at the thought of how little Jakub would be squeezed to death in one of those wagons without an adult to protect him. "Is there anything we can do?"

"I made some inquiries and it turns out that the principal might unknowingly have saved his neck." He paused to take her hands into his. "We should register him properly with the authorities, though. Officially adopting him as a war orphan. There are too many for them to verify backgrounds, so it's just a matter of our word."

"We're going to lie to the authorities?" Irena gasped.

"We'll have to, if we want to keep him safe."

Irena tore her eyes open. Her Luka, the upright, correct, honest man was suggesting they commit perjury and pretend to their government that Jakub was actually their relative? It was one thing to lie to other parents, vaguely hinting that he was a distant cousin's son. But walking to the registration office and filing adoption papers, swearing he was theirs?

"Won't they punish us?"

"They'll never find out." Luka stared at the wall behind her. "It's... we'll break the law, but..."

She knew what he was struggling with, since he loved the boy as much as she did. "What if we can pass him into good hands?"

"But to whom? You haven't seen and heard what I have. Those transports are hell."

"The Red Cross people? They could accompany him to his destination."

"They're swamped with work. I talked to one of their workers at the hospital, and she said it's not clear where these people will end up, except that it'll be a refugee camp somewhere in Germany."

Irena shuddered. Her sweet boy alone in a camp, far away from her and Luka to watch over him. He'd lived with them for over a year now, without news about his mother or other relatives. Would he have to spend his childhood in the orphanage of a refugee camp waiting for a person who might never show up? She violently shook her head. "No."

"No to what?" Luka put his hand on hers.

"We'll make sure he can stay with us. Whatever it takes, even if we have to lie to the authorities," she said with fierce determination, fueled by motherly love.

Luka nodded. "The Red Cross hasn't found his mother yet and they might not ever. We must choose between giving him a loving home with us or sending him into uncertainty."

The decision was easy. The very next day they went to

register Jakub, receiving official documents, identifying him as their son.

Weeks passed, then months. Nobody knocked on their door and slowly Irena stopped hitching her breath at every unexpected visitor. Luka had urged her to visit the Red Cross office two more times, but it was always with the same result.

"No, we haven't found his parents yet. You must be patient, there are so many children still separated from their families."

Irena had no problem with being patient. For all intents and purposes Jakub was her son and she prayed this would never change.

Jakub had brought so much joy into their family. She delighted in waking him in the morning, making breakfast for him, kissing him goodbye, and then waiting for him with a hot meal when he came home from school. It seemed that God had finally answered her dearest wish and given her the child she'd always wanted.

Some days she sensed a slight pang of guilt, because she should put more effort into searching for his mother, or at least find someone with whom he could secretly talk German to keep the memory alive. On the other hand, life in post-war Poland was hard enough: she had her hands full with working at the hospital, attending to the household and caring for the two men she loved. There simply weren't enough hours in the day to do everything.

On the last day of Jakub's first year in school, he rushed through the door, beaming from ear to ear, while waving his record card in the air. "Look at my grades!"

Her heart overflowed with love and she kissed him on both cheeks, before she took the document into her hands. "Amazing! Straight As and one B. That deserves a celebration."

"A trip to the zoo?" he asked with shining eyes.

"I'll have to talk with Luka about it." Jakub had been wanting to visit the zoo for quite some time, but so far they hadn't found the opportunity, because Luka worked almost around the clock. She hoped he would be able to take a weekend off to do something to celebrate their son's stellar report card.

That night, when Luka returned home, Jakub was already asleep, and Irena was waiting for her husband with a hot meal.

"Today was the last day of school," she said.

"I know." Luka sighed. "I wish I could spend more time with both of you. It's just that the new administration fired everyone with German roots, so we're more short-staffed than ever and it doesn't look as if that is going to change anytime soon."

She valiantly ignored her disappointment. "Jakub's teacher said he is one of the brightest children in his class. Just look at his grade report."

Luka took up the report, reading thoroughly through the grades and the additional remarks, a huge smile spreading on his face. "That's my son! I'm not surprised at all. Remember how fast he learned to speak Polish? If he keeps showing interest in medicine, he might even become a doctor."

Irena knew Luka wanted to retire from the hospital into his own practice and would have loved to have a son to follow in his footsteps. She had not let herself think long-term, since the threat of someone coming to take Jakub away from them had always been looming over their heads. "Do you think... I mean... do you believe...?"

Luka knew what she was trying to say. His thumb rubbed over her palm. "I don't know. Nobody does. All I can say, is, that with every passing day the chances of the Red Cross finding his mother must be diminishing. We can only take it day by day."

"It's so hard. When I hear the other parents talk about the future, planning for their sons to follow in the footsteps of their fathers... I never dare to let myself dream. It's such a fragile situation, since he can be whisked away at any moment. I feel like we're living on borrowed time."

Luka suddenly looked very old. "It is all we have. Therefore we should enjoy each day, hoping it won't be our last one with him."

"You're right." She cocked her head to one side, deciding to take advantage of his own words. "Jakub wants to go to the zoo to celebrate his stellar grade report. I told him I'd have to talk with you first."

"I don't think..." He stopped himself mid-sentence, gazed at her for quite a while, before he agreed. "I guess I should heed my own advice and enjoy the time we have together because it may end soon. I'll see that I get two days off next week and then we can go to the zoo together, and perhaps to the lake. It's about time I taught him to swim."

"He'll love that," Irena said.

"And you?" Luka asked her.

"I'll love it, too. As long as I can be in the company of the two men I love, I'll always be happy."

Irena had never learned to swim and was afraid to go into the water, but she'd gladly sit on the bank on a picnic blanket and watch Luka and Jakub having fun. It would be a rare occasion for them to spend a summer day like any other family.

31

"Sophie. Sophie, where are you?" Emma burst into their assigned living hut, waving a piece of paper in front of her.

"She's outside drawing with chalk. What has you so excited?" one of the women asked.

"We are leaving for Aachen on the train tomorrow," Emma told them, giddy with excitement.

They had been in the transit camp for more than six months. Her initial elation to finally have arrived had been gradually chipped away by the harsh conditions. It wasn't the fault of the British, who did their best. Yet, living in these Nissen huts among dozens of other refugees, with no privacy whatsoever tore at her.

The International Voluntary Service for Peace worked hard to give the children something akin to a home. They had even installed a tent school with more or less regular classes.

Still, the camp wasn't a good place to raise a child, especially a traumatized one like Sophie who'd lost first her brother and then Hans, when his family moved on to Aachen. She had difficulties making friends with children her age and had often complained it wasn't worth trying, because anytime she got to like another girl, her new friend inevitably left mere days later.

It was true. Families came and went, some moved on to live with relatives in West Germany, others were transferred to different camps or taken on stints to work if they had skills needed for the reconstruction of the country.

Emma, though, had never learned anything but being a good housewife and mother—both things that didn't seem much in demand right now. With so many men dead or prisoners of war, the authorities gave priority to anyone who had learned a trade like baker, seamstress, teacher, or basically anything but cooking, cleaning and raising children.

She pressed her lips together, bitterly realizing that her reward for adhering to the Nazi ideology of being a good German woman was being cast aside. A dinosaur nobody needed in this new country under Allied rule.

She walked outside and found Sophie behind their hut, alone, drawing elaborate paintings with chalk onto the ground.

"Sophie, come here," she called out.

Her daughter raised her head, giving her an utterly forlorn gaze. "What is it?"

"I have good news." Emma had expected Sophie to come running toward her, if not with delight, at least with curiosity, but she merely nodded.

Sophie took her time to gather the tiny pieces of chalk, got up, smoothed down her dress and trotted over. It broke Emma's heart to see her formerly happy, obedient, sweet girl so destitute. The dress she'd been given upon their arrival at the camp was too small again, barely covering her knees and the sleeves ending a few inches from her wrists. It wasn't their material poverty, though, that struck Emma. The complete lack of interest in her daughter's eyes drove a stab deep into her mother's heart.

"Agatha's cousin finally found a neighbor who has agreed to

take us in," she said, hoping to return the spark into Sophie's eyes.

"Aha."

"Aren't you happy?"

"About what?"

"That we'll leave this camp to live in a real home?"

"It's not going to be a home." Sophie stomped with her foot. "I'm not stupid. These neighbors aren't the good-hearted people you make them out to be."

"Please, Sophie, you don't even know them." Emma didn't recognize her soft-spoken daughter anymore.

"I don't need to. If they were decent people, they'd have given in to Agatha's begging months ago, don't you think?"

"There can be any number of reasons why..." Emma hesitated. They'd started out full of hope, but Luise's first letter after arriving at her mother-in-law's cousin had sounded like a cold shower. Apparently she had only begrudgingly accepted the three of them into her home and had outright refused to even consider the notion of taking in Emma and Sophie, too.

According to them, they weren't the welfare, claiming the refugees should have stayed where they came from. Emma would have loved nothing more, though that wasn't an option. After the downfall Stalin had claimed her former home country for his new satellite state Poland.

From the news, and the gossip the never-ending stream of newcomers at Friedland brought with them, the Poles hadn't wasted time in ousting anyone with German roots from their newly acquired territory. Those who hadn't fled on their own account, were driven out with whips and truncheons.

"I'll tell you why they suddenly found goodness in their hearts," Sophie said, squinting her eyes at her mother. "Because the victorious powers forced them to. They are imposing quotas on every village to host a certain number of refugees. They go around, inspect the houses and assign people, whether the owners of the house agree or not."

"How do you know?" Emma paled. She'd had no idea that her eight-year-old daughter could be privy to the more sordid details of the current goings-on.

"Everyone knows. People talk. It's even been announced on the radio." Sophie planted herself a step away from her mother, crossing her arms in front of her chest. "I'm not a baby anymore."

"No you're not." Emma gave a sad smile. "Whether our new hosts are taking us in voluntarily or not, I'm sure it'll be a lot better living with them, than in the camp. We'll have our own room that we don't have to share with other people, access to a kitchen to cook our own meals, and you can go to a real school."

"To be spat at by children who think I should return to where I came from!" Sophie yelled.

"My darling, who told you such nonsense? The children will accept you without problem, we're Germans after all."

"Not to them. We're strangers who've come to take away what belongs to them. Several of the pupils in the camp school said so. They went there and came back, because it was unbearable."

Emma couldn't believe that was true. Even if it was, there wasn't anything she could do about it, because she wasn't willing to stay in Friedland a single minute longer than required. If other children teased her at school, Sophie would have to suck it up and live with it. That was just how life was.

"In any case, we'll board the train to Aachen tomorrow." Emma was about to turn on her heel, when she hesitated and added, "Aren't you looking forward to seeing Luise and Hans again? I'm sure Hans will be happy to see you."

"Hans is a baby. Do you expect me to be happy that the only friend I'll have is a five-year-old?" Sophie sulked.

"Why don't you wait and see. I'm sure it'll be a lot better than you assume." Emma left, since she had lots of things to prepare. Although their possessions were few, she needed to leave her new address with the Red Cross search service, say goodbye to the women she'd made friends with and try if she could get new shoes and a dress for Sophie from the clothing store.

32

POZNAŃ, AUGUST 1947

Jakub had been looking forward to this day. His seventh birthday. The only slight issue was it being during school holidays, his best friend Alek was away visiting his grandparents in another town. Instead Irena had allowed him to invite two other boys from his class in the afternoon.

As soon as he woke in the morning, he raced down the stairs to make a skidding halt in front of the table that showcased a round cake and two packages wrapped in brown paper.

"Are these my presents?" he yelled.

Irena came out of the kitchen, carrying a cup of hot chocolate and two cups of coffee. "Yes, they are. Happy birthday, Jakub!" Luka walked behind her and hugged him. "You're a big boy now."

"Oh. Can I open them, please?"

"Of course you can." Irena put the cups down on the table. "But don't you want to drink your hot chocolate first?"

Who cared about hot chocolate when there were unopened presents on the table? He shook his head. "Can I, please?" Giddy with anticipation he could barely keep himself from tearing them open. When his parents nodded, he carefully opened the wrapping, because he knew Irena would smooth it down and store it in the drawer next to the stove for later use.

"How wonderful is this!" he exclaimed and help up a self-made kite made of fine wooden rods and thin red cloth. It even featured a long tail that consisted of paper bows. "Can I test it right away?"

Luka laughed. "I took the entire day off, so we can walk to the lake and let it fly on the bank before your guests arrive in the afternoon."

"It's wonderful. Thank you so much." Jakub was delighted and continued to unwrap the second package that contained a wristwatch. It was used and much too big for his wrist, nevertheless he instantly loved it. Ever since he'd started school last year he had wished for a wristwatch.

"Shall I help you put it on?" Irena asked him.

He nodded and admired the wonderful watch on his arm. Now he'd never be late again. Luka explained to him how he had to wind it up every few days to make sure it ran properly.

Jakub looked at the two people he loved so much, completely overwhelmed with joy and hugged Irena. "Thank you so much, *Mamusia*."

"*Mój synku*," she said and for some strange reason she suddenly had tears in her eyes.

"What's wrong, *Mamusia*?" he asked.

"Nothing. It's just... you never called me mother before."

He squinted his eyes, since that seemed so strange to him. He knew he had another mother somewhere, his mami, who had disappeared during the war and nobody had been able to find her.

As far as he was concerned, now Irena was his mother. He didn't want her to be sad, especially not on his birthday. So he declared in a cheerful tone, "Now I want to drink my hot chocolate!"

She smiled again and the three of them sat down around the

table to have a piece of cake. It was a special treat, since rationing was still tight and sugar was scarce.

Jakub, though, didn't care. He had a new wristwatch, a kite and two people who loved him dearly. What else could a seven-year-old boy want?

At night, after an exhilarating day playing with the kite and having two friends over for his birthday party, he fell into bed, utterly exhausted. But sleep was elusive. Somewhere in the back of his mind, a memory nagged at him. Something he'd forgotten was resurfacing and not letting him rest. For the longest time he stared into the darkness, hearing the sounds of a busy city outside. As he finally fell asleep, he had a dream. It was on his fourth birthday and he was playing with Hans, his former best friend.

The other boy didn't have a face, though he clearly saw his checkered sweater and the cap on his head. Why would Hans wear a cap on a hot day in August? The dream continued, but when he woke up in the morning, the only thing he remembered was the cap on Hans' head.

"How did you sleep, Jakub?" Irena greeted him when he trotted into the kitchen.

"I had a strange dream. My best friend Hans came over to my birthday and he wore a cap. Why would he wear a woolen cap in summer, *Mamusia*?"

She mustered her thoughts for a while, sighed and beckoned him to sit at the table. Then she settled next to him and explained. "When I found you at the hospital, you didn't know your birthday, just that you were four years old and had been for quite a while. Later, a pediatrician estimated your age and we settled on August fifteenth, because we needed to put a date onto your papers."

Reeling from shock, he choked on his milk. "You mean you don't know my birthday? What if we find out it wasn't yesterday? Do I have to return my presents?"

"No, *mój synku*, for all intents and purposes your birthday was yesterday. And if we ever find out the truth, we'll..." she paused, "we'll simply celebrate twice. What do you think?"

The idea of having two birthdays brightened his mood, especially because he would age twice as fast and would soon be a grown-up. Then he could become a doctor like Luka and his parents wouldn't have to work so much anymore, since he would provide for them.

33

AACHEN, GERMANY, OCTOBER 28, 1949

Today was Jacob's ninth birthday. Emma looked out the window and up at the sky. Big fluffy white clouds floated along happily, unaware of the turmoil in her chest. It had been almost five years since she'd last seen her son, but the crippling grief had never left her.

After arriving in Aachen, Emma and Sophie had slowly gotten their bearings. Despite everything that was happening in their lives, she visited, without fail, the local Red Cross search service every single month to ask whether they'd found her son. Because she wouldn't give up hope, ever.

The one photograph of him she possessed was faded and worn. Last year she'd bought a frame, for fear it would otherwise fall apart. Silent tears ran down her cheeks as she traced her finger across his sweet and chubby face.

How must he look now? A nine-year-old boy. Would he still have the white-blond curls she'd ruffled so often? Would his bright blue eyes still shine with excitement? Or were they dimmed and sad, because he vegetated in a dark and loveless orphanage after experiencing unimaginable evil? In her soul there was no doubt that he was still alive. To think otherwise was too frightening, too painful. So she clung with every fiber of her soul to the idea that he lived and it was only a matter of time until the two of them would be reunited again.

Two hands landed on her shoulders and she leaned back against the warm male body behind her. "What's put that sad look on your face?" Martin asked.

Martin worked at the local shoe shop and after casually greeting each other for several months, he had finally asked her for a date. At first Emma had been reluctant, since she had been a widow for just two years. Still grieving for her killed husband and for her missing son, she hadn't been in the mood for flirting.

Luise, who lived down the street, had finally convinced her that she needed a man to provide for her, and a father for Sophie, who wasn't coping well with the circumstances of her new life.

She grew to like Martin, despite not feeling passionate love for him like she had for Herbert. Back then she'd been young and foolish, without a care in the world. Now, she was a single mother of a rebellious teenager, who barely earned enough as kitchen help for the British occupiers to keep them afloat. She couldn't afford the luxury of love.

Martin treated her well and showed the right amount of strictness to keep Sophie on track. So when he'd asked her to marry him a year ago, she'd said yes. She and Sophie had moved into his two-room apartment, which was a significant improvement over the single room they'd lived in with Agatha's neighbors, sharing a kitchen and bathroom with them, which had been a challenge to say the least.

She turned to look at her new husband. "Just thinking."

"About Jacob?"

"How did you know?"

"Today is his birthday. How could you not be thinking about him?" Martin replied before placing a kiss on her forehead. Her husband had been exceedingly patient with her efforts to search for Jacob, running from pillar to post, making telephone calls, writing letters, filling search forms and more, but she worried his patience with her obsession to find her lost son would eventually wane.

She fought the sadness away, because she should be grateful for what she had. A kind and caring husband, a fine apartment for their family, her daughter... and... She looked down at her growing belly. Soon Martin's child.

It would bind them together even more, giving him the much-desired child of his own and her the security to be accepted not only by him, but by his entire family as well.

Sophie's behavior had improved considerably since they'd moved in with Martin and she didn't have to bear the constant condescension of their involuntary hosts. Since her husband, a native citizen of Aachen, had adopted her daughter, the teasing and bickering at school had immediately stopped and Sophie had changed from being the ostracized refugee to a regular girl.

The one thing Emma wasn't happy about, was that Sophie refused to even mention Jacob's name. Whenever Emma talked of him, she rolled her eyes and said, "Mami. Accept it. He's long dead or they would have found him already."

Emma let her head drop to Martin's chest and relaxed in his embrace. "I still can't shake the feeling that it's my fault he's missing. At night I lay awake contemplating whether I shouldn't have left him in the hospital to begin with. Or whether I should have stayed in Posen to search for him."

"You did what you had to do, to get yourself and Sophie to safety. Also, there was nothing you could have done, since the SS guard wouldn't let you return," Martin reminded her.

Emma winced. She'd never told Martin, or anyone for that matter, what had really happened after fleeing from Posen. Not even with Agatha, who had endured the same treatment, did she acknowledge what the Russians had done to her. It was best to bury the memory deep down in her soul, from where it could never surface again.

"That's what I keep telling myself. I had to think about Sophie, and Luise... and myself. It sounds so selfish when I say these words out loud..."

"There's nothing selfish about it. It was war and you were given a horrible dilemma. The decision you took was incredibly tough, but it was definitely the right one. You couldn't do anything for him, but you could save yourself and Sophie."

"I'm still feeling bad."

"I have a surprise for you." Martin smiled.

"For me? It's his birthday, not mine."

He looked at his wristwatch and said, "Turn on the radio."

"The radio?" She gave him a confused look. It was ten minutes to two p.m. She walked over to switch it on and caught the radio speaker as he said, "The soldier Franz Wolters, born June eighteenth 1912 is searching for his wife Martina Wolters, who last lived in..." Emma looked up at her husband, wondering why he wanted her to listen to the daily search program for missing persons on the radio.

"Psst... Listen," he said, putting a finger on his lips.

There were two more missing person announcements and then the speaker said, "Emma Kroger, widowed Oppermann, is searching for her son Jacob Oppermann, born October twenty-eighth 1940 in Lodz. He was last seen in Posen, former Reichsgau Wartheland. He has blond curly hair and blue eyes. You heard the search service. We ask listeners who can provide information about the whereabouts of those named to contact their nearest search service office."

She broke out into a bright smile. "You did this? For me?"

"Yes."

"How did you manage? I've tried to get Jacob into the announcements for months, but it's next to impossible, because every day there's only several and hundreds of thousands of missing persons waiting."

He put a hand on her shoulder. "My boss knows someone at the German Red Cross in Munich and when I told him I wanted to give you the announcement as a birthday gift for Jacob, he pulled some strings."

"Thank you so much." A wave of love poured into her body, even as the unborn child under her heart gave a hard kick, as if affirming its father's words.

"Let's hope someone has seen him. In any case, the radio station claims they have a success rate of fifty percent."

Emma felt powerful emotions surging in her, threatening to overthrow her composure, therefore she said, "I'll be with you in a moment," and walked toward the window, looking out into the sky, sending a silent prayer.

Wherever you are, Jacob. Please know that you were and are loved. I hope one day I can hold you in my arms again, but until then, I pray that you have someone else to shower you with love and affection. Happy birthday, my darling boy. I love you. Always. Mami.

34

POZNAŃ, SPRING 1951

"*Mamusia*, can I go and play football, please?" Jakub came running into the house, throwing his school satchel into the corner.

"Take off your shoes and put your satchel in your room," Irena said. "Do you have homework?"

"*Mamusia*, today was our last day of school before Easter recess. We never have homework during vacation."

Irena looked up, so proud at her son who was in fifth grade already and had never once given them grief with bad grades or inappropriate behavior. Luka was very strict about schoolwork and often practiced calculation with him. He also took him to help at his doctor's practice, teaching him the names of the bones in the human body, along with other things a future doctor might need to know. Because there was no doubt that Jakub one day would follow in Luka's footsteps and take over the practice his father had opened up after retiring from the hospital with its demanding night and weekend shifts.

"Still, put your satchel in your room, wash your hands and set the table. Lunch is almost ready."

"Do I have to eat? My friends are waiting for me."

"They'll have to wait until you're finished with your meal."

"But what if they start the game without me?" Jakub whined.

"I'm sure their mothers will make them eat first, too."

He pouted, but took off his shoes and did her bidding. Irena had to hide her smile from him. She could understand his excitement for the week of vacation, but he'd be the first one to complain when he got hungry.

When he'd arrived at their house during the war, food had been a constant problem, for at least one or two more years. Thankfully that time was behind them. In communist Poland there were many hardships still – going hungry, though, wasn't one of them.

The choice of foodstuff to buy might be limited, but there was always enough bread or potatoes to satisfy even the biggest hunger.

"Will Papa join us?" Jakub asked her as he entered the kitchen.

"I suppose so." Since Luka had stopped working at the hospital, he joined them most days for lunch and dinner. He still worked long hours, and made house calls at nights and on the weekends, however, he spent so much more time with them than in the early years.

Irena herself continued to work part-time at the hospital and sometimes she helped Luka when a second person was needed. The sound of the key in the door told her Luka had returned and she said, "Quick now, your father is here."

Then she distributed *pierogis* onto three plates and gave two of them to Jakub to carry to the table.

"Hello, darling." Luka came inside and gave her a kiss, before he tousled Jakub's hair. "How was school?"

"Good, Papa. We're in recess for the next week."

"I know and I have managed to take the weekend off, so we can go and visit Grandma. How would you like that?"

"Wonderful! When are we going to leave?" Jakub jumped up and down with delight. Luka's mother lived about one hour by train away in a small village and Jakub loved going there, spending his time roaming the woods and fields with some of the village boys.

As Irena watched her two men eat with hearty appetites, she thought how very lucky she was. In her bleakest hour, God had bestowed this wonderful boy on her, whom she loved like her own flesh and blood. After everything she'd been through, Jakub had returned the sunshine into her life. She closed her eyes and sent a silent prayer to God for giving her this precious gift.

During the past five years Jakub had truly become a part of their family and she couldn't imagine a time without him. Once a year they took a picture of him to give it to the Red Cross search service, but apart from that, she barely spared a thought about his past.

Sometimes she felt a pang of guilt, because he seemed to have forgotten about his birth family. However, neither she nor Luka knew anything about them, so they hadn't been able to keep the memory alive for him. Anyway, what good would it do to make him miss a family he'd never see again?

Jakub finished his meal in record time and asked, "Can I go and play with my friends now?"

"You may," she said and looked after him as he took off running. "Be home at six!" she yelled after him.

"He's grown so much," Luka said.

"Yes, he's a big boy. We need to buy new clothes for him again."

"I really don't know where he gets that height from, neither of us are very tall." Luka looked at her and then laughed. "I tend to forget."

She put her hand over his. "Me too. God has answered our prayers by sending him to us."

35

AACHEN, SPRING 1952

"Mami, there's someone at the door for you," Sophie's voice floated to the back of the apartment.

Emma took a quick glance at her toddler Liesl, before she switched off the new electric iron, and patted her hair to make sure she was presentable as she walked toward the front door.

She was surprised to see two people, a woman and a man, standing there, wearing Red Cross uniforms. A multitude of emotions rushed over her as she tried to read their expressions. The last time someone had come looking for her, it had been to tell her that her first husband had been killed in action. At the memory, the wall erected around her heart came tumbling down and she swayed under the impact. Barely able to keep herself composed, she considered slamming the door shut in their faces, because she wasn't ready to hear similar news about her son.

No, no, no. After all these years and her continued efforts to find him, she would not allow these people to crush the one thing that kept her alive. According to Martin, her quest to find Jacob had become an obsession, and even Luise had warned her to move on, or she'd soon find herself not only without her son, but without her daughters and husband, too.

Emma balled her hands into tight fists, until her nails dug painfully into the flesh of her palms as she remembered the candid, unpleasant, treacherous discussion with her best friend.

"It's been seven years, don't you think it's time to let go?" Luise had said.

"How dare you! He's my son! I won't rest until we're reunited, even if it's the last thing I do."

"It may well be. Don't you see how much damage you're causing with your obsession?"

"It's not an obsession! Why doesn't anyone seem to understand? Would you just give up on your child, knowing they were out there somewhere?"

Luise had given her a sad smile. "You don't actually know that, now do you?"

"What are you insinuating? That he's dead?"

"Not at all. Just that you're damaging all your relationships because of him."

"Aha, now it's my fault that nobody understands me?" Emma had been exasperated.

"Of course not. I'm just trying to make you realize that you're alienating both your husband and Sophie by putting Jacob above everything else."

"Please leave. I don't need so-called friends who don't support me," Emma had said outraged. It was the last time she'd talked to her former best friend. Obviously, she'd later regretted her harsh words, but had been too proud to apologize to Luise.

"Frau Kroger?"

The words returned her attention to the two visitors in front of her.

"Yes. How can I help you?" she asked, eyeing the pair up and down.

"Could we please speak with you for a moment?" the man asked.

"Of course." Emma turned back into the apartment and called out, "Sophie, would you please watch Liesl for a few minutes. I'll be in the living room." Then she invited the Red Cross officials in.

"Please, have a seat." She beckoned at the sofa they had recently bought. Due to the economy soaring in the past few years, Martin had opened his own branch of the shoe shop. He now earned considerably more than before, enough to afford his family a rather comfortable life.

"What brings you here?" she asked, even as anguish attacked her. She would not, no, she could not, accept a negative outcome. Jacob was alive. He just had to be.

"It's about your missing person filing." The woman handed her a picture of a boy who looked to be about eleven years of age. "We believe we've found your son. Do you recognize him?"

Despite sitting, Emma swayed, as a thousand emotions attacked her at once. Was this the answer to all her prayers? She stretched out a shaking hand, almost afraid to take the picture, since she wouldn't survive another disappointment.

The boy looked so grown up, a serious expression on his face. His white-blond hair had settled into a darker blond tone, but the eyes were unmistakably his. She traced her fingers across the photograph, shaken to the core. It was him. It must be him. *My darling boy.* Her finger caressed his cheeks, imagining the cute dimples whenever he smiled. Her mind ran away into the future, imagining, how he rushed into her open arms and she swirled him around, holding him tight, never letting him go. Finally, she'd be whole again. Happy. Overjoyed.

"It's him, no doubt," she said.

"He's living in Poland under the name of Jakub Pawlak, but was registered with the search service as Jakub Opaman."

"Opaman?" Before marrying Martin, her last name had been Oppermann.

"Yes, we realize it's not an exact match, which we believe is due to a bad pronunciation." The woman gave Emma an apologetic gaze. "Your son was very young during the war and might not have been able to properly spell his name. We encounter similar issues all the time and it makes our work so much more difficult, resulting in very long times trying to match missing children with their parents."

Emma nodded. She knew all about the quest to find missing persons, especially children. The Red Cross wasn't at fault here, since they strived for the best every day. Their work was greatly hindered not only by bad data, especially regarding small children, but also by the tightening of the Iron Curtain. At times it had been almost impossible to get information across the borders, and in some instances even children that had been properly identified had had to wait months or even years to receive traveling papers.

She knew first hand how difficult it was, since she'd tried fruitlessly for years to receive a traveling permit for Poland to go and search for him herself. The blockheaded bureaucrats at the Polish trade mission in Frankfurt am Main had been unimpressed by her pleas and had refused her a visa time and again.

In the beginning, Martin had supported her, but he'd drawn the line when she requested him to ask his boss for an affidavit, claiming she was an important sales representative of the shoe store chain, traveling to Poland on the official purpose to export much-needed shoes.

"...he was reportedly picked up in an abandoned hospital the night before the Russians conquered the city of Poznań. He's been interviewed and has mentioned his mami and a sister called Sophie."

"It's definitely him." Emma interlaced her fingers to calm herself. What her heart had known from the moment she saw the photograph was now supported by facts. Nobody could argue this might be a coincidence. "I knew he wasn't dead."

"We're fairly sure it's him. Even his birthday is close to the one you provided."

"Only close?" The elation she'd felt earlier was replaced with anxiety.

This time the man raised his voice. "This is nothing unusual. Small children often don't remember their birthday. They know their age, and whether it's in summer or winter, or perhaps the month."

"But I drummed his birthday into him, along with his name and address." She suddenly had the need to defend herself. "Since he was too young to be issued papers, I practiced with him what to do if he ever got lost."

"Please, none of this is your fault." The woman seemed to understand her. "I'm sure you did everything you could. Your son was under a lot of stress, having been separated from you. We don't know what he experienced at the hospital."

Emma blanched at the memory of the killed patients she'd seen.

The woman continued. "Many children will forget things when traumatized. We also have to count in the language barrier."

Emma nodded, fidgeting harder with her fingers. On the one hand she wanted to scream with joy, but on the other hand she couldn't allow herself to be too optimistic, since Jacob was still somewhere in Poland, where the heartless communist bureaucrats had full say over his fate. Finally, she asked, "So, what happens now?"

"Well, we have a few more questions to ask. For example, he mentioned a friend called—"

"Hans! He used to be his best friend and is living in Aachen, too," Emma interrupted her, finally starting to believe that her time of waiting was over.

The woman smiled. "That's right. And that's good news. Is there anything else you can tell us? It's a momentous decision to take him from his foster family and reunite him with you, so we don't want to make a mistake here."

"He's not been in an orphanage?" A big burden fell from her shoulders, since the idea of him being raised by cold-hearted, strict nuns along with dozens of equally miserable children had been one of her biggest fears.

"No. A nurse found him in the hospital after it was evacuated and took him home with her. Apparently she returned the next day, but found only destruction. She's been raising him ever since. She and her husband have even adopted him."

"Adopted? How can that be? He's my son!" Emma barely restrained herself from reaching across the table and strangling the woman. For the love of God, how could the government allow someone to adopt her son? He wasn't an orphan, he had a mother. Her. And she had certainly never consented to him being adopted by some random people.

Chills ran down her spine, as she considered the implications. If this couple had legally adopted Jacob, would they agree to return him to her, his birth mother? Did she even have the right to get him back? Knowing the coldhearted bureaucrats at the Polish trade mission, she already feared they'd laugh up their sleeves, claiming her son was now a Polish citizen and under no circumstances would they allow him to pass the Iron Curtain.

Blinking several times to dispel the troubling images, she suddenly heard the male Red Cross worker say, "Please, Frau Kroger, it's not as bad as it seems. You must understand the circumstances. For the Pawlaks, who are Jacob's foster parents, it wasn't safe to harbor a German boy, so they pretended he was a distant cousin's child. They were afraid the Red Army would harm him otherwise or the Polish authorities would force them to send him to one of the transit camps all on his own."

Emma sank back into the cushions of her armchair, over-whelmed by whirling emotions. "But..." Would it have been better if he'd been sent to a displaced persons camp? Would she have found him earlier... years ago, maybe?

The woman leaned forward. "This must come as a shock to you, but trust me, it was the correct decision for him at that time. You've been to the Friedland camp yourself. It was such chaos after the war, the poor boy would have suffered so much more. At least in Posznań he was with a couple who gave him loving care."

A tear stole into Emma's eye and she furtively swiped it away, since she didn't want to seem ungrateful. "How is he getting here?"

"Our co-workers in Poland will visit his family." Emma flinched at the word 'family' and pressed her lips into a thin line so as not to interrupt the woman. "Together with the informa-tion you just gave me, they'll verify all the details one last time. Then we'll request a special permit from the Polish government that will allow Jacob to emigrate."

"Emigrate?" Emma hissed in a breath. Everyone knew that the countries behind the Iron Curtain did not let their citizens leave, and apparently her son had become their citizen through the adoption. Again, a debilitating anguish seared through her cells. "What if they don't allow him to leave?"

"There's no reason to worry. The Red Cross has good contacts with the authorities and we've reunited many children with their birth families. It's a mere formality and will take a few months at most."

A few months? Emma gasped, but then scolded herself. She'd waited seven years, a few months more wouldn't make a difference. "Can I write a letter to him?"

"Of course," the woman said and took out a sheet of paper from her purse. "This is the address of the Red Cross office in Poznań. They'll see that your letter will be delivered to him."

She seemed to sense Emma's disappointment and added, "We do this to make sure protocols are followed as we don't want to anger the authorities and risk losing their cooperation in the repatriation of missing children."

She barely noticed the two people leaving. In unusually rude behavior she simply stayed in the living room, staring at the piece of paper with the address in Poznań.

Was her most fervent wish coming true? Would she soon hold her little darling in her arms again? After seven long years!

Suddenly Sophie was standing in the middle of the room, rocking her baby sister to and fro. When she saw Emma's face, she frowned. "What did those people want?"

Emma needed several seconds to realize what her daughter was asking. "They found Jacob," she gushed. "Isn't that marvelous news?"

"Really? After all these years? And they're sure it's him?"

"Yes, everything fits. His description, the location where he was found, that he has a sister called Sophie and a best friend Hans."

"And? Are we going to visit him?"

"Visit?" Emma stared in disbelief at her daughter. "No, he's coming home."

"He's going to live with us? Here? We don't even have a room for him." Sophie was all practical.

"Those with the smallest houses are the ones who can always find space." Emma wasn't concerned with practicalities. "He and you can share your room."

"But... he'd better share with Liesl, she's almost his age by now."

Emma wrinkled her forehead, scrutinizing her daughter's face, who seemed to be serious about what she'd said. "You realize that he's grown too, don't you? He's not a four-year-old anymore, he just turned eleven."

"God no!" Sophie seemed honestly shocked. "I can't possibly share a room with a boy that age!"

"He's your brother."

"A brother I don't even know." Sophie sighed dramatically, put Liesl down on the floor and stomped from the room, leaving her mother feeling utterly bereft, hoping that her husband would be more enthusiastic.

36

POZNAŃ

Irena arrived home from the hospital at the same time Jakub came running down the road.

"Hello, darling, how was school?" she asked after tousling his curly blond hair.

"Good."

"Do you have homework?"

"No, *Mamusia*. I already finished it in class."

She gave him a stern gaze, while she fished out an envelope from the mailbox. The Red Cross logo was in the upper corner, and she quickly slipped it into her pocket.

"Can I go play football?" Jakub asked his usual question. He'd joined a football club years ago and spent all of his leisure time on the field, either training or with his friends.

"After lunch. And first I need to make sure you actually did your homework."

He pouted at her. "I did, *Mamusia*. What's for lunch?"

Jakub was a bright boy, who rarely received bad grades at school, but he also had the habit of not doing his homework properly, because he knew he could wing it in class; a habit that exasperated his parents and his teachers alike.

After finishing their meal, Jakub changed into training gear and ran off to meet his friends at the football field. Irena washed and dried the dishes, before she took out the envelope with shaking fingers. It was addressed to her and Luka, but apart from the Red Cross logo it didn't bear a sender's address.

She yearned to rush over to Luka's practice to open it together with him, but then remembered that it was his afternoon of making home visits, so she'd most probably not find him at the practice anyway.

With a deep sigh, she opened the envelope and took out a piece of paper.

Esteemed Pan and Pani Pawlak,

We're happy to inform you that your missing person report has resulted in finding the mother of Jacob Oppermann, who has been verified to be the same child as Jakub Opaman...

The rest of the letter swam before her eyes. She had to sit down at the table, unable to comprehend. She didn't know for how long she'd been sitting there, when she heard a rap on the door and got up to open it. In front of her stood one of Luka's patients, an elderly lady.

"What can I do for you?" Irena asked her.

"I came to bring you this, as a thank you to your husband." The woman held out a freshly baked apple cake.

"Thank you so much." Irena took the offered gift and couldn't help a sigh, when she thought how much Jakub loved to eat cake.

"Is everything alright?" The elderly woman's face showed genuine concern.

"It's nothing really, just a sad case at work." As much as Irena might need a sympathetic ear, she refused to burden this woman with her own sorrows. Not to mention the fact that almost nobody, except for the Red Cross officials, knew that Jakub wasn't who they pretended him to be.

"Well then, please give my thanks to the doctor, without him I wouldn't be here anymore."

"I will. Thank you so much for the cake."

Irena returned inside and busied herself with housework. There was always more than enough to do. Doing laundry, sweeping and mopping the floors, starching and pressing Luka's white coats, preparing meals.

During dinner she absentmindedly followed the conversation between Luka and their son, not uttering a word herself. Luka cast her several worried glances, but didn't, however, ask her about it. At least not until Jakub was in bed and the two of them settled on the recently acquired two-seater in the living room.

"What has you so depressed?" he asked.

She gave a sigh and handed him the letter that she'd been carrying all day in her apron. Her voice was feeble as she imparted information that had left her devastated. "They have found Jakub's mother."

"They have?" Contrary to hers, his voice was professional, not betraying his emotions as he grabbed the paper to read it. "They want us to visit their offices together with Jakub. It's a formality apparently, but they want to make a last check..."

Tears rolled down her face and her entire body began to shiver violently. "Can't we just ignore the letter?"

He looked at her, his eyes full of heartbreak. "They'd simply send another one. Or come visit us. No, I'm afraid we have to go. We knew this day might come."

"But... what will we do without him?" Irena sensed the vehemence of the loss. Memories of feelings she thought she had long overcome bubbled up, making it difficult to breathe. This felt so similar to the devastation after losing her baby, yet somehow so different.

God had uplifted her from misery by sending Jakub as the answer to her desperate prayers, just to cruelly take him away again. It seemed as if her entire life was tumbling to pieces like a tower made of building blocks, knocked down by the hand of a curious child.

How would her soul survive this second great loss? How would she be able to keep going? The emotion overwhelmed her with such power that she suddenly saw stars in front of her eyes, and then nothing.

"Are you alright?" She was lying on the floor, Luka's beloved face hovering over her.

"What happened?" she asked.

"You fainted. Stay there for a minute longer, I'll get you a strong drink." He rushed off into the kitchen. As she stared at his back, the feeling of loss increased evermore, pushing down on her lungs, her heart, her mind and her soul, making breathing a superhuman effort.

When Luka returned, he helped her sit up and held the glass for her while she sipped the clear liquid. It burned down her throat, kindling a fire in her stomach, reviving her spirits, but also the all-consuming pain.

"Do you feel better?" he asked, stroking her back.

"I love him so much."

"I do, too. As does his mother, I suppose. It says she's been searching for him all these years, that she's desperate to reunite."

"But she abandoned him! She never returned to search for him!" Irena spat out, although she knew she was being unjust. The situation at the end of the war had been chaotic to say the least, and many children had been separated from their parents, by no fault of either party. After the war had ended, the hostilities against Germans had been such that they'd feared for the life of Jakub, an innocent four year old, and she knew an adult would have fared far worse.

In her heart of hearts, Irena had hoped and prayed his mother was dead, or would at least assume her son was dead, never to show up and destroy their happy little family by ripping Jakub from their midst.

Alas, her prayers had not been heard and after so many years, the worst had happened: Jakub's birth mother wanted him back.

"We have to go to their office. We always knew this could happen."

"But now he's our son too! We adopted him, that has to count for something, doesn't it? They can't force me to give him up. He's my son! I love him!" Irena cried.

Luka hugged her close. "Irena, you know we can't do that. We have to do the right thing, or we'll never be able to look Jakub in the eye again. He deserves to know his birth family."

"I can't lose him," she sobbed into his chest.

"He was not to be ours forever, just for a time. We should be grateful for the joyful years we had with him." He pressed her tighter against him. "I'm sure he can visit and we can write letters."

"It's not the same." Eventually Irena's sobs subsided. They sat holding each other for a long time, until he said, "We should go to sleep. We both need to get up early in the morning."

Irena sighed and nodded her agreement. There was nothing else she could do. As she lay in her bed, she cursed the day they'd gone to the Red Cross office to register Jakub as a missing child. If they hadn't, this awful letter would never have shown up.

As she listened to Luka's rhythmic breathing, the tears returned and she silently cried into her pillow, feeling the loss of her beloved son already, as if they'd taken a limb from her.

. . .

The next morning, she hugged Jakub extra tight and pressed a kiss on his cheek, as she sent him to school.

"What's wrong, *Mamusia?*" He scrunched his face at the unusual smothering.

"Nothing, my sweet darling. I just want you to know that I love you more than anything in the world. Don't ever forget that."

Like any eleven year old he hated being mothered and nodded with a peculiar expression. "Can I go now?"

"Yes." Irena stood in the room, watching him as he put his satchel on his back and ran out the door, down the street to meet his friends. She'd miss him so much.

Then she went to the Red Cross office, where they were already waiting for her.

"*Pani* Pawlak, good to see you. We have received a photo and a letter from the probable mother and wanted you to iden-tify the boy, if possible."

The woman handed an old, faded image of a one-year-old boy to her and Irena's heart stopped beating for several seconds. This was her chance to deny everything. To tell the woman the boy in the photo wasn't Jakub, that they had to continue search-ing. That she could keep her son.

But the moment she held the photograph in her hands, she knew she couldn't do this. There was no doubt it was him. The same curly hair, the vivid eyes, the cute dimples in his cheeks. He was much older now, but even a blind person would see it was him.

Her instinct screamed to run away and hide, do anything to keep the inevitable from happening. At the same time, deep down in her soul she realized the other woman, Jakub's birth mother, must feel the same pain and grief as she did. She had to do the right thing, even though it felt as if she was issuing her own death sentence.

Her heart shattered into a million pieces as she handed the

picture back and said in a toneless voice, "It's him. There's no doubt about it."

"That must be such a relief for you," the Red Cross worker said in a much too chipper voice.

"It's not. I love him so much." Irena barely bit back the tears attacking her.

"Oh." The young woman apparently had never considered that there was another side to the reunification of missing children with their birth families—especially after such a long time.

The adoptive parents who'd cared for them, laughed with them, cried with them, suffered through their little problems, held their hands when they were scared, wiped their foreheads when they were sick—those mothers and fathers who'd loved their charges with all of their heart and would now be robbed of their treasured children.

"What now?" Irena's voice sounded clipped even to her own ears.

"We'll arrange for everything and will let you know." The young woman smiled. "Here's a letter from his mother. She's addressed it to you and your husband. It's written in Polish."

"Thank you." Irena didn't trust herself to read the letter in front of other people, so she pocketed it and left the Red Cross office. Outside the sun was shining down on her, but she didn't notice. Her soul was bathed in a stark blackness, one that was even worse than on the day she'd lost her baby.

With every step she took, the burden pressing down on her seemed to become heavier, until she finally reached her house and slumped down on the bench next to the tiled stove—Jakub's favorite place, where the two of them had sat countless times.

She took out the letter and began to read.

Dear Pan and Pani Pawlak,

Please excuse my less than perfect Polish. I haven't had much opportunity to practice since leaving Lodz.

I want to thank you from the bottom of my heart for all you have done for my son. Since that fateful day when I had to leave Jacob at the hospital so he could receive the medical treatment he needed to live, I have worried every single day about his well-being. But, it's hard to explain, somewhere deep in my heart I knew he was still alive. And I prayed every night that he wasn't alone or in some loveless orphanage.

I have relived those days in Posznán over and over again, trying to come up with something different I could have done. You can't imagine my relief when the Red Cross told me he'd been raised in your family and never lacked for anything.

Please don't believe I left him there by choice. I returned to the hospital the next day, despite soldiers trying to herd me onto the evacuation trains. When I finally reached it in the late afternoon, it had been evacuated already.

I won't tell you the disturbing things I saw there, but I want you to know that my gratitude toward you for saving him from this fate is without limits. I will forever be indebted to you for saving my sweet boy's life.

I know you must be full of emotion after all these years, therefore you'll understand that I dearly love my son. It is my wish to have him come to Germany and be reunited with me and his sister. My first husband, his father, was killed during the war. I am now remarried and have another daughter (aged two). The day Jacob will join us and complete our family, will be my happiest day. He's the missing piece of the puzzle, the sorrow that has kept me awake at night for the last seven years.

Thank you so much for loving my son and acting as surrogate parents in my absence. I hope one day I can meet you in person and thank you. Words are not enough.

Emma Kroger

As she finished the letter, Irena couldn't hold back anymore and broke down sobbing on the bench. Shivers wracked her body, tears streamed down her face. One dropped onto the letter, leaving a smear. She didn't care. Nothing mattered anymore, now that she knew that Jakub really would be ripped from her.

It wasn't much consolation that his birth mother seemed to love him dearly and would treat him well. All that counted was the horrific ache in her heart that spread across her entire body from head to toe, immobilizing her, turning her into a heap of sobs.

37

Jakub returned home after football training. "Evening, *Mamusia*. What's for dinner?"

"*Zrazy*."

He raised his head to sniff the distinctive smell of beef roulade, served with potatoes and red cabbage. It was his favorite dish and his mother usually reserved it for Sundays. "Hmm... that smells great."

"Have you done your homework?" she asked, her voice sounding slightly hoarse.

"I haven't had the time..." He prepared himself for the inevitable scolding, because he was supposed to finish homework before going to football training. Yet, nothing happened. His mother only shrugged and said, "Well, then wash your hands and finish it. Dinner will be ready in twenty minutes."

It was the first time she'd ever let him off the hook so easily and he bounded upstairs, taking three steps at a time, conveniently forgetting to wash his hands, so he'd finish his homework in time. By no means did he want to miss *Zrazy*.

When he walked downstairs not much later, both his

parents were standing in the kitchen, murmuring in low voices. A sudden queasiness took hold of him, because this usually meant they had found out about one of his shenanigans and were going to scold him. He wracked his brain for what he could have done this time, but came up empty. They couldn't know about the frog he'd hidden in a classmate's satchel, or could they?

When his father turned around and looked at him with a very grave face, his heart sank to his boots. This was serious. Much more serious than a hidden frog. But why the *Zrazy*? Or hadn't they known about his mischief when she'd started cooking? Whatever it was, he squared his shoulders, hoping he'd get away lightly.

"Jakub, we need to talk to you about something very important. Let's sit at the table," his father said.

This was truly worrisome, he could feel it in his bones. He braced himself for the worst. Silently he followed his parents into the living room and settled at the table that was already set for dinner.

His father steepled his hands on the table and gave him a long, scrutinizing look. "You remember that you came to us after Irena found you at the hospital, right?"

"Yes." Jakub looked between his parents. That was old news. His mother had abandoned him and fled the country. He didn't even remember her name, much less her looks. The only thing he sometimes recalled was the horrific angst he'd gone through before meeting Irena, and the feeling of utter desperation that not even his stuffed toy Affie had been able to alleviate.

"This may come as a surprise," his father cleared his throat, apparently fighting to find the proper words, which was very unusual for him. "Today the Red Cross confirmed that they have found your mother."

"What? After all these years?" Jakub's breath hitched in his lungs. That despicable woman who'd left him to fend for himself now had the guts to show up?

Irena took a calming breath and then said, "Your real name is Jacob Oppermann. The Red Cross believe it took so long because we misspelled your last name on the search form."

"She has married again and her name is now Emma Kroger. She's living in Aachen, West Germany, with your sister Sophie and a new child, called Liesl." Luka produced a piece of paper and added. "She has written a letter."

Jakub stared at the envelope as if it was going to bite him. His father nudged it toward him and nodded. "Go ahead. Read it for yourself. *Mamusia* and I will answer any questions you have."

He hesitantly unfolded the letter and read the first paragraph until the enormity of what he was doing reached his brain. No, he would have no part in this game! He threw the letter to the floor.

"Jakub, darling..." Irena tried to calm him down.

"Who does this woman think she is? She left me in a strange hospital with people I couldn't even understand." Despite knowing he wasn't allowed to speak to his parents in such a disrespectful way, the wrath broke through his defenses and he shouted. "I hate her! She abandoned me! I don't want anything to do with her!"

Luka raised his voice. "Jakub, I need you to calm down. I understand you're angry, but it wasn't her fault."

"So now she claims it was my fault?" He jumped up, trying to hide his tears, as his entire world was being ripped to pieces. What did he care about this woman he hadn't seen or heard from in years?

"Please, sit back down." Luka pointed to the abandoned chair.

"I'm sorry, Father." Jakub somehow managed to cling to his

manners and sat back down, although his anger was like a beating drum in the room.

"There's more, I'm afraid. She wants to have you back and the Red Cross will arrange the formalities and reunite you with her."

"What? You want to get rid of me, too?" he cried out, losing the struggle against his tears.

Irena got up and stood behind him, stroking his back. "We don't want to, but we must. She's your birth mother. She has the right to have you back."

"I'm not going. You can't send me to live with a stranger! You can't! I want to stay with you..." He started sobbing inconsolably, while his mother—the one he saw as his real mother, who'd cared for him all these years—stood behind him, wrapping her arms around his shoulders and murmuring soft words into his ears.

He didn't hear any of it. The only sensation was the big, burning hole in his chest as he relived the horrors of those days back in the hospital, when he was all alone. The fear, the anger, the guilt, all these emotions returned and washed over him, turning him into a sobbing mess. No, he would not go through that again. He'd not let a stranger take him from the only parents he knew, the ones who had loved him all these years and whom he loved back with such force it hurt every cell in his body.

After a while the sobs subsided, leaving him in a state of despair. Not even his mother's comforting words or the *Zrazy* she served him could penetrate the dark cloud that had settled over him. He didn't want to leave them to join some family he barely remembered.

It was only after he finished the meal and helped his mother wash the dishes that he noticed she was crying too. It broke what was left of his heart. Why did the world have to be so cruel? Why couldn't he simply stay with them, when none of them wanted him to leave?

His father entered the kitchen and said, "Jakub. I think you and I should have a talk between men. Grab your jacket."

Jakub did as he was told, respect for his father calming down his inner turmoil, at least for the time being. Outside, they fell in step and walked down to the lake in silence, a trip they'd made hundreds of times together, but never in such a dreadful mood.

It wasn't until they were halfway there that his father raised his voice. "Both I and your mother are completely destroyed over this news. You know that we love you more than anything else in the world.

"In the beginning I was worried when Irena brought you home from the hospital, because I feared we might be punished for helping the enemy, even if it was only a four-year-old child. But you were so sick, you wouldn't have made it through the night alone in the cold ward.

"And when Irena returned with you the next day to look for your mother, she witnessed things... We never knew whether the Germans or the Russians did them, however we both knew that she had done the right thing by rescuing you."

Jakub swallowed and pushed his hands deeper into his pockets. Aged just eleven years, he'd almost surpassed his mother in height and came up to his father's shoulders.

"Since we couldn't have children of our own, after..."

"After what?" Jakub turned his head to look at the man who'd been his father for all these years.

"Before we met you, Irena was pregnant with our first child. We were so happy... but then... she got rounded up by the Nazis one day and was beaten so severely, she lost the baby and almost died herself. To save her life, the doctors had to remove her ability to ever bear children again."

"I had no idea." Jakub was stunned by the revelation about the woman he called *"Mamusia"* and loved with all of his heart.

"It's not something we talk about. After that, she was so depressed for a long time. And with the war going on... times were hard. Finding you was the answer to our prayers, as if God himself had given us a gift. A child to love and cherish." Luka cleared his throat. "Soon we came to consider you as our son and... we love you so much."

Jakub's mind was whirling with all the revelations that the day had brought him.

"We always knew your birth mother might be found one day, and we would have to give you back. However, this didn't stop us, and especially Irena, from opening her heart and loving you unconditionally, the way only a mother can. She was never deterred by the threat that her heart might get broken if you had to leave. She was so incredibly happy to call you her son, for however short or long a time that might be."

They had reached the lake and Luka beckoned his son to sit on one of the benches.

"As the years passed, the possibility of finding your birth mother became ever more distant. Meanwhile, the political climate changed and the hate for the Germans seemed to increase evermore. That was the reason we adopted you and told everyone you were the orphaned child of a distant cousin, to keep you, and us, safe from persecution."

"I see." Jakub had no idea what else to say, since his entire world had been turned upside down during the past hours. Of course he'd known he was adopted, and used to speak German, but just now he finally understood that he wasn't a Pole, but one of the Germans everyone hated so much. A frightening thought occurred to him. Would his friends still talk to him when they knew he was German?

Then his shoulders sagged. It didn't matter. He might not

ever see his friends again, if his parents, who weren't really his parents, sent him away.

"Do I really have to go and live with this woman?" Jakub asked.

A sad smile showed up on Luka's face. "As much as I wish it was different, I'm afraid you'll have to go."

"I don't want to. I like it here just fine," Jakub protested.

"Unfortunately it's not for you or me to decide. Now that the authorities know, the bureaucratic cogs have started moving, and there's no way to stop them." Luka stayed silent for quite some time, staring at the water, before he finally spoke again. "Consider it as a chance. West Germany is much better off than Poland right now, and things will only get worse here with the communists ruling everything. You'll have more prosperity than Irena and I could ever offer you—"

"I don't care about money." Jakub kicked a pebble with his foot and watched it roll onto the grass.

"And freedom. In West Germany you can take up the profession you want, read any book you desire, travel wherever you wish to go." Travel was highly restricted in communist Poland and normal citizens were rarely granted a visa for a capitalist country.

Finally Jakub's mood lit up. "Can I come and visit you?"

"We'd love that."

Slightly mollified, Jakub said. "I still don't want to go, but I don't want to cause you problems either."

"You can write as often as you wish and we will answer every single one of your letters."

It wasn't the same as actually being with them, but it presented a ray of hope and Jakub decided to consider this an adventure. If he didn't like his new family at all, he could always just run away and return to Irena and Luka. He wouldn't tell his father about this plan, though, knowing he wouldn't approve of it.

"When do I have to leave?"

"We don't know. It will be several weeks, I assume. You'll need to get an exit permit and who knows what else."

At least it seemed he could stay with the people he loved most in this world for some more weeks and that he would get to say goodbye to his friends. Jakub sighed. "I'll go then. But if I don't like it in Aachen, I'll return to you."

Luka gave him a sad smile.

38

ABOUT TWO MONTHS LATER

Irena did her best to hang onto her fragile emotions. She was standing on the platform waiting for the train Jakub had to board.

Luka stood behind her, while Jakub clung to her hand. She glanced at him, noticing he was doing his best not to cry, but every once in a while, a tear slid down his cheek and he would hurriedly wipe it away.

A Red Cross official was going to accompany him throughout Poland and East Germany until the inner-German border, where she'd hand him over to her West German counterpart, who'd take him safely to Aachen.

"All aboard," came the call ten minutes later.

Jakub turned and wrapped his arms around Irena in a death grip. "I don't want to go, *Mamusia*."

Irena couldn't hold her tears back, because she feared she'd never see her son again. She smoothed her hands over his head. "I know, my darling. I know. I love you so much."

Luka stepped in to say, "Make us proud, son. And don't forget to write. We'll wait to hear from you."

"Yes, Father." Jakub was surprisingly calm as he hugged Luka.

The Red Cross worker picked up Jakub's small suitcase and tapped his shoulder. "We need to board the train."

Jakub nodded and followed her. Before he stepped onto the stairs leading into the train, he turned back to them and called out, "I love you *Mamusia* and Papa. I'll never forget you."

"Write as often as you can!" Irena called back and blew him a kiss, even as she fumbled with her other hand for Luka, because she feared she'd crumple into a sobbing pile if he didn't hold her up.

Jakub disappeared onto the train and reappeared again at the window of his compartment. He pushed it down and gazed out, waving at her. But much too soon, the locomotive started up and pulled the train out of the station taking her beloved son away from her.

Irena lost the fight against her tears and buried her head in Luka's shoulder, bawling inconsolably, until he gently led her away.

"He's gone," she whined. "I don't know how to cope without him. I just don't. I love him so much."

Luka had no words of comfort to offer. She knew it was the right thing to do. Jakub had never been hers, he'd only been borrowed from his real mother, for her to shower him with her love, to raise him and care for him.

And now what she had feared all those years had come true. The same way he'd suddenly popped up in her life, now he was gone.

"It's not forever," Luka said in an attempt to calm her. "He might be able to visit."

But they both knew it was next to impossible to cross the Iron Curtain, even for a tourist stay. If his mother had lived in East Germany, it would have been a realistic option, but now that Jakub was in the enemy capitalist world?

Still, she clung to the notion of him coming home every summer to visit, since that was her only way to endure the horrible loss searing through every cell in her body.

"Come, people are already looking at us." Luka put an arm around her shoulders and pulled her away from the platform, away from the place where she'd last held her son in her arms.

"How am I going to live without him?" she murmured.

"We will get through this together. We still have each other," Luka soothed her.

"I know. But it hurts so much. I want to board the next train and go after him." She knew that wasn't possible, because they'd never get a visa for a capitalist nation.

"He's not dead. He will write letters."

Instead of giving her comfort, Luka's words sent another violent wave of pain rushing through her and she cried out, "He even got a new birthday! On what day should I send him a present?"

"You're irrational with grief." Her husband, although grieving himself, was his usual composed self. He grabbed her tighter and led her home, where he settled her on the couch and then walked into the kitchen to boil water for tea.

When he brought her the tea, he also handed her a pill and said, "That will calm you down. Take it and sleep."

"I want to die," she bawled.

"You have to be strong. For me." Luka looked at her with so much love and pain in his eyes that she finally realized she wasn't the only one completely out of her mind with pain.

"I already miss him so much."

"I do too."

39

AACHEN

For the hundredth time that morning, Emma picked up a cloth and dusted the living room cabinet. She wanted everything to be perfect when Jacob arrived.

"When do you think they'll be coming?" she asked Martin, who'd taken the day off from work for this special occasion.

He gave her an indulgent smile. "The train should have arrived about an hour ago, but apparently they had to go to the Red Cross office to sign some papers first. I gather he should be here any moment now."

"Wouldn't it have been better to meet them at the train station? Perhaps we should go there and have a look? Just in case."

"It's their protocol to do it this way. Presumably they don't want a public scene on the platform."

Emma turned around to scrutinize the living room to check that everything was spick and span. Jacob should feel right at home with them. She'd even re-arranged the living quarters and moved Liesl into Sophie's room—much to her older daughter's chagrin—so he would have his own room.

After another glance at the clock on the mantelpiece, she

walked to the window and looked down onto the street. Nothing. She turned to look at her husband who sat in an armchair, reading the newspaper. How on earth could he sit still and read during such a momentous time? Her own nerves were frayed up to the last thread.

"What if they can't find our house?" she asked.

Martin gave a sigh and dropped the newspaper. "The Red Cross has visited four times already, it's highly unlikely they'll suddenly forget where we live."

"But... they should have arrived already. Do you think something has happened? An accident, maybe? Or the train was held up somewhere?"

"You need to stop fussing. He'll be here any moment now." Martin was as calm as usual, which Emma resented slightly. It wasn't his long-lost son, so he didn't understand.

She picked up a feather duster to clean the hard-to-reach places behind the radiator, when the doorbell rang. Panicked, she stopped mid-movement and stood frozen in the room.

"Don't you want to get it?" Martin asked.

"Me?" She stared at him, suddenly unable to move.

Before she could say another word, he sighed, folded his newspaper and got up. Emma heard him open the door, followed by an exchange of words. That tore her from her stupor and she discarded the feather duster as if it were poisonous, quickly rubbing her hands on her skirt, while glancing into the cabinet's glass pane to make sure her hairdo was impeccable.

She had wanted Sophie to be present for the big moment, but Martin had put his foot down and said she wasn't going to miss school for this, since she'd see enough of her brother in the years to come.

At first Emma had resented his decision, but now she realized he'd actually done this because he knew she needed time just for her and Jacob. She had enough problems dealing with her own emotions, she didn't need a teenager prone to drama around.

Footsteps clicked on the hallway's linoleum floor and then he was there.

"Jacob," she called out, instantly recognizing his face, despite the many years since she'd seen him last. She swiftly closed the distance between them and wrapped him in her arms. "My sweet, sweet boy. I missed you so much!"

He stiffened in her embrace and as soon as she let go, he took a step backward, standing awkwardly in the room. In heavily accented German he said, "*Guten Tag*, my name is Jacob Oppermann."

Shock numbed her limbs, her eyes darting between him and the Red Cross worker. It was only now she noticed that it wasn't the young woman she knew, but an elderly man. He stretched out his hand and spoke in the accent of her native region around Lodz.

"Good day, Frau Kroger. My name is Gottfried Heller. It's a pleasure to be able to assist with this family reunion. The Red Cross requested my presence, because Jacob..." he gazed at the boy "... doesn't speak German."

A shockwave attacked Emma, making her sway on her feet. What this man said was impossible. How could her son not speak his mother tongue?

"Shall we sit down?" Herr Heller asked.

Emma nodded, not really comprehending what was going on. It wasn't until Martin whispered something into her ear that she remembered her duties as hostess and asked, "Can I offer you something to drink? A glass of lemonade, maybe?"

"Yes, please," Herr Heller said and then turned to Jacob to ask him the same in Polish.

On her way into the kitchen to fetch the prepared soft drinks from the newly acquired refrigerator, she felt as if she was walking through a thick cloud of mist. When she returned she listened only with half an ear to Heller's explanations, while intently studying Jacob's face.

This first meeting was so different than the one she'd imagined. In her dreams it had been filled with love, joy, and excitement. In reality, though, it was nothing but awkward. Jacob looked as if he'd rather be anywhere else than here and she believed she could see defiance in his gaze.

"... I'll visit you every day to help with the language," Herr Heller said.

Finally she shook off the confusion that held her in its grip. "That is so very kind of you, but that won't be necessary. I speak some Polish. It's a bit rusty for lack of use, but will do."

He nodded. "That is a relief to know. In any case, Jacob should receive German lessons."

Emma shook her head in disbelief. Her own son had to re-learn his native tongue. Never in her wildest dreams had she thought this might happen. Then she turned toward Jacob and told him in Polish, "Welcome home. I'm aware this must be difficult, but I'll help you to remember your German. Let me show you your room."

He answered in a very stilted tone. "That is very kind of you, *Pani* Kroger."

Him addressing her as "Mrs Kroger" stabbed her heart and she said, "You don't have to call me *Pani* Kroger, I'm your mother."

"Irena Pawlak is my mother. You are the person who abandoned me," Jacob said with so much ice in his voice, she all but recoiled from him.

"Would you at least call me Emma? Please?"

He gave a nod and picked up his small suitcase before he asked, "Where's my room?"

When she'd left him in his room, she returned to the living room, where Herr Heller and Martin were conversing. What should have been the happiest day in her life had turned into an utter disaster.

"Please don't be disheartened, Frau Kroger," Herr Heller said. "It often takes a while for the children to adjust to their former families. This is one of the reasons why the Red Cross engages volunteers like me. To help the transition process. Jacob has been torn from his life in Poland and everything here is new and strange for him. Give him some time."

She gave a loud sigh.

Martin talked with Herr Heller for the next thirty minutes about formalities, but Emma couldn't concentrate, since too many conflicting emotions whirled in her chest. Thankful that she could rely on her husband, she leaned back, asking herself whether she should have done anything different.

Was Jacob right in his accusation that she'd abandoned him? If she had gone to the hospital earlier? Demanded to stay with him overnight? Should she not have left him there and taken him with her to the refugee camp? Or should she have stayed in Posen and let Sophie flee with Agatha? Could she have done anything to find him earlier? Should she have known he would have forgotten his German and taken precautions?

She bit on her lips, suddenly exhausted.

Some minutes later, the two men got up to bid goodbye, but it wasn't until Martin nudged her shoulder that she remembered her manners and stood to shake Herr Heller's hand. "Thank you so much. We really appreciate your help."

"He'll come around soon enough. The trip was strenuous. Just give him some time."

40

Things were even worse than Jacob had imagined. Apart from Gottfried Heller and the woman who claimed to be his mother and forced him to call her Emma, nobody spoke Polish in this whole damn place.

His new "father" Martin seemed nice enough, but rarely spoke a word. He was out at work most of the day anyway. And his sister Sophie, whom he barely remembered, compared to the bitchiest, most unpleasant girls in his class back home. With her he was actually glad that he didn't understand what she said.

Even his new classmates were horrid. They stared at him, pointed their fingers at him and said bad things behind his back. He didn't have to understand their language to know they poked fun at him.

At home, he'd been a good student, but here, the only subject where he excelled was sports. If the boys in his class let him play. Usually they made sure he never got the ball when he was in their team. After yet another awful day at school and extra German classes in the afternoon, he returned home to find Emma in a rush.

"Oh good, you're back. I need to run an errand, can you please keep an eye on Liesl? It won't be long."

"Yes," he agreed. It wasn't like he had friends to meet with anyways. At least Liesl never made derisive comments about him. He took the little girl by the hand and asked in Polish, "What do you want to play?"

Despite the language barrier she always seemed to understand him. Her eyes lit up as she babbled on, leading him to the corner in her and Sophie's room where her building bricks were stored.

"Build me a tower!" she demanded and he obliged willingly. Once he was done, she thrashed it to pieces, laughing happily at the mess she had created.

Jacob rebuilt the tower, being reminded of happier times when he and Luka had done the same. Luka had taught him so many things. He quickly pushed the memories away, because thinking about his parents always threatened tears to spill.

"Don't be sad," said his half-sister and climbed on his lap.

He couldn't help but feel comforted by her presence. If nobody else in this place liked him, at least she was a ray of sunshine in his life. He made an effort to talk to her in German. "It's so hard."

"Not hard. Do it again. I not knock over." She gave him her sweetest smile, obviously thinking he was sad, because she'd destroyed the tower he had built.

"Why don't you build it and I thrash everything?" He nudged her to help him build another tower.

Things didn't improve much over the next months. With the exception of his little sister Liesl, nobody seemed to like him. Even Emma constantly nagged at him for one thing or the other. She always corrected his pronunciation and grammar, to the extent that he'd given up speaking German altogether.

By now he understood most of what was said, but refused to answer in their language, since he didn't want to give her, or his teachers, the feeling they had won. If Emma hated him so much, why had she insisted that he come here? Why hadn't she left him with his parents, who actually loved him, and where he'd been happy?

Most nights he retired to his room directly after dinner. There he lay on his bed, staring at the ceiling and wishing himself back home. Big fat tears rolled down his cheeks as he dreamed of his friends in Poznań. He imagined himself with them, playing football or going to the lake after school and cursed his bad luck for having to be so miserable here.

He was dreaming about his *Mamusia* making his favorite meal *Zrazy*, when loud voices caught his attention. That would be Sophie and Emma arguing again. From the day he arrived, the two of them had been fighting on a daily basis. He shrugged, completely uninterested in his sister's shenanigans, however, his ears perked up when he heard his name.

Silently he got up and walked to the door on stockinged feet to open it ajar. There was a break in the argument, then a sigh and Emma's voice. "What has gotten into you? You've become obstinate. You're talking back all of the time. Staying out after school. Not doing your chores. Why?"

"Why does it even interest you? All you ever talk about anymore is Jacob. 'Jacob this. Jacob that. I'm worried about Jacob. I have to learn German with Jacob. I'm afraid Jacob isn't feeling well.' What about me? Does anyone in this house care about me?"

"Of course I do, sweetie."

"No. You don't. Nobody does. I'm only good enough to babysit Liesl and help with chores, while Jacob gets treated like a prince. Why don't you get yourself a maid instead of a daughter? She wouldn't mind people trampling all over her."

"Sophie, please. That's not true. Jacob has had such a hard

time since he arrived here—"

"See? Jacob again. Why are his feelings so much more important than mine? Why do you always fuss over him and barely spare a thought about me? I bet you wouldn't notice if I dropped dead right now, until you needed someone to clean the mess because your precious Jacob can't be expected to raise a single finger in this house!"

There was a long pause before Emma answered. "I realize I have put too much on your shoulders, because I considered you grown up, but now I realize you're still a child who needs me. I'll make sure to have more time for you. Perhaps we can ask someone to babysit Liesl once a week and do something, just the two of us?"

Emma's voice seemed exceedingly tired, exhausted even. Guilt washed over Jacob. It was his fault that Emma and Sophie were constantly fighting. Because of him, Emma had so much extra work and was always tired.

"I wish he'd stayed in Poland with his adoptive parents whom he seems to miss so much. Everything was better before he showed up," Sophie said.

An exasperated sigh was the answer. "You can't genuinely mean that. He's your brother."

"Why not? We were happy without him, weren't we? I really wish he'd leave again."

Jacob had heard enough. He softly closed the door and curled up in his bed to cry. After a long time, he dried his tears, sat at his desk and took out pen and paper. Then he wrote a letter to his *Mamusia*, who actually loved him, and told her how very awful he felt, begging her to somehow bring him back home.

He sealed the letter and the next morning took it to the post office. Then he entered the school building with a much lighter heart, because he was sure Irena and Luka would come to his rescue. Together with them, he'd be happy again.

41

Emma waited anxiously until Martin came home from work. After dinner, when she'd put Liesl to bed and her older children had retired to their rooms, she told him what had happened.

"Sophie is just jealous, I'm sure she'll come around," he said.

"But Jacob's so miserable, too. He thinks I don't notice, but he cries himself to sleep every night."

"He's a boy. He'll soon learn not to cry." Martin rubbed her shoulders.

She wished she could be as nonchalant as he was, but the heartache of her children seared her soul with pain. "I do want him to be happy."

"It's just a phase of adaptation that he has to go through. It'll serve him well later in life." Like most men, Martin had no time to waste for emotions.

"He hates it here and said so himself. Did you know he told his German teacher that his only Christmas wish is to return to his parents in Poland?" Then she voiced the guilt that had been accumulating in her chest for months. "Do you think I was selfish in making him come to live with us?"

"Selfish? We're sacrificing a lot to offer him a comfortable life. Each of us has had to relinquish things we used to have. Sophie has to share her room with Liesl. I work overtime to make up for all the extra cost, and you... you have your hands full with three children instead of two, and a household to run, up to the point that I rarely get time alone with you."

Emma sighed. He was voicing the same complaints as Sophie. "Do you feel that I'm neglecting you?"

"I wouldn't have put it that way, but yes, you're often absentminded these days. I thought having Jacob here would make you happy. It seems the opposite has happened. You're worried all the time."

"It's just... I feel so inadequate. He misses Irena and Luka so much, he doesn't see me as his mother, he and Sophie don't get along, and he still hasn't found friends at school. It seems the only person he likes is Liesl."

"Well, that's a start, isn't it?"

She thought for a moment and then asked, "Do you think we should send him back?"

"What?" His face was full of surprise.

"You said it yourself—everyone was so much happier before he arrived."

Martin sighed and walked over to the cabinet to pour them two glasses of schnapps. "Here."

"Thank you." From experience she knew not to interrupt, because he was pondering an answer. He was like that, never talking out of an impulse. It didn't take long.

"Look. I realize this situation is difficult, for everyone, including you. I also realize that you want to do right by him and are worried about his emotional state. However, his life here is so much better than in Poland. He has possibilities he'd never have over there, starting with prosperity, a free choice of career, traveling, freedom. I'm sure the Pawlaks would agree that he's better off with us than with them."

"But..."

"No buts. No person in their right mind would return a child to behind the Iron Curtain. It would be exceptionally cruel to take away his entire future, just because of a few adaptation problems in the present."

Emma nodded wearily. She was consumed with guilt, but deep in her soul she'd never wanted to return Jacob to his other mother.

Martin swallowed the schnapps and poured himself another one. Then he looked at her intensively. "Even if we wanted to return him, it's likely not possible."

"It's not?"

"No. Poland, all communist nations in fact, have tightened their rules again. It's basically impossible to get a visiting visa, let alone one to stay."

"He came here."

"That was an exception. Arranged by the Red Cross, based on international contracts and only because we could prove he's in fact a German citizen, who'd gone missing during the war. Do you actually believe the Polish government would take him back? An alien national from the archenemy? A German and a capitalist?" He scoffed. "There's no way in hell these corrupt Stalinist puppets would do that. Although..." He paused, looking at her with squinted eyes. "They just might. But if they do I can assure you, they'd use him as the prime example of a failed attempt to defect to the class enemy. They'll pass him around, making him famous as the boy who wanted to escape from the communist paradise and then hated it so much he had to return. They'll make him the poster boy of everything that is bad in the West and blame his return on our rotten morals. Do you really want this? Do you want Jacob to be used as a publicity vehicle for the Commie bastards?"

"Martin!" she hissed, as she didn't appreciate him using that kind of language.

"It's true, isn't it? They give us nothing but problems. In any case it's completely out of the question to send Jacob there, even in the improbable situation that they'd allow him back in. He is here to stay and we all have to accept that as a fact."

"I guess you're right."

It wouldn't solve any of her problems, but at least it softened her guilt. There was nothing she could change, since the horse had already bolted from the stable.

42

Irena jumped with delight when she found a letter from Jakub in the mail. Though he was writing regularly, his letters always felt stilted and distant. She blamed it on the unusual medium of communication, since he wasn't used to writing letters to anyone, much less to his parents.

She made herself a cup of tea and settled on the bench by the tiled oven, before she opened the envelope and unfolded the paper.

At the sight of his neat handwriting, a wave of love rushed through her body. No matter how far away, he'd always be her beloved son. She still missed him terribly every single day, but had come to accept the fact that he had a much better life ahead of him in West Germany with his birth mother. And she was grateful for the years God had allowed her with to be with Jakub, caring for him and raising him to become a fine young man.

Dearest Mamusia,

I can't tell you how horrible my life here is. Nobody likes me. My classmates make jokes and say mean things behind my back and my teachers do nothing. They all think I'm stupid, because my German is still not very good.

Despite understanding their language quite well, I have now stopped speaking it, since everyone makes fun of me when I say something wrong. Emma, the woman who claims to be my mother, scolds me every day for every little mistake I make.

And Sophie, my sister. I can't even begin to tell you how awful she is. She hates me with all her soul. Just tonight she told Emma that she wishes I had never come to live with them.

Please, Mamusia, if you love me at all, can't you come and take me back?

Jakub

Her hand holding the letter sank to her lap as her heart broke all over again. All she'd ever wanted was for her beloved Jakub to be happy. Had they committed a horrible sin by sending him away? Should they never have registered him with the Red Cross? Or pretended Jakub was a different boy after they'd adopted him?

She was still sitting with the letter on her lap when Luka came through the door.

"Dear God, Irena, what has happened?" He knelt down beside her and she wordlessly handed him the letter.

"That doesn't sound good," he murmured.

"It's all my fault. I have failed him."

He settled beside her, wrapping an arm around her shoulders. "You haven't. We had no choice. We had to return him to his rightful mother."

"But he's desperate."

"Yes, I realize that."

"Can we take him back?" she asked with a hopeful note in her voice, since that would fulfill her dearest wish.

"You realize that's not possible, don't you? Poland now is effectively a huge prison where nobody can move in or out."

Heavy sobs wracked her body. "Isn't there anything we can do?"

"I will write him a letter, reminding him to stay strong and take it one day at a time."

"Can't we give him a phone call?"

Luka rubbed his chin. "We can, but since it's international we'd need to go to the post office and do it from there. Maybe next week we could go?"

She wiped away her tears and nodded. "Yes, let's do that, but write the letter immediately."

43

Jakub waited every day for Irena to come for him. A week passed and nothing happened. He received a letter from her, which had clearly been sent before she'd received his cry for help. Mail between Poland and Germany was slow and unreliable, at least that was how Emma and Martin explained the long delays.

So he decided to take matters into his own hands. One morning, Emma told him she had to visit Martin's elderly aunt in another town and wouldn't be home until evening.

"Sophie will stay with her friend in the afternoon. For you I have prepared lunch. It's in the fridge and you just need to heat it up. Will you cope?"

"Yes. I'll be fine," he said, wondering why she didn't suggest he joined her.

"Now, don't dawdle or you'll be late for school. I'll see you in the evening."

"Goodbye." He missed the way his *Mamusia* had always kissed him on the cheek and tousled his hair before sending him off to school. Emma did neither. She was like a stranger to him.

Sitting in class, he decided this was too good an opportunity to let pass. As soon as classes were over, he raced home, tossed the contents of his satchel onto his desk and filled it with his most beloved possessions. He grabbed what little money he had, walked down into the kitchen and made himself sandwiches, which he stuffed into the satchel as well, plus a bottle of water.

With one last gaze at the place he'd come to hate so much, he took his jacket off the hook, tied it around his waist and closed the door behind him. Then he walked to the train station, where he bought a train ticket to Cologne, which he knew to be one hour by train to the east. From there he'd figure out what to do next. If he was clever, the conductor wouldn't notice and he could stay on the train until its final destination Berlin. From there, he might even walk to the border.

On the map in his school atlas it looked like a very short distance. Since he was a good runner, he was optimistic that he'd easily be able to walk forty or fifty miles in a day. So he should arrive at the border way before anyone would think of searching for him that far away.

If Emma even noticed that he was gone when she came home tonight, she'd surely not assume he'd left for good. If she did, she might secretly be relieved to get rid of him and not bother to search at all.

He valiantly willed anxiety and sadness away and squared his shoulders. As soon as he was in Poland, everything would be fine again. He'd place a phone call to the post office, where everyone knew him and then his parents would come to get him. Already looking forward to returning home, he relaxed in his seat, watching the landscapes pass by.

Everything worked according to plan, until about three hours into the train ride. Suddenly a new conductor came along and asked for his ticket. It took him only one glance to know that Jacob had long passed the destination he'd paid for.

Jacob pretended to have been asleep, but the conductor became suspicious. At the next stop he handed him over to a

colleague, who took him to the station police. Now he sat opposite a rather intimidating policeman, interrogating him.

"Where were you headed?" the policeman asked.

"I told you, I was visiting relatives in Aachen and am now
on my way back home."

"Where's your home?"

He wanted to say Poznań, but thought better of it. The
policeman wouldn't believe him anyway. Thinking quickly he
answered, "Cologne."

"Your address?"

"I... I don't remember."

The policeman cast him a suspicious glance, though
dropped the topic. "What's your name again?"

They had taken his name twice already and he'd been
clever enough to give them his Polish name, since he didn't want
them running to Emma. If he could convince them to just let
him go, he'd walk to the Polish border if he must.

"Jakub Pawlak."

"That's a Polish name."

"Because I'm a Pole. I came here to visit relatives in
Cologne and need to go back to Poland."

"Didn't you just say you visited relatives in Aachen?"

Sweat was running down his back. He'd never thought it
would be so difficult to run away. Why did this man even care?
Nobody in Aachen liked him anyway. They'd all be better off
without him. "Well, yes. Those are different relatives. I first
visited those in Cologne and then the ones in Aachen."

"All on your own?" The policeman gave him a friendly nod.

Jacob, though, was on the alert. "It's not that far, so my aunt
gave me the ticket."

"How old are you?"

"Eleven."

"And your birthday?"

He gave the date of the birthday he'd used most of his life, since he still hadn't quite accepted the fact that he was actually born two months later.

"Well. Your aunt must be out of her mind with worry. Don't you think we should let her know where you are?"

"No!" Jacob yelled. "I mean... she won't be home right now. And they don't have a telephone."

"Now that is a problem." The policeman scratched his head. "Your aunt doesn't have a telephone and you don't remember her address. Do you at least remember her name?"

Before he could stop himself, Jacob shook his head.

The policeman stapled his hands. "I tell you what. You're not the first runaway to end up in front of me. I'm sure your mother is sick with worry. Why don't you tell me her name and address and I'll send a policeman to her house to let her know you're safe? How does that sound?"

Jacob burst into tears. "You don't understand. She's not my mother. She abandoned me. I was happy with my parents in Poland. Everything was fine until the Red Cross arrived and made me go to her. She doesn't even like me. My sister Sophie hates me, all my classmates hate me. Even my teachers do. Why can't you let me return to Poland? I was happy there! *Mamusia* and Papa, they will be delighted to have me back." He knew they would.

The policeman got up and called something into the hall-way, before he returned to the table to ask a few more clarifications about how Jacob had ended up with this woman he didn't call mother.

Between sobs, he recounted his entire sorry story. At one point, the door opened and a young woman came inside, carrying a mug of hot chocolate and a slice of bread with butter. "You must be hungry."

"Thank you," Jacob said, before he devoured the food. He hadn't realized how hungry he was. "What time is it?"

"Almost ten p.m.," she answered.

"You may be the strangest case that's ever come into my station," the policeman said after the young woman was gone. "I hate to tell you, but there's no way for you to return to Poland. The borders are closed. Poland has been closed off for years, and just recently the East German government has completely sealed off the inner-German border. No traffic allowed, except for government functionaries or the odd merchant."

"I came here less than six months ago."

"That was with the help of the Red Cross, right?" The policeman rubbed his chin. "I guess there were special programs to reunify missing children like you with their families?"

"I wasn't a missing child! I was happy with my parents at home."

"I don't doubt you were, but the fact is you can't go back, even if I was willing to help."

Jacob let his forehead fall onto the table and sobbed for a long time, until the policeman said, "If you tell me the name and address of your mother in Aachen, I'll inform her and we'll return you on the first train in the morning."

There was no point in being obstinate or difficult. If the policeman was telling the truth, and Jacob had no reason to doubt him, he'd never see his beloved *Mamusia* again. He would have to return to his miserable life with the family he did not like.

Another wave of sobs hit him hard. Once they subsided, he wrote down Emma's name and address.

Though, the policeman had given him a lot to think about. Perhaps he hadn't made his best effort to try and find the positive in his situation?

44

Emma paced the room with frantic steps.

"Please will you calm down?" Martin said.

"How can I? Jacob's gone and none of his classmates know anything."

"I'm sure he'll show up soon, he probably forgot the time." Martin was the voice of reason, the complete opposite to Emma, who feared she was going to lose it.

"It's dark already."

"We have street lamps. And he knows his way."

"How... can you be so... so... indifferent?" she yelled at her husband.

"I'm just trying to stay reasonable here. Statistically ninety percent of runaways return within twenty-four hours—"

"You can't actually expect me to be comforted by statistics?" Emma flopped on the couch, her entire body shaking at the realization that she might lose her little boy a second time. She wasn't sure she could survive such a blow—going through the angst, the heartbreak, the guilt all over again.

It was silent in the room except for the tick-tock of the clock on the mantelpiece. Tick-tock. Tick-tock. Her eyes were magically drawn toward the hand indicating the seconds. It felt as if her very lifeblood was draining with every movement of the hand. Tick. Tock. Tick.

She sprang up to pace the room again. She stopped in front of Martin, who sat seemingly undisturbed in his armchair, reading the newspaper. She cocked her head, scrutinizing him. He wasn't the love of her life. That had been Herbert—sweet, funny Herbert who had to die on the battlefield somewhere in Poland.

Nonetheless, she loved Martin. She loved his calmness, which had given her a much-needed pillar to lean against during the turbulent times after their arrival in Aachen. He'd supported her every step through the lengthy process to find Jacob and then bring him home, and she'd never fully appreciated his efforts to take on another child who wasn't even his.

During the past months she'd mistaken his calm for indifference, which had caused her much grief, however, as she gazed into his face now, she realized he wasn't unfazed at all. A steep frown of worry creased his forehead and from the lack of movement of his pupils she knew he wasn't reading at all.

"I'm so sorry." She knelt next to his feet, putting her head on his knee.

"Don't be sorry."

"It's all my fault. I should have left him with the Pawlaks. He was happy there."

Martin sighed. "Personally I don't think so, but even if it were true, it's too late for regrets. The Iron Curtain has fallen. The last loopholes have been sealed. The entire communist bloc is de facto a heavily guarded prison where nobody can get in or out." He put down his newspaper and glanced at the clock. "It's midnight. We should call the police."

"The police?" she shrieked. "Jacob's not done anything criminal."

"We'll report him missing. If someone picks him up, they'll know who he is. I should take a recent picture of him."

"No, you can't do that," she murmured. "He's not missing. We just found him. It's not the war anymore. I can't do this again. I..." She broke out into sobs, grateful when Martin gently forced her onto the couch.

"You'll stay here, in case he returns, while I go to the police station." He put on his coat and hat, took Jacob's photo from the mantelpiece, slid it into his pocket and left.

The moment the door closed behind him, Emma felt as if her entire being exploded. She was so occupied with her pain that she didn't hear steps coming into the room until Sophie stood in front of her, her eyes wide with shock.

"Mami, why did Papa leave?"

"It's nothing."

"Is Papa coming back?"

"Of course he is."

"Then why are you crying?" Sophie insisted.

Emma wiped her tears away. "It's Jacob. He hasn't come home yet."

"Jacob! That boy again! He causes nothing but trouble! Why can't he return to where he came from?"

As she heard her daughter spew such hate, which she'd obviously picked up at school, where prejudices against refugees from the East were rampant, she had an epiphany. "I believe that's exactly what he's trying to do. He ran away to return to his former life."

"Really?" Sophie's mouth hung wide open.

"I think so."

"Then he's a lot braver than I thought." Sophie snuggled up to her mother on the couch. "Don't worry. He'll be back soon enough. If nothing else stops him, in the end the border will. I heard the East Germans put up spring guns all along the inner-German border."

A dizziness overcame Emma at the imagination of her sweet boy shredded into bloody pieces when stepping on a land mine.

Sophie seemed to have noticed, because she put a hand on Emma's arm. "Don't worry, Mami, he'll be picked up long before."

"I hope."

The two of them must have fallen asleep, because suddenly Martin stood in front of them with a huge grin. "They found him. He was on a train to Berlin, intent on traveling to Poznań."

"Thank God! Where is he?"

"Still in Dortmund. A police officer will accompany him back to Aachen in the morning and return him directly to us."

"Dear God, thank you so much!"

The next morning a police car stopped in front of the door and a very subdued Jacob stepped onto the sidewalk. Emma rushed downstairs to meet him halfway.

He stopped before her and murmured, "I'm so sorry for causing you grief," before he headed to his room.

Realizing his inner turmoil, Emma didn't try to stop him. Instead she invited the policeman, who came accompanied by a social worker, to join her in the living room. "Thank you for bringing him back home."

"You're welcome. Your boy has some serious issues."

Emma nodded. "I know. He and I got separated during the last days of the war and the Red Cross just found him six months ago. It's been a tough time."

The female social worker nodded. "We see this quite often, especially in young children who barely remember their parents. It sounds cynical, but those who grew up in loving families in Poland have a much harder time than the ones found in orphanages. It'll take some time, but he'll come around."

Emma hoped this was true.

Once the officials were gone, she knocked on Jacob's door.

"Come in." He stood at his desk, his ears burning with shame, as he gazed down to his feet. "I'm sorry, Emma. I never wanted to cause anyone grief."

Her heart spilled over with love for her boy, who was hurting so much. "Don't worry, my darling. I'm just relieved to have you back in one piece." She looked at his face that showed his confusion, his anger, his pain and his sadness. "I knew you were suffering, but I never realized how much you loved your foster parents."

It had taken a while to accept this truth, since she'd never considered the possibility that her son could call another woman "Mother" or that Jacob and his other mother could love each other as unconditionally as she loved him.

Jacob cocked his head. "My *Mamusia*, Irena, was there for me when nobody else was. She rescued me from the hospital and brought me to her home, despite the hardships that must have meant for her. I was so angry at you for abandoning me back then. It was such a frightening night, I'll never forget it. And I never forgave you for it."

She wanted to protest, but before she could say anything he stopped her with a gesture.

"But I realize now it wasn't your fault. You were probably as terrified as I was."

"I was, sweetheart. Don't believe that I didn't try to fetch you. The one time I managed to sneak into the ward, you weren't there. So I left Affie for you. Whatever happened to him, by the way?"

"I left him with *Mamusia*, so she would have someone to keep an eye on her and comfort her during my absence."

A wave of love surged through Emma's veins at such a considerate gesture. She longed to take Jacob into her arms, but resisted, since she wanted to give him the freedom to take the first step.

Jacob continued. "I don't remember much about the first years after the war, just that Irena took me to the Red Cross office several times to inquire after you. But when the years passed and nothing happened, I forgot about my past." Those words stabbed Emma's soul and she held her breath, waiting for what would come next. "I was so occupied learning Polish, going to school, having friends, playing football. My life was good." He looked at her with such sadness, it tore into her soul. "Yes, we didn't have any of the luxuries you have like a refrigerator or a telephone in the house. We couldn't afford to buy new shoes or flashy clothing, but we always had enough to eat and I was happy."

"I'm so sorry," Emma said. "It just never occurred to me... I always assumed you were missing me as much as I missed you. That you were waiting for me all this time, suffering miserably. Therefore I couldn't understand your reluctance when you came here. It hurt me deeply when you refused to call me Mami. Because I had never stopped loving you, I assumed you were the same, but..." She paused to organize her emotions and choose her next words carefully. "What should have been the happiest day in my life, the day we were reunited, turned out to be catastrophic and it only went downhill from there. Whatever I did or said, nothing seemed to be able to get through to you. It broke my heart, because I never intended you to be unhappy. I only ever wanted the best for you." She bit her lower lip to keep herself from crying.

"Nobody ever asked me what I wanted," he whispered.

"I realize that now," Emma said. "The guilt of failing you once again and making you unhappy ate at me. So much, I seriously considered sending you back to the Pawlaks."

"You did? Really?" A bright smile appeared on his face, only to disappear a second later. "The policeman said it wasn't possible though."

She so dearly wanted to reach out and caress his cheek.

"Unfortunately that's right, yes. Martin and I talked at length about this. In the current political circumstances, it simply isn't an option. There's no way for you to return to Poland." She gave a sad shake of her head. "So I hoped you'd somehow come around."

"You should have told me. I wasn't even trying to blend in, since I hated everything here, and I believed nobody liked me, not even you," he admitted.

"Oh, Jacob, that's not true. I've always loved you, from the moment I knew I was pregnant with you. Throughout all these years without a life sign of you I never stopped loving you, not even when everyone else advised me to move on and accept that you were dead. I never lost hope that I'd find you again, one day." She smiled and stretched out her hand to ruffle his hair. "I almost wish I hadn't found you, because then you'd still be happy."

"Don't say that." Jacob was clearly fighting for composure. "I never realized that you'd suffered, too. I assumed you had forgotten about me, if you weren't dead."

"How could I ever forget you?" Emma said, and finally, he stepped closer and wrapped his arms around her. It was a clumsy embrace, which warmed her heart more than anything else had in the past years.

"I'll make an effort to be happy," Jacob whispered.

"Together we'll get through this." She dabbed at her eyes before she continued, "By the way, I wrote a letter to the Pawlaks, asking them if there's a way to call them to a public phone, so you'll be able to talk to them at least a few times a year. And with time, the travel restrictions might be lifted again and as soon as they are, I promise you can go visit them. How does that sound?"

"That's wonderful... Mami, thank you so much."

Her heart filled with joy, because he'd called her Mami,

nevertheless she said, "You don't have to call me Mami, if you don't want to."

"But I do. I realize it's time for me to make a real effort." He gave her a lopsided smile, "I do remember a few things from before we got separated, mostly how happy I was at our home. You reading a book to me and Sophie at night before tucking us into bed. I want to have that feeling again."

45

POZNAŃ, FEBRUARY 1989

Jacob stepped off the train in Poznań together with his two daughters, Maria and Claudia. He'd been looking forward to this moment ever since the Polish government had allowed free travel between their country and West Germany two months earlier.

His heart was beating violently. Maria noticed his nervousness and took his hand in hers. "Is Irena meeting us at the train station, Papa?"

His oldest daughter had just turned twenty years of age and attended university in Aachen. He'd waited and timed his first visit to the woman who'd been his mother for seven years to coincide with Maria's winter recess, because he wanted Irena to meet both of his daughters. Although, to be honest, he also needed their support for this momentous trip.

As much as he still loved Irena, he was also afraid to see her again, worried they'd grown too much apart and the meeting would be a shocking disappointment.

"No, we'll have to take a taxi, since Irena doesn't leave the house much anymore," Jacob said. He'd kept in touch with his foster parents for the last thirty-seven years. First mostly by letter only, until several years ago, when they had finally gotten telephone service in their house.

International calls were prohibitively expensive, yet he'd made it a habit to call them once a month and keep them updated on the changes in his life. Luka had been over the moon when Jacob had decided to study medicine and they had exchanged long discussions by letter about medical topics.

In the sixties, just in time for his graduation as a doctor, Jacob had bought two identical Super 8 cameras and sent one to Luka, giving them the opportunity to exchange films about their lives, and thus feel closer together.

Almost thirty years later, a widower and father of two grown children, he still cherished the monthly call with his foster parents and always looked forward to it.

The sudden change of political climate and the granting of freedom to travel by the Polish government had been a gift sent from heaven, since he hadn't in his wildest dreams expected to hold Irena in his arms once again. The changes had come too late for Luka, though, who'd died just a year before at the age of seventy-five.

The taxi drove through the streets of Poznań while Jacob strained his eyes to recognize something familiar. The streets looked so drab and desolate—a stark contrast to the new, shining cities in West Germany. Finally they stopped in front of Irena's house.

He stepped out, so completely taken in by his memories, he forgot about everything else. The house looked so much smaller than he remembered it as. Nevertheless, a warm, cozy feeling spread through his veins, mixed with anxiety. Any moment now he'd meet the woman again whom he had loved all his life despite a distance of a thousand miles and an Iron Curtain between them.

The sound of a coughing exhaust shook him from reminiscing and he turned around to watch the taxi drive away.

"No worries, I paid him," Claudia, his younger daughter said. Maria stood next to her and between them they carried their suitcases, including his.

"Thank you." He reached for his suitcase, but Maria gently pushed him away. "Why don't you go and ring?"

He knew they wanted to give him some alone time with Irena and was grateful for it, since he didn't want them to see the tears he felt coming. Gathering his courage, he approached the front door.

Irena must have heard them coming, because even before he rang the bell, the door opened and there she was. Aged, with white hair and wrinkles in her face, but unmistakably her. All of a sudden he was transported back in time.

"*Mamusia*," he whispered, wrapping her into his arms. It was a strange reversal of roles, since he towered her by almost two heads.

"*Mój synku*," she murmured the endearment she'd used for him when he was little. "This must be the happiest day in my life, to see you again."

"I missed you so much. Every single day." It was true. Despite having grown to love not only his birth mother Emma and his stepfather Martin, but also his sisters Sophie and Liesl, nobody had been able to take Irena's place in his heart.

"I missed you too, my sweet boy." After a while she looked up and saw the girls lingering behind. "These must be your daughters. What beautiful girls. Come in!"

Both his daughters had taken a crash course in Polish when it became clear they'd be allowed to visit. They were by no means proficient, but spoke enough for a basic conversation.

As they greeted Irena in her native language, he could see her eyes shining with pride at the girls she considered her grandchildren.

"I'm so happy to finally get to know you in person. But come in, I'll show you your room. The three of you will all have to sleep in Jakub's old room." She spoke too fast to hide her nerves, so Jacob took her hand.

"Everything will be perfect."

"I don't have much."

"You have more than enough love," Jacob said. Upstairs in his old room, which had been converted into Luka's study, his gaze fell immediately on a rather worn out stuffed animal. "Affie!"

"He comforted me all these years whenever my longing for you threatened to overwhelm me." Irena's voice was but a hoarse whisper.

"I knew he would." Jacob was fighting for composure. To distract himself, he sniffed the air. "I smell a home-cooked meal."

Irena cast him a smile. "I made *Zrazy* for you."

"What a treat! You can't get decent *Zrazy* anywhere in Germany, not like the one you make."

"Mamusia, are you sure I can't convince you to sell this house and move to Germany with me?" Jakub had been trying to talk her into that very thing for the duration of his two-week visit, but she was standing firm on her decision.

"No, now stop pestering me about it and go join those lovely girls of yours. I so enjoyed getting to meet them. You are a good papa." Irena patted his cheek.

"You could see them a lot more often, if you lived with us," he insisted.

"Jacob, you don't teach an old horse new tricks. I want to die on Polish soil and be buried next to Luka. Do not take that away from me."

"I'm just worried about you living alone. You're not getting younger either."

"I'm fine. What would I even do in Aachen without speaking a single word of German?"

He nodded, remembering how awful he'd felt during his first year. For her it would be so much harder since she'd lived her entire life in the same place. "At least you have a telephone and I can send you money via bank transfer every month, so you'll never lack anything."

"I get along just fine," she protested.

"Things are changing. Communism is dead and Poland will undergo drastic changes we might not even envision. It's the least I can do for you. Please let me." He knew she was just scraping by, because with the turnaround the Polish zloty had lost its value and all the shiny new things imported from the West were only attainable for the very rich, or those who paid in hard currency.

"Well then, if you insist."

"I do. I'll come to visit again in summer."

"I can't wait!"

She hugged him tight until Claudia said, "Papa, if we don't leave for the train station right now, we're going to miss the train."

"I love you, *Mamusia*."

"I love you too, my son."

"I'll see you soon." Jakub gave her one last hug, kissed her cheek, and then ran to the taxi and slid into the back seat. He looked out the window until the little house disappeared from view.

It had been a long time coming, but as he boarded the train, he was finally completely at peace with himself. He might be German by birth, but a piece of his heart would forever be right here in Poland with Irena.

A LETTER FROM MARION

Dear Reader,

Thank you so much for reading *The Orphan's Mother*. If you did enjoy it, and want to keep up to date with all my latest releases, just sign up at the following link. Your email address will never be shared and you can unsubscribe at any time.

www.bookouture.com/marion-kummerow

Inspiration for my novels often hits me when seeing an evocative photo, or reading a snippet of history. Jacob's story was no different.

A while ago I visited the Friedland Transit Camp Museum, at the former inner-German border near Göttingen to do research for my book *Endless Ordeal*, which follows a Wehrmacht soldier into Russian captivity after the war. During my six-hour visit in the museum I found much more than just the needed facts about prisoners of war coming through this camp between 1945 and 1955.

The Red Cross missing person search service impressed me deeply. You must know that several million people across Europe were uprooted, meandering through the region, searching for families, friends, relatives and a home. Hundreds of thousands lived in refugee camps for months or even years, and there, the Red Cross started their "filing system".

Over the years they refined the service into a sophisticated operation, even publishing year-books with the photos and short biographies of the missing persons. You can read more about my visit and the search service on my blog post here: https:// kummerow.info/friedland-camp/.

There you'll also see the image of a small child with a bag and a sign around the neck, which deeply moved me. The accompanying exhibition told about the fate of several thousands of unaccompanied children arriving at camp Friedland from behind the Iron curtain to be reunited with their birth families.

In the last room hung short profiles of several people next to a picture of them. Some were soldiers, others war criminals, but one of them caught my eye and jogged my imagination.

It was the story of a boy (I don't remember his name), who had gotten separated from his mother during their escape, had been adopted by a Polish couple and was returned to his mother ten years later. His reaction when he was told he would be sent home, was quoted on the profile: "I'm not going to live with that strange woman."

As you can imagine, I was instantly intrigued. Jacob/Jakub was born. Apart from the cornerstones of his life, everything else about him is fictional, as are all characters in this novel.

I chose Lodz/Littmannstadt and Posen/Poznań as Jacob's home towns, because they are located in a region where Poles and Germans had mingled for centuries, living more or less peacefully together. The correct spelling is Łódź, pronounced like "wuj", but in this book I opted for the anglicised version, purely for the ease of reading.

Lodz was conquered by the Red Army on January 19th 1945, whereas Poznań was the venue of the Battle of Poznań, lasting almost one month from January 24th until February 22nd.

Initially the Polish people welcomed the Russians as liberators, although many of them quickly changed their opinion, as you know from history.

Great thanks go to a fellow writer and native Polish speaker who kindly agreed to check the Polish expressions for accuracy. She alerted me that the word *Mamusia,* mother, has to be declined. In this case I opted for readability over grammatical accuracy, because most everyone who doesn't speak Polish would be confused if she was suddenly called *Mamusiu.*

The Radio Search Service was installed in 1946 by the NWDR (Nordwestdeutscher Rundfunk, the main broadcaster in north-western Germany), who broadcasted a daily ten-minute-transmission in cooperation with the German Red Cross. The announcements were free of charge.

In the book Martin surprises Emma with having Jacob announced as a missing person, but in reality, the German Red Cross made the lists and forwarded them to the radio station. I don't know how they chose which persons were read on air.

According to a press release, a total of 67,946 children had been reunited with their parents by the end of 1951 as a result of the radio announcements.

When I wrote this book, the war in Ukraine hadn't started and I had never believed in my wildest dreams that we would see those cruelties again. Undifferentiated bombing of military and civilian targets, even hospitals. Deliberate brutality against civilians, shooting of defenceless people, widespread atrocities like torture and rape, all of this I believed to have been a thing of the distant past. It breaks my heart to see the images and hear the stories. The trauma will stay with the Ukrainians for generations to come.

Last but not least my heart is with the children. They always suffer most in a war, without ever having had a say in it. How many thousands will have lost their parents by the time this ends? How many will end up in a situation like Jacob, separated from his mother? Some may find loving foster parents like

Irena and Luka Pawlak were for him, others might have a harsher fate in orphanages or living with unkind relatives.

Mothers might be sent to camps and Gulags in Russia, never to show up again on our side of the newly installed Iron Curtain. Even as I write this, thousands are hauled away to "filtration camps" with uncertain outcomes. Given the other stories from eyewitnesses we must fear for the worst.

Therefore, it is my dearest wish that every one of us does what little we can to bring peace and joy into this world, to alleviate pain and hopefully, soon, put an end not only to this war, but to all wars in this world.

It must be possible for humanity to live in peace with each other. That is my dream.

Again, thank you so much for reading *The Orphan's Mother*. I hope you loved it, and if you did I would be very grateful if you could write a review. I'd love to hear what you think, and it makes such a difference helping new readers to discover one of my books for the first time.

I love hearing from my readers—you can get in touch on my Facebook page, through Twitter, Goodreads or my website.

Marion Kummerow

https://kummerow.info

facebook.com/AutorinKummerow
twitter.com/MarionKummerow

Made in the USA
Coppell, TX
28 August 2022

82220749R00163